PRAISE FOR *THE ENG...*

"Readers who adore romcom with laye[...] [...] with the latest Krista Phillips novel. With a fresh voice that Melissa Tagg and Jenny B. Jones readers will adore, this book is filled with characters you want to love as much as you want to take them out to coffee and set them straight. This new voice takes romantic comedy and adds a layer of life and depth that make this book a truly enjoyable read. No light fluff here. If you're expecting another reality TV romance, this book will delight you as it surprises you."

—Cara Putman, award-winning author of
Shadowed by Grace and *Beyond Justice*

"Full of Phillips's characteristic humor and keen insight into what makes humans tick, *The Engagement Plot* is a romantic escapade to tickle your fancy, warm your heart, and stir your imagination."

—Valerie Comer, *USA Today* bestselling author
and two-time Word Award winner

"Romantic comedy at its best! Phillips blends the perfect amount of humor, romance, and faith into this delightful story about two people discovering what the true price of love really means."

—Jessica R. Patch, author of the Seasons of Hope
contemporary romance series

"Delightfully fun and fresh! Phillips dazzles with pitch-perfect humor and a unique twist on reality-show romance. Sweet, snappy, and wonderfully sincere, *The Engagement Plot* is everything a romantic comedy should be and more!"

—Amy Leigh Simpson, author of
When Fall Fades and *From Winter's Ashes*

The ENGAGEMENT Plot

Krista Phillips

SHILOH RUN PRESS

An Imprint of Barbour Publishing, Inc.

Print ISBN 978-1-68322-316-0

eBook Editions:
Adobe Digital Edition (.epub) 978-1-68322-315-3
Kindle and MobiPocket Edition (.prc) 978-1-68322-314-6

Cover Design: Kirk DouPonce, DogEared Design

Published by Shiloh Run Press, an imprint of Barbour Publishing, Inc., P.O. Box 719, Uhrichsville, Ohio 44683, www.shilohrunpress.com

Our mission is to publish and distribute inspirational products offering exceptional value and biblical encouragement to the masses.

ecpa Member of the
Evangelical Christian
Publishers Association

DEDICATION

To my alley cat sisters, past and present—you have walked
this writing journey with me since almost the
beginning. You all mean the world to me!

CHAPTER ONE

*B*lizzard-like conditions are expected to last through the evening. Stay inside, folks. If you're out there on the roads, well, just don't be."

Hanna Knight clicked the POWER button on the radio as she inched the Dodge Ram pickup down the snow-covered highway. Embarrass, Minnesota, was only a few miles farther. She should have never left the farm knowing a storm was brewing, but she'd thought she could beat it home.

Obviously not.

She'd driven in worse before, though.

Hanna tapped on the brakes and squinted to see through the white flakes that waged war on her windshield. Was that something in the ditch ahead?

As the truck neared, she made out a pair of red taillights. The closer she got, the clearer the back of the car became. A rental agency logo was barely visible on the back of the snow-drowned Lexus. Just her luck. She'd have to play good Samaritan to some moron who didn't have enough sense to stay inside during a classic Northern Minnesota blizzard.

Be nice, Hanna. It wasn't the moron's fault the weather was grating on Hanna's nerves.

As long as it wasn't another reporter. Those were the only strangers she usually saw on the road to the farm lately. And even they were becoming rare, thank goodness.

On a normal day, she'd have headed on by, alerted her dad, and let him come back and help pull the car out. Picking up strangers on the side of the road, even (and maybe especially) stranded ones, wasn't the safest activity in the world. But the snow was turning into blizzard conditions faster than she was comfortable with, and there might not be time.

Her pulse picked up speed as she guided the truck to the side and threw it into PARK. Hanna grabbed her pink stocking cap and slipped it over her head then checked the rearview mirror to make sure her blond hair wasn't sticking out all over. If it was a reporter, no sense having another horrible picture show up in the grocery store checkout lanes.

The moment she thought it, guilt plowed into her conscience. Caring about her hair when a person could be scared and hurt? A year ago, she wouldn't have given it a second thought.

Hanna grabbed the emergency kit from the glove box and her rifle from behind the seat—just in case—and hopped out of the truck. Icy wind cut against her body, and she tightened her muscles to keep from being blown over. Head down against the oncoming snow, she trudged around the front of the truck.

After she made sure the driver was safe, she'd give him or her a good talking-to for trying to drive in this weather. Probably him. This was something a guy would do.

She was a bit stupid for making the run to Ely when she knew bad weather was brewing, but that was different. She'd cut teeth on icicles during winter and had been driving in the snow since she was fifteen.

City Slicker, on the other hand, probably couldn't say the same.

She shimmied down the ditch, ignoring the cold wet of the snow seeping into her jeans, and pounded her gloved fist on the tinted driver's window. "Hello? You okay?"

No reply. Just great.

She reached for the ice-covered door handle, but it refused to budge. The car had been there at least a half hour by the looks of it, but minus twenty-degree weather could freeze a car pretty fast, and the person inside with it.

She set the emergency kit on top of the car, then, rifle in hand, ran back to the truck, sliding to a stop at the back, and grabbed a crowbar. When she reached the car again, she used the end of the bar to chip away the ice forming along the door and handle then tried to open it again. The black metal shifted then refused to budge.

Short of breaking a window, she had no clue what else to try. And the butt of her rifle through the window didn't bode well for the driver.

Coffee. She'd been sipping a nice hot travel mug full of heaven's liquid on the way back, and it was still over half full. Maybe it would melt the ice just enough, although it was a long shot.

Hanna trudged up the incline again and returned with the stainless-steel thermos. She poured the coffee slowly around the car door and handle, careful to avoid the glass so it didn't shatter. *Please, Jesus, let this work.*

Bracing a foot against the car, she leveraged and pulled with all one-hundred-twenty-five pounds of her weight. Her efforts were rewarded when the door finally popped open, and she went sprawling into the snow. Ignoring the wetness clinging to the back of her blue jeans, she heaved herself from two feet of snow and bent down to assess the person huddled in the car.

"Sir, are you all right?"

The man had wrapped himself in a blanket—at least he'd done

that right—so she couldn't make out his features, but she did notice a slight nod of his head.

"We aren't gonna get this car out of here tonight, so why don't you get in the truck so you can warm up?"

The body shifted but didn't get out. Probably from shock and cold. She shrugged off her coat, which she knew would already be warm, and threw it over him. The biting cold nipped at her skin through her oversized Vikings sweatshirt, but she was still much better off than the poor guy in front of her.

She reached in and grabbed his legs, swinging them out of the car and into the snow. His leather shoes were no match for the knee-deep snow drift. "I don't have the muscles to carry you, but if you can walk, just lean on me, and we'll do this together, okay?"

Putting her back into it, she grabbed his arms and pulled. After two tugs, a grunt from her, and a moan from the man, he stood. Together, though his steps were stilted, they made it to the cab of the truck, where she all but hoisted him in.

She ran back down to his car, grabbed the keys from the ignition, and locked the door. Not like anyone was going to steal it out here, especially in this weather, but with his dress pants and shiny, expensive-looking loafers, he looked like one who might worry about such stupid things.

Hanna hopped into the truck and cranked the heat on full blast then turned to the man, who still shivered under a combination of the blanket and her coat. "I'd offer you coffee, but I used it on your car to get the door open. Here, let me get that cold blanket off so the heat can reach you."

The man jerked away from her as she tried to remove the blanket. Stubborn cuss. "I just wanna help. You have to be freezing."

He shook his head.

Fine, let him suffer. Men.

Slamming the truck into gear, she headed down the road toward the little town of Embarrass. Some might balk at the term *town* considering it wasn't much more than a post office and community center, but it had been her home since she was born. These people loved her regardless and were some of the few in this world who hadn't turned their backs on her over the last six months.

Just on the outskirts, she turned down the gravel road that led to her dad's farm. How sad was it that she, at twenty-seven, lived back at home yet again?

She'd have given anything to be back in her cozy little apartment in Duluth, teaching a group of giggly kindergartners in the nearby elementary school. They probably had a snow day today, so she'd be sipping hot chocolate and binge-watching something on Netflix.

Shaking the memory out of her brain, she determined to focus on the invalid next to her. "We're almost there. Dad will be able to help you into some warm clothes once we get inside. They may not be all fancy like you're used to, but they'll be warm."

The stranger nodded again, or, at least, that was how she interpreted the shift of the blanket.

As she parked the truck in her usual spot, Hanna laid on the horn, then jumped out of the cab when her dad opened the door to the old farmhouse.

His thick Scandinavian accent shouted out as he pulled on a coat and hustled down the steps. "Hanna, what's going on?"

She gritted her teeth against the bitter, snow-filled wind. "Picked up a straggler on the side of the road half-frozen. You wanna help me get him inside?"

Dad was already headed toward the passenger side. "You're gonna freeze to death without your coat. No, you go on in and start some soup and coffee. I'll see to him."

Her teeth started to chatter as she trudged through the

snow-filled path to the front deck of the house. She didn't love the idea of leaving Dad to help the man inside all by himself, but there wasn't much she could do to help if she froze, too.

Hugging her arms to her chest, she headed into the house and let the warmth embrace her once she closed the door.

The familiar house stood as it always did when she got home in the winter. Floorboard heaters going at full blast. Cookstove that heated the living room filled with burning wood. She stood for just a minute in front of the old black stove, allowing the warmth to thaw her fingers.

But Dad would be in here with the crazy rich guy any minute, so her comfort was going to have to be put on hold.

Ignoring her wet clothes, she grabbed a pair of Dad's flannel pajamas and long johns from the basket of clean clothes she'd planned to fold later, laid them out in the guest bedroom just off the living room, and headed into the kitchen.

She poured two large cans of chicken noodle soup into a pot then took a break to try and unstick her jeans from her legs. She really should have changed into dry clothes first. But before she could head upstairs, the front door opened.

Wet jeans would just have to wait a few minutes longer. Flipping on the burner, she yelled toward the front of the house. "Need any help?"

"Nope, you stay put."

Hanna wrinkled her forehead at his demanding tone. Her dad was usually laid back and easygoing, rarely commanding her to do a thing. Of course, she was an only child and was used to pitching in. Shaking off her confusion, she tossed the soup cans into the trash and put on a pot of coffee.

When the soup started boiling, she inhaled the warm aroma, letting the steam from the broth thaw her insides the rest of the way.

She ladled it into three bowls and set them on the table along with spoons and toast. As she grabbed for a TV tray in case the stranger wasn't able to walk to the table, a throat cleared behind her.

She turned, and the tray clattered to the floor.

In front of her stood a slightly blue-hued, oversized flannel-clad William Preston, CEO and handsome bachelor who had won the hearts of America's women. That was, until seven months ago when he'd stomped on her heart and left it to freeze to death by humiliating her in front of millions of people.

CHAPTER TWO

*W*ill stood on wobbly legs swathed in foreign flannel and tried to look confident, all the while knowing he appeared anything but.

His toes were frozen, his fingers numb, and he couldn't even feel his rear end when he'd sat on the bed a few minutes ago. He'd never known one could be so very, very cold.

Jim Knight, a man he'd only talked to on the phone previously when asking for his daughter's hand in marriage, came up behind him and slapped him on the back with a bit more force than necessary. "Sit down and eat, Will. You need some warm food in that belly to thaw you out."

Will forced himself not to wince, although a large handprint was now probably engraved in the ice that was the middle of his back. "Yes, si–ir." Why wouldn't his teeth stop chattering? This was not the impression he wanted to make when he saw Hanna again.

He hadn't known what to expect, but in his dreams she would run out of the small farmhouse, gasp, then throw herself into his arms, last year's slip of the tongue forgotten.

Then he woke up and hoped she wouldn't take the ax she used to chop wood and swing away at his head. He wouldn't blame her either. If anyone deserved a good decapitation from an ex-girlfriend—if she could even be called that—it was him.

Forcing his feet forward, he gripped the chair with a shaky hand and lowered his icy bum onto the padded seat. He didn't allow himself to glance at Hanna again, given the look of shock and disgust he'd seen on her face when she finally realized who he was.

A familiar pit of remorse lodged in his stomach.

He gripped the spoon and moved it slowly to his mouth so he wouldn't douse his lap with the bubbling-hot soup. The broth slid down his throat, gradually thawing his insides.

After a few spoonfuls, the shaking subsided, and he allowed himself to peek at the woman who slid into a seat across the long oak table that looked straight out of *Little House on the Prairie*. Her eyes focused on the bowl in front of her, but the older man was staring as if Will was a rogue cowboy come to pillage them and ruin his daughter.

Jim finally put his spoon down and sat back, arms folded over his broad chest that spoke of years of manual labor. "What are you doing here, young man? Don't you think you've caused my Hanna enough grief?"

A noodle stuck in his throat, but he managed to swallow it anyway. What was he doing here? Twenty-four hours ago he would have said he wanted to reconcile, to right the wrongs he'd done to Hanna, but it was becoming increasingly clear just how difficult that would be. "I came to apologize."

Glaring but gorgeous blue eyes finally met his. "You think you can fly on up here, almost get yourself killed, say a quick 'I'm sorry,' and I'll fall over myself to forgive you? Dream on, William Preston."

Jim cleared his throat. "Hanna, careful."

Her gaze moved to her father, and an unspoken conversation went on between the two.

Jim was the first to look at him, while Hanna's gaze slipped back to her soup. He already missed seeing those sea-blue eyes, even if they were shooting icy darts his direction.

"Will, you can stay the night here in the guest bedroom. We'll talk more in the morning. Weather is supposed to be bad for a few days. It was pure stupid of you to even try to drive here in this mess."

He opened his mouth to protest and remind the man that his daughter had been out in the storm as well, but the cold that still clung to his numb toes reminded him that he was the idiot who slid headfirst into a snow embankment, not Hanna.

Instead, he nodded. "Thank you for the offer. I'll be out of your hair in the morning." It wasn't what he wanted. He'd hoped to have a few days to talk to her, to explain. To apologize.

He glanced out the window, winter still wreaking havoc on the world just on the other side. Maybe the snow wasn't so bad after all—

Hanna pushed back her seat and stood, revealing wet jeans that clung tightly to her curves. The annoyed glare she cast him said it all. "Oh yes, when your car is piled in three feet of snow by then. What are you going to do, walk back to Duluth to hail the next airplane out of here? That'll be a fine sight to see. Wait, you probably have a private jet to take you wherever you want. Maybe it can land out on the frozen lake."

Her dad stood and put an arm around her, whispering something in her ear. She glanced back at Will, scowled, and marched up the set of stairs he hadn't noticed before in the corner of the kitchen. There must be two sets of them, because he'd also seen larger ones when he came in the front door. While the old farmhouse looked pretty big, deterioration could be seen in the peeling paint and decades-old decor.

His picture-perfect condo in Nashville flashed in his mind. Such a contrast. They'd always been opposite, even from the first day of taping for *The Price of Love*. He, the CEO bachelor looking for love, and she, the small-town teacher with morals tighter than some of the other contestants' skinny jeans.

Why everyone had wanted him to pick her, the one who fit in the least with his life, was beyond him.

He wouldn't have had to listen to them. He could have picked Stephanie.

But he didn't. For the life of him, he couldn't figure out why, except that there was something about Hanna he couldn't let go of.

Jim turned around, arms crossed in front of him. "She won't sleep a wink tonight because of you."

Guilt landed directly on his shoulders, where it belonged. The show aside, he'd hurt an amazing woman who didn't deserve it any more than she deserved to be saddled with him, a sorry excuse for a fiancé, not to mention CEO. "I'm sorry. I hadn't meant for this to happen. All I wanted was to—"

"I know. You wanted to say you're sorry. Not sure how you couldn't say that with a phone call or a well-worded letter on that fancy letterhead of yours."

He would have loved to shoot off an e-mail to fix this and go on his way. But his board of directors had other ideas. No way could he admit that just yet, though. "I honestly thought I was doing the right thing. I couldn't get Hanna out of my head, and my heart told me to come."

Which made no sense. It had just been business. That's it.

Jim's eyebrows hiked up so high they almost touched his receding hairline. "Your heart? You telling me you still have feelings for my daughter?"

A spark lit in his belly, but Will doused it immediately. He couldn't have real feelings for Hanna. They'd only known each other on the show for, what, six weeks? And until the end, he'd been dating a slew of other women.

But those other women hadn't plagued his dreams almost nightly.

Plus, she was a painful reminder to him of a time long before that stupid reality TV show.

Picking her had been strategic. Purely—mostly—strategic. And had backfired exponentially. "My feelings for Hanna are complicated. But regardless of that, she's important to me, and I've hurt her. I want to make it right."

Despite the plans his board had in mind, that much was true.

Hanna's father studied him for a moment then stood and stretched his hands over his head. "I don't know about you, but I'm beat. We'll talk more tomorrow after we get a little sleep."

Will stood and held out his hand. "I appreciate you letting me stay. I know this isn't ideal, but—"

Jim ignored the outstretched hand and folded his arms over his chest. "Son, let's get a few things straight. First, I don't care who you are. Hanna and I, we don't let strangers die of hypothermia out in the cold. Second, you and I are good. You've apologized, I've accepted, and we'll get on with it. The good Lord expects nothing less of me. You'll have a little harder time with Hanna, although I have faith that she'll come around, too. Third"—his index finger dug into Will's chest—"under no circumstances while you are stuck under my roof will you put the moves on my daughter, you hear?"

He swallowed hard. "Yes, sir."

"Now, while you're here, help yourself to whatever you need. Our home is your home."

CHAPTER THREE

*H*anna plopped down at the desk in her room and buried her face in her arms. *God, please, please just make him leave.*

This couldn't be happening. Maybe she'd wake up and it would all be a dream. Lifting her head, she pinched her arm, her nails digging into her skin.

She sighed when the world remained intact while her arm sported nice, nail-trimmed red marks.

It was nothing compared to the knife wound in her heart that had just started healing—put there by none other than the half-frozen man who now sat downstairs at the kitchen table.

What had possessed him to come all the way up here from Nashville, anyway? She could have asked him, but honestly, she wasn't sure she wanted to know the answer. Her defenses were not to be trusted when it came to Will, and he needed to leave, sooner rather than later. He was a smooth talker and had a way of getting under her skin and climbing into her heart before she even knew he was there.

But not this time.

She would not be taken in by him.

Tugging open her laptop, she clicked on the bookmark she'd

made months ago, clenching her jaw when the now-familiar You-Tube video popped up on the screen.

She'd watched the humiliation over and over the first few months. Analyzing every word, trying to figure out just where she'd gone wrong.

Her journal had a running list of over a hundred things she could have seen, should have seen, and would have done had she seen who Will really was—a lying player who only cared about dollar signs and his precious image.

But today, she needed to watch it one last time to remind herself.

She picked up the laptop, flopped onto her bed, and after taking a deep breath, clicked PLAY.

Collin, the show's host, strode along the white, sandy beach, looking suave and casual in khakis rolled up to his calves and a half-buttoned Hawaiian shirt. "Welcome back to the finale of *The Price of Love*. Now, I know you're all chomping at the bit to find out who William picked to spend his happily-ever-after with. Will it be Sultry Stephanie or Holy Hanna, as you viewers have dubbed them? Well, it's time to find out."

The camera faded out then focused on Stephanie, bathed in a long red dress with a slit that almost reached her bikini line.

Hanna grabbed a pillow and hugged it to her chest to calm her racing heart. If only he'd picked Stephanie. For that matter, why hadn't he? She'd asked herself that question a thousand times. While Hanna had been the viewers' "choice" for him, all the social media outlets had agreed: Stephanie was much more William's type.

Hanna focused back on the screen, where the woman in red walked down the pebbled trail toward a waiting William Preston. He stood, dressed in a black suit that accented his broad chest and shoulders. The Caribbean Sea danced in the background of the breathtaking Jamaican beach as if the waves were trying to show off for the viewers. The camera zoomed in on Stephanie as she stepped up to Will, a haughty look of expectancy on her lips. Then she winked, the classic move that had given her the sultry label. "William."

He reached out and held her hands then smiled. "Stephanie."

A moment later, she pulled Will to her and raised her lips, but he gently pushed her back and shook his head.

His it's-not-you-it's-me speech lasted a few minutes, followed by tears and scalding words of anger and a few bleeped-out words from Stephanie.

He tried to follow her to talk, but she threw her coin at him, the trademark of *The Price of Love* show, and flung herself into the waiting taxi.

Hanna took a trembling finger and moved the cursor to skip the next part, but she snatched it back. No. She'd watch the whole thing in all its humiliating glory.

After more dialogue by the host, Hanna appeared on the screen, walking down the path toward William, her fingers clasping on to her coin for dear life.

The tangible *price* of love that seemed so corny now but was such a big deal to her at the time. The coin was a little gold piece with a heart in the middle, surrounded by the words *The Price of Love*. It was a nod to the theme of the show—rich guys who were too busy with their careers to date, coming on the show to find women in hopes that they could weed out the ones who were in it for the money.

Each week, after crazy, over-the-top dates, the contestants presented the wealthy man with their *heart*, and the guy chose to accept it or not.

But after all those weeks of dating and having her coin accepted, it hadn't occurred to her that she was trying to give her heart to a man who wasn't even close to worth the cost.

She clenched the covers of the bedspread. *This is good for you, Hanna. Remember.*

Yes. She had to remind herself. Of his deception. Of what a smooth, fake jerk he could be.

Of how naive she'd been.

This last episode, she had pulled out all the stops to look her best, unlike some of the previous ones where she'd opted for sweats and an old T-shirt around the house, a stark contrast to the other contestants who constantly tried to look their best for the camera. No, at this last ceremony, every detail was perfect. Her long blond hair was down, just how William had liked it. She'd had it curled and just the sides swept up into glittery combs.

Her gown went against everyone's suggestions, but it was one of the few dressy outfits she'd worn on the show that was *her.* Past women chose to wear long evening gowns for that final potential proposal, but she wasn't most women. The ivory, embroidered dress came just above her knees with a high boatneck that was modest yet classy.

She remembered all the rhinestone numbers they'd tried to fit her with, but when she'd glimpsed this one in a storefront in Duluth, she'd known it was the one.

Then again, she'd also thought Will had been the one, too. She'd been right about the dress but oh-so-wrong about the man.

William took her TV-self's hands. She remembered the thud of her heartbeat, the sensation of that stupid coin pressing between their hands, the fear that her sweaty palms would repulse him, and the calm reassurance of his hands squeezing hers.

His eyes had locked in on her, and she'd known immediately he was going to ask her to marry him.

Her stomach had filled with butterflies, but all that remained now were the dead corpses of squashed bugs.

On the screen, she accepted the ring with eyes full of tears, and then William took her face in his hands and kissed her, the coin dropping to the ground, forgotten and probably swept up and thrown away by the cleaning crew later.

Her heart thrown in the trash—oh how appropriate.

Hanna's stomach twisted into a hard, sickening knot. With shaking hands, she scrolled forward a few minutes past all the lovey-dovey fake stuff to the part she needed to see the most.

Collin appeared again, this time lounging on the beach in a chair, looking cool, calm, and irritating. "Now, the happy couple will be letting us know their plans soon, but I thought we'd have one final chat with the bride and groom before we say good-bye, letting us know their feelings in their own words. Remember, they haven't been able to see each other for the last two months while the show aired, so these were filmed separately. You can see them together in public for the first time tomorrow morning on the *ALIVE* morning show."

Hanna's face, happy and delusional, popped up on the screen. She gushed about how much she loved Will, how she was sure that God had led them to each other, even in this odd way that didn't seem normal to most people. How they didn't know their plans just yet, but that obviously with Will's job as a CEO, she'd agreed to relocate from Minnesota because she could teach kindergarten anywhere. Future Preston babies? Oh, someday she'd love that, but let's not rush things just yet. She answered Collin's questions with well-worded answers, relying on the same steady brain that allowed her to handle five-year-olds with ease.

Next, William's handsome face filled the screen, his smile eager.

Hanna clenched her fists at the image of the man who had made her think he was her dream come true in flesh. He was larger than life, the epitome of the handsome, professional businessman.

Too good to be true. It had been there all along—it was the clue she had needed to see to send him packing before he could do damage to her heart.

It tied closely with the "Sure I believe in God, I was practically born with a Bible in my hand" line he'd given her more than once right before he quickly changed the subject.

His deep voice echoed from the computer. "Hanna is like no woman I've ever met. Some women walk into a room and fireworks go off, threatening to explode and torch the place at any moment. Hanna walks into the room, and there's peace. You just can't help but smile when you're around her, and it makes you want to be around her more."

The host chuckled. "So, what, no fireworks, though?"

William laughed along with him. "Oh, there are fireworks, don't get me wrong. But the kind that consume your heart, not threaten to blow up in your face."

The camera panned out to show both William and Collin. Collin leaned forward in his seat, elbows on his knees. "All right, the question we all want to know. You and Hanna have had no contact since the end of the show, of course. But you were allowed a weekend off camera with each of the final women as a last shot to get to know them. On behalf of all America, the question we're dying to know the answer to: Just how holy is Hanna?"

William shifted his position in the chair and fiddled with the lapel on his jacket. "I—Hanna and I had an amazing weekend. Let's just leave it at that."

Blood pounded in Hanna's veins as she watched the moment for the thousandth time, her heart begging him to clarify, even though she already knew what he was going to say.

Collin raised his eyebrows. "Amazing, huh? As in—?"

William laughed and winked. "Amazing. Definitely."

The host shook his head and shrugged. "I guess Holy Hanna isn't quite as holy as we all thought she was. Well, it was great chatting with you, Will. We wish you and Hanna the best of luck."

Will just smiled and nodded. "Thanks, Collin."

With a shaking hand, Hanna closed the laptop and shoved it to the side.

Amazing.

Definitely.

Who would have thought those two words would completely ruin her world?

A piercing ache attacked her skull as well as her heart. She buried her head into her pillow, allowing tears to flow, tears she'd promised herself she was done with months ago.

She'd gone on that stupid show at the pressure of her best friend, who'd signed her up as a joke. But when she'd decided to go for it, she'd sworn that no matter what, she wouldn't compromise who she was for the sake of a show.

The press and social media had dubbed her Holy Hanna. She'd been so angry at first. But then Dad, sweet, wonderful Dad, reminded her there's nothing wrong with being holy.

Well, evidently there was.

Because once that aired, her life had been flushed down the toilet, right along with her reputation.

She didn't really want to take a trip to the sewer to retrieve it.

⌒〰⌒

Will squinted through the darkness, eyeing the carpeted floor of the guest bedroom. Even though the tan shag had obvious wear and tear from years of use, it still looked more comfortable than the rock-hard mattress he was sleeping on.

Correction. One actually had to be in a state of slumber in order to be labeled "sleeping." "Lying in agony" described it more accurately. Every limb of his body, now defrosted but not happy about the drastic change from close-to-frozen to toasty warm, screamed at him.

Maybe if he lay still long enough, he'd fall asleep and dream he was on his nice Tempur-Pedic back in his downtown Nashville condo.

After a minute of listening to nothing but the howl of the wind outside and a grandfather clock somewhere in the house tick-tocking the seconds going by, sleep was still a distant dream. Instead, his botched mission ran through his thoughts as he struggled to figure out a solution to get it back on course.

Reconciliation with Hanna looked far from reach. And the board of directors' hope of a renewed relationship? Plain laughable. He'd have to throw down some thick charm and extreme lies to even come close.

Charm he could do. Lies, however, weren't really his thing any-more. A vague stretch of the truth was what had gotten him into this mess in the first place.

Besides, he'd climbed his way to the top through old-fashioned hard work, unlike some other people he knew. No way would he stoop to what others wanted him to do, specifically his CFO, Doug Perry. If the man suggested one more scheme to improve sales num-bers that reeked of potential scandal, Will would have no choice but to go to the board of directors and request he be replaced.

He should have done it months ago, but since he was in hot water himself, he hadn't wanted to bring even more negative atten-tion to the issue.

But his job was on the line now. He had to think of something.

Will stretched his legs beneath the homemade quilt and cringed at the cracking sounds his body made. His stomach decided to moan its complaint at the same time.

He'd skipped breakfast as well as lunch yesterday to make it to the airport on time, and then because he'd been in a hurry to get the rental car and drive out here before the storm got too bad.

The little bit of soup he'd had for dinner served to warm his insides but didn't come close to satisfying his hunger.

It went against every set of manners his mother had instilled in him to rummage through someone else's cupboards for food, but sleep was a long shot and food a necessity.

Throwing back the quilt, Will clamped a hand on top of the dresser next to the bed and hauled himself upright.

His muscles froze for a moment, but with gritted teeth, he forced his way across the guest room and peeked outside the door. Not a creature was stirring.

His body finally adjusting, he tiptoed in the direction he hoped was the kitchen. The pitch darkness of the house was blinding, but he didn't dare turn on a light.

Feeling for the wall, he sucked in a breath when his toe connected with a piece of furniture—maybe an end table?—he'd forgotten about.

He leaned against the wall and bit the inside of his cheek, trying not to yell the four-letter words that threatened.

When the throbbing subsided, he limped the rest of the way, thankful when he finally found the edge of the counter with his fingers.

He opened the fridge and squinted at the bright light that blasted his eyes, then blinked to adjust his vision. A bag of sliced turkey caught his eye. Didn't turkey have stuff in it that made you sleepy? Jackpot.

He grabbed the mustard and mayonnaise and set them with the turkey on the island before closing the fridge. The room settled into darkness again.

Now for the bread. A bread box maybe? He started to feel his way around the counters, his fingers meeting a large stand-up mixer, a butcher block of knives, then a cutting boa—

His hand stilled on the wooden board when the kitchen stairs started to creak. The sound was so soft, maybe he imagined it. But then it came again. And again.

His heart kicked up speed. Someone was coming downstairs.

Hide. He had to hide before they saw him. Hanna had always teased about the guns her dad kept around for hunting and possible burglars and how he wasn't afraid to use them.

Not a gun guy himself, Will would rather not be acquainted with Jim's rifle anytime soon, and definitely not by way of a bullet in his body.

Turning, Will put his hands forward and felt for the island. The jar of mayo met his hand. He grabbed the sandwich makings, tucked them under his arm, and turned to tiptoe back to his room.

On the third step, he collided with a petite body, the contents in his arms crashing to the floor, replaced by a shrieking woman.

CHAPTER FOUR

A man. In her kitchen.

A hand. Covering her mouth.

Something mushy. Squishing between her bare toes.

Hanna gripped the shoulders of the intruder, debating whether to use the knee to the groin technique or the fingernails in the eyeballs.

Before she could decide between the two, the man wrapped an arm around her and lifted her to sit on the island. A voice whispered in her ear, sending warm tingles down her neck when she recognized it. "Hanna, it's me. Please don't scream again, or you'll wake up your dad."

Fat chance. Her dad could sleep through a pack of wild wolves invading the house and howling all the while. The man wouldn't wake up until 6:00 a.m. on the dot, no alarm clock needed. Still, the voice offered relief. Her brain fuzzy from sleep, she'd almost forgotten Will was here.

But what was he doing in their kitchen in the middle of the night? And what was all over her feet? "Light. Turn on a light, Will."

The hands that still held her hesitated. "Where's the switch?"

"Left corner, behind the table."

He left her, and a minute later, the fluorescent bulb flickered overhead.

The floor was littered with a broken jar of mayonnaise, a bottle of mustard, thankfully contained, and sandwich meat.

Hanna wiggled her toes, which she could now see were covered in creamy mayo. How her feet escaped the shards of glass sprinkled into the white substance, she wasn't sure.

Will walked back, still tiptoeing.

"You don't have to tiptoe. Dad can't hear a thing when he sleeps."

He shot her a glance, a crooked smile appearing on his broad lips, the ones she used to think were terribly kissable. "I'm more worried about bloodying my feet. These socks are thick, but not that thick."

Good point. "What were you doing up this late anyway?"

He ran a hand through his frazzled dark hair. Usually he kept it manicured, a little long shag in the front, but clean-cut. This bed-head look definitely suited him. "Your dad said to make myself at home, and I hadn't eaten all day."

She crossed her arms over her chest. "And the soup?"

He shook his head. "Let me rephrase. The soup was the only thing I've eaten in the last twenty-four hours. And while it was good, my growling stomach wouldn't let me sleep. What about you? Why are you up so late?"

The evening before rushed through her mind—seeing Will in her house, invading her space, reminding her of the future she used to think they'd have together—and her anger stirred again. "Same thing. If you'll remember, I didn't get to finish my dinner."

He slung his hands on his hips. "Since it was my fault, how about I make us both a sandwich?"

The sight of him in red flannel pajamas and thermal socks almost made a smile creep up on her lips and would have if she didn't have the urge to jump off the island and pummel him. Hanna started to hop off, but he rushed to her. "No you don't. Can't have you cutting those cute toes of yours."

Cute toes? The memory of his charm invaded her good sense. He always was one for open flattery, a fact she used to love about him. And she'd never admit it to a soul, but the compliment made her heart skip a beat. Or maybe just half a beat.

He picked her up by the waist as if she were a child and carried her a few feet away from the wreckage before setting her safely onto the vinyl floor. "Go sit at the table."

She scowled. Did he really have the gall to order her around?

Well, he deserved to have to serve her anyway. She held her chin up and marched to the table, knowing she looked like a drama queen but not caring in the least. A good hostess would make the sandwich for him, clean up the mess, and insist he take a load off, especially since his muscles had to still ache from their freeze. She, however, was determined to be the worst hostess ever and make him pay. If he hurt, served him right.

An invisible finger tapped a warning on her heart. If Jesus were present, He would probably have an eyebrow raised in her direction.

But she shrugged off the reminder. Seventy times seven, blah, blah, blah. It's what her dad tried to tell her earlier, and she hadn't listened then either. Didn't a girl have a right to be mad and get a teeny bit of revenge first?

The guilt continued to crowd in around her, though, as much as she tried to ignore it.

She turned to see Will, on his knees, cleaning up the floor.

Okay, fine. He seemed to be trying anyway. Walking gently on her heels, she made it to the sink and grabbed a rag to wash the mayo off her toes. When her feet were mostly clean, she eyed the bread box. It wouldn't hurt to at least get the bread out. And maybe it would appease God a little, too.

Two freshly made sandwiches with potato chips sat on paper plates at the table by the time Will stood from the floor. She'd need to take a good mop over it in the morning, but at least he'd tried.

He looked at the sandwiches and frowned. "I told you I'd get that."

Had he not even noticed her working around him for the last five minutes? Men could be so oblivious. "I was hungry and tired of waiting." No use having him think he was out of the doghouse quite yet. Because he so, completely, was not.

He nodded and headed to a spot at the table.

"Actually, that one's mine." She bit the side of her lip at his puzzled expression. "I like pickles; you don't."

A flicker of desire flashed across his face, but it disappeared just as fast. "Okay. Thanks."

She should have piled his sandwich full of pickles.

They ate in silence, Hanna examining every inch of the familiar kitchen table her dad had made out of wood from their property. Anything to avoid glancing at the man next to her.

"Hanna?"

She finally peeked at him and saw that he'd only eaten a few bites of his food while she was almost done. "Hm?"

"I'm sorry."

Her heart constricted at the words she should be grateful for. She popped a chip into her mouth and chewed for a moment then swallowed. It would be the right thing to say, "I forgive you," and be done with the matter. Three simple words. But the pain that warred inside her heart couldn't allow it. She just wasn't ready. "You should be."

"I didn't mean—"

Fire burst in her veins, and her fist slammed against the table. "Don't you dare." For the first time since he arrived, she looked him in the eyes—the deep brown depths that less than a year ago she swooned at the sight of and wanted to stare into forever. "Don't you even dare tell me that you didn't mean what you said."

He closed his eyes and lowered his head. "I wasn't going to—"

Her anger launched with as much power as a NASA space shuttle. "Do you know what I had to go through, Will? Do you? The stares? The whispers? The guys who suddenly had interest in me for all the very wrong reasons?" She jumped to her feet and paced the floor, her arms hugging her middle. "You knew how important it was for me to keep my values intact. We'd even talked about it on the show. And what did you go and do? You tell the whole world how great I was in bed. Which, if you recall, you wouldn't even know as you never actually got me there."

"Hanna, I—"

"No. You don't get an out on this one, William. 'Amazing. Definitely.' I believe those were your exact words. I'm sure you figured I would be flattered or something."

He stood up and tried to grab her hand, but she snatched it back. "The name of the show is pretty accurate. *The Price of Love.* Well, I paid a price for it, all right, and it wasn't worth even a penny. I'm sorry if you thought you could waltz back in here, give me your apology, and everything would magically be okay, but it's not going to happen."

His pink cheeks told her he'd thought just that. "Collin egged me on, but it's no excuse. I was an idiot. I want to make it right, Hanna. I don't know how, but I will."

Hanna grabbed her paper plate and tossed it into the trash. She walked over to the stairs and stood for a moment, her fingers gripping the wooden stair rail. Could she forgive him? Just like that? Is that really what God was asking of her?

She dug deep into her heart but found no will, no desire to do so. All that lay there was the scarred remains of her heart. Turning back, she saw Will staring at her, a raw, pleading look in his eyes that slammed against her conscience.

"Please, Hanna. Let me try."

"You're seven months too late, Will." The words burned like sandpaper against skin as she spat them out.

His shoulders slumped, and Hanna forced herself to turn and go up the stairs, ignoring the shards of guilt stabbing at her.

Maybe, with any luck and a few extra prayers, he'd be gone in the morning, and she could start the process of getting him out of her mind—and heart—for the second time.

The next morning, after glancing out her window and seeing the backyard covered in at least two feet of snow, she heard male voices coming from the kitchen. Evidently, neither God nor Dad was joining her on the get-rid-of-Will bandwagon.

She paused at the top of the stairs. Maybe she could just go back to bed.

"I hear you up there, sunshine. Get on down here. Pancakes are on." Her dad's voice was like fingernails pinching her last nerve. How could he betray her and make friends with the enemy? And how dare said enemy intrude on her Saturday morning pancake ritual with her father?

A whiff of fried bacon taunted her nose and lured her to ground level despite her gut reaction to run back to bed and hide out for the rest of the day.

She stopped short at the sight of Will in her frilly pink apron, manning the skillet. He flashed his famous smile, dimples and all. "Bacon's hot. Take a seat."

She'd rather dump the sizzling bacon grease down his pants. "Is there anything I can do to help?"

Her dad flipped another pancake, sending the circle flying high in the air. "Nope, you just sit down and relax."

The traitor. She hoped it smacked him in the face.

Instead, it landed perfectly on the pan, like always. Darn.

She moved to disobey and get plates, but the table caught her eye. Three sets of dishes already graced the table, complete with silverware and goblets her mother had always saved for special occasions.

How she wished Mom was still here. Momma had no tolerance for stupid men, and Will would have been put in his place long ago.

"Mom's special glasses? What for?"

Her dad shrugged as he flipped another cake. "We haven't used them in a long time. Thought this morning was as good as any."

The man was a bona fide liar. Mom would have served Will his breakfast on a napkin if he were lucky. "At least let me pour drinks."

Despite traitor-dee and traitor-dum's insistence that she take a seat, she poured orange juice into each glass. By the time she finished, pancakes sat on a huge platter in the middle of the table, and bacon and eggs were heaped in a bowl.

Just one look at the food and she could sense her scale prepping for her weight gain. "I don't understand why we couldn't just do good old oatmeal this morning. We need to get out and shovel the driveway before we're completely snowed in."

Dad served himself four pancakes and a heap of scrambled eggs. "No need. Will and I took care of it this morning."

Oh, joy. The guy was trying to work his way into her good graces. No way was that going to happen. "Have you seen about Will's car yet?"

"Nope. Figured we'd ride out there after breakfast and see if we can get it out ourselves since the snow seems to have tapered off for now."

"Good luck with that. It was stuck pretty good last night."

Hanna sat the rest of the meal in silence while the men exchanged manly small talk about cars and the latest politics. She only barely restrained herself from plugging her ears and singing *la-la-la-la* at the top of her lungs.

Childish? Yes. But did she care? No. She did, after all, have a degree in elementary education. She was skilled in all things childish.

It didn't help that Will looked ridiculously handsome now that he'd gotten rid of the flannel pajamas and was no longer wearing the pink apron. He'd tamed his short brown hair and changed into a flannel button-down shirt that looked like one of her dad's old ones, prior to his belly having developed a paunch these past few years. While it wasn't Will's normal Armani dress shirt, he still looked annoyingly handsome.

"...took off for two weeks."

Will's words perked Hanna's previously tuned-out ears. "What about two weeks?"

Her dad frowned at her. "Will, here, was saying he's taken two weeks' vacation, so he's in no hurry to go home. Told him while he's stuck here, I might initiate him into some ice fishing."

Oh, golly gee. What luck. "But, Will, surely you want to leave as soon as possible. Embarrass is a far cry from what you're used to in Nashville." If he didn't leave, she would. Carly would let her sleep on her couch. Heck, she'd get a hotel room if she had to.

Two weeks cooped up with Will? Not happening.

He shrugged, his eyes focused on the pancake doused in syrup he was cutting. "Never been ice fishing before. Thought it might be kind of fun." He lifted a bite to his mouth, glanced at her, then winked.

Big. Honking. Jerk. She squinted her eyes at him and gave him the dirtiest look she could muster.

He just wiggled his eyebrows and bit a piece of bacon.

Her dad cleared his throat and glared at both of them. "Now listen, you two. We're adults here. No need to act like two-year-olds."

Hanna slammed her fork down. This had gone too far. Her father was supposed to be on her side. "Dad, you know what he—"

"Hanna." The harsh reply from her father startled her. Her dad never yelled. "Will is a guest in our home. I understand the bad blood between you two. But God has dropped him in our lap, and we have to make the best of it. For the moment, I think a little reconciliation would do both of you some good. I'm not expecting you two to get all kissy-kissy in the next five minutes. In fact, if you do, I'll throw you both out in the snow and lock the doors. But flinging knives with your eyes isn't going to solve a thing. Apologize. Now."

Apologize? She closed her eyes, but in her heart, she knew her dad was right. She'd gone too far. Even if the jerk did deserve it. "Fine. Sorry, Will. You're welcome as long as you need."

He nodded. "Forgiven."

That was just peachy. He was forgiving her. How did things get turned around so fast?

Her father put a napkin on the table and stood. "Will, if you're ready, we'll go take a look at that car of yours while there's a break in the snow."

Will stood, still a little stiff if Hanna read his jerky movements correctly. His body was probably screaming at him from his freeze the day before, not to mention if he really helped shovel snow this morning.

She should offer him some pain meds but, instead, gave him a limp smile and wave. "Well, you both enjoy. I'll just clean up here."

The men left, and she watched through the kitchen window as Will hobbled to the truck.

She sighed. Okay, so withholding meds from a guy in pain wasn't her finest moment. What had gotten into her?

She'd give him some when he got back.

Hanna gathered the dishes and filled the sink with water. Nothing like hot, soapy water to help clear a girl's head.

"Lord, seriously, if You could just keep the whole snow spigot turned off long enough for Will to leave—and maybe miraculously melt the snow around that car—that'd just be amazing."

Because the sooner Will left, the faster she could get back to the process of forgetting about him again.

She was happy without him. Life was moving on. People were forgetting about her—them—finally. She already had a few leads on teaching jobs starting in the fall.

The RESET button was being pushed, and she could pick up where she'd left off a year ago after she'd signed up for that stupid show.

Yes, she was very much content with where her life was heading, and Will just needed to skedaddle on out of here so she could get on with setting everything back to rights.

After putting away the last dish in the cupboard, she hung up the dishrag and headed for the den. It would be awhile before they returned, hopefully with good news, so she grabbed a novel—a non-romance unlike what she used to read pre-Will—and settled on the couch.

She was starting chapter three when Dad and Will stomped through the door, looking like abominable snowmen. She dog-eared her spot and set aside the book. "Any luck?"

Her dad shook his head. "Nope. We'll need a tow truck, and have you looked at the weather lately?"

God, please— "No, let me see if any news is on." She picked up the remote and clicked to the weather channel.

A map of the United States appeared on the screen, and it was as clear as if they'd written, "Ha, ha, Hanna! You're stuck with him!" at the top of the map.

The whole northern portion of Minnesota and North Dakota was covered in bright pink, and a blizzard warning scrolled at the bottom of the screen.

CHAPTER FIVE

*S*unny beaches.

Warm sand sifting between her toes.

A dip in the pool to cool her sun-kissed skin.

A nice fruity nonalcoholic drink with a cute little umbrella in it just for fun.

No snow forcing her archnemesis to stay at her house for an undetermined period of time.

Hanna opened her eyes, her daydream replaced with flurries of self-pity.

The sight of Will and her father playing checkers at the kitchen table made her want to scream. Didn't they realize her agony over here? Couldn't they mope around and be glum with her?

Scratch that. She'd rather them be far away from her right now. Especially Will.

Her dad turned in his chair toward the den and raised his eyebrow. "Hanna, you gonna play the winner?"

Considering he was a master at checkers, and maybe it would make Will go to another part of the house for a while, the idea held promise. "Sure."

He scooted his chair back and stood. "Good, because this young man just beat the pants off me. Besides, it's past my bedtime."

The big stinkin' liar. It was barely eight o'clock. And her dad never, ever lost at checkers.

She stretched and faked a yawn. "I don't know. Now that you mention it, I'm kinda beat myself."

Will's expression turned to a smirk. "Afraid I'll win?"

Hanna gave her best snarl back at him. "No, I'm afraid I'll make you cry like a girl when I wipe the floor with you."

He cocked an eyebrow. "I'll take my chances."

Trying not to stomp too hard, she walked to the table and slouched into the chair her dad had just vacated. "Fine. But I'm red."

Wordlessly, Will began arranging the board with red on her side. When finished, he nodded to her. "Ladies first."

She tried not to snort her irritation at his fake gentlemanly manners, but the noise left her nose before she could stop it. Still, she moved her first piece and raised an eyebrow to him.

The game continued in silence, jumps, moves, kings, until all that remained on the board were three red kings and two lonesome black pieces.

Hanna smirked. "Give up yet?"

He studied the board and responded without looking up. "Do pigs fly?"

"They'll be flapping their wings long before you win this game."

Will tapped a checker with a finger while staring at the board. Surely he didn't think he could really beat her at this point in the game? The man was quite stubborn, though, as she recalled.

He looked up from the board and caught her eye. "What about a truce?"

The man had some gall. He was in the losing spot. There was no way he could win, yet he wanted her to call it even? She looked him in the eye, ready to give him a piece of her mind.

His burning gaze stopped her short.

He wasn't talking about the game anymore. And given that she had no desire to talk about the thoughts running through his head, she pushed away from the table. "Fine. It's a tie. I'm going to bed."

A voice laced in desperation beckoned her back. "Please, Hanna? Can we please just talk about it?"

She stood against the island in the kitchen, her hands grasping the edge of the counter. Talking wouldn't help. It would be like ripping duct tape off an already gaping wound. "What you did to me was wrong, Will. No amount of talking will help."

Out of the corner of her eye, she saw him stand from the table and take a step closer. "I know it won't solve everything. But I don't know what else to do."

Did he really think they could just talk through this? He'd crushed and humiliated her then left her heart crumbled. He needed to be reminded of that. "Wait here."

Running up the stairs, she went to her room. Lying flat on the ground, she pushed aside the lacy, homemade bed skirt and stretched her arm far underneath the full-size bed until her fingers grazed cardboard.

After pulling it out, Hanna stared at the old shoe box.

When she'd first started it, the collection had been an obsession. Her dad had told her to ignore it all. But something drove her to keep every single one. In a way, it had been a reminder to her. Every piece within confirmed that letting the walls of her heart down was a horrible idea.

At one point, she'd almost started believing the lies. What if there was some truth to them? What if she'd done something that had not only tarnished her name but God's as well?

But slowly, the news had slowed to a trickle until now, where there was little if any mention.

She hadn't opened the box in over a month. Had slid it under the bed, deciding the past was best left where it was. In the past.

The box in hand, she turned, more determined than ever, and made her way back downstairs.

Will still sat at the table, the checkers game put away. He glanced up, and she vowed not to let the puppy-dog look in his eyes stir her heart into pudding like it used to.

He eyed the box. "What's in there?"

She slammed it down on the table in front of him, bracing herself for the memories sure to come flooding back. "Open it and see."

Will stared at the box, more than a little nervous about its contents.

Lifting the lid, he frowned at the crammed papers inside.

He picked up the one on top, a tabloid article. The heading read HANNA'S NOT SO HOLY AFTER ALL. Thumbing through the others that included newspaper clippings and online printouts of blogs, he felt bile rise in his stomach, and he wanted to puke. He'd done this to her. Sure, he'd seen a few papers at the time but hadn't let himself read them. Had turned his back at the sight of them, not wanting to know the full impact of his stupidity, except for how it affected his business.

But the truth was spelled out in black and white, and in the case of one magazine article, in full color.

REALITY CHECK: VIRGINITY ISN'T ALL IT'S CRACKED UP TO BE.

AMERICA'S REALITY SWEETHEARTS SEAL THE DEAL, BEDROOM-STYLE.

HOLY HANNA'S FALL FROM GRACE.

DENIAL, THY NAME IS HANNA.

Will put the papers back in the box and started to close the lid, but Hanna shook her head and opened it again. "Not so fast. That stuff you knew about." She dug to the bottom and pulled out a thick rubber-banded stack of letters. "There are also e-mails and letters from pastors, women's ministry leaders, and a host of other people all calling me to repent from my sin and turn away, offering their assistance. A few fun ones even told me how I was going to burn in hell because I disgraced the Christian religion and Jesus Himself. I had to change my e-mail address and shut down my Facebook account."

Will gripped the side of the table. He wanted to take her in his arms, hold her, and tell her how very, very sorry he was, but it wasn't enough. It would never be enough to erase the pain and humiliation he'd caused.

How do I fix this? Think, Will, think.

At his heart, that was Will. A fix-it man. He researched problems. Found solutions. And empowered others to implement while he oversaw. It's what made him a great researcher. It's what helped him rise through the ranks and achieve the level of CEO at the rare age of thirty-five.

But this problem was proving to be the hardest one yet.

"Hanna, I don't know what to say. I had no idea."

She snorted. "Of course you didn't. You were too busy shacking up with other women at the time."

He stood so fast the chair toppled over behind him. "That's not true. I haven't slept with anyone since—"

"Since you told everyone you slept with me?"

He closed his eyes in shame. A few months ago, he'd have denied her words, claimed that he hadn't said it, that the press just took his jesting and ran with it. But deep in his gut, he had to admit that his arrogant words claiming they'd "gotten to know each other *real* well" had been meant to spark the host's imagination. "Yes."

"For some reason, I have a hard time believing that."

Not that he blamed her. His history wasn't the most stellar. And the media hadn't been kind to him either. "Believe what you want, Hanna, but I promise you, I haven't."

She shrugged, her fingers letting loose a pile of papers, sprinkling clippings all over the table. "I guess it doesn't matter if I believe you."

Will watched as she walked back into the den, picked up the remote, and flipped the TV on as if she didn't have a care in the world. Looking back at the clippings and letters, Will clenched his jaw.

He would make this right.

He just had no clue how.

A gasp from Hanna brought his attention back to the den. She sat frozen on the couch, the remote lying on the floor, her mouth gaped open.

"Hanna?" He walked closer, but she didn't respond.

Then he saw the entertainment news channel on, their faces plastered across the screen. Fear furrowed into his gut. "What are they saying about us?" He grabbed the remote and clicked up the volume.

"*. . .over six months ago that America's reality TV heartthrobs turned into enemies after the CEO of Foster and Jones, William Preston, claimed to have gotten the oh-so-religious, would-be virgin, Hanna Knight, to be, shall we say, not quite so religious in the bedroom during their free weekend on the reality TV show,* The Price of Love. *But could this feuding couple be getting back together again?*

"*Sources tell us they may be secluded away together up in the frozen North Minnesota area, waiting out a massive blizzard that slammed the area yesterday. And given the pictures of Hanna's suspicious baby bump a month ago, this might not have been the first time Will has journeyed up North. Could we be hearing baby rattles soon instead of wedding bells?*"

He clicked the Power button as the news switched to some other, most likely untrue, celebrity gossip. His hand gripped the remote so tight, he felt the plastic threaten to buckle, but it was either that or throw the stupid thing across the room.

How dare they put such idiotic, untrue news on TV like that?

Well, the part about them secluded in a snowstorm was accurate, but how had they found that out? His mother, Hanna, and Jim were the only ones who knew where he was.

And the board of directors. Surely they wouldn't. . .

But then again, their edict for him to come up here and "fix" things had been pretty clear. As in, emergency board meeting scheduled after the latest dip in sales figures came in for last month.

Clearly, they didn't feel he was up to doing the job himself.

Neither did he. But this was over the top, even for them.

Hanna sniffled beside him, and he choked down his anger when he saw the tears cresting over her eyes, leaving a sorrowful path down her cheeks. Every inch of him desired nothing more than to take her in his arms and hold her. Well, that wasn't completely true. Quite a few inches wanted to jump through that old TV screen and blacken a few TV producers' eyes.

Then yet another inch wanted to wring his own neck because he knew if it wasn't for his big mouth and ego, they wouldn't be in this mess in the first place.

Not able to stand it any longer, Will sat and put an arm around Hanna and tugged her to him. To his utter amazement, she came willingly and burrowed her face against his chest.

Memories of their whirlwind relationship jammed into his thoughts with the same force as the bitter wind that slapped against the farmhouse, all brought back by the incredible sensation of having Hanna in his arms. Her silky blond hair tickling his chin, the scent of whatever fruity shampoo she must use luring him.

The last time they'd been like this, Hanna hadn't been crying because she was sad. She'd been sobbing because she was so happy. They'd picked each other, and their future together was finally theirs to live. He'd even proposed to her on national television, much to the delight of their fans and the groans of all the show's critics who claimed there was no way to fall in love in so short a time with cameras rolling and millions of people watching.

His board had been happy then, too. Their plan had worked.

He, however, hadn't been quite so ecstatic. As much as he liked Hanna, the whole show was a sham. His love life used to increase sales. He'd already felt uneasy about the whole thing. Maybe that's why it had been so easy to go with the flow in that stupid final interview.

There was one moment he thought it all might work out. After the final taping, they'd spent one wonderful, glorious evening together, just the two of them. No cameras to capture their every movement. No microphones to record their every word. No producer to dictate the scene. And most of all, no other women waiting for their turn at a date. It was perfect.

Then the show began to air. And his careless words ruined it all.

CHAPTER SIX

regnant. The world now thought she was having a baby. Hanna snuggled in closer to the flannel shirt beneath her face. She wanted to call herself all kinds of a fool for letting him hold her, but she couldn't relinquish the warmth she felt being in his arms again. His hand rubbed her back while she listened to his heart beating strong and steady against her ear.

For a moment, she allowed herself to dream. What would it have been like had Will not been such a prideful, arrogant jerk? Would they still be engaged, planning a wedding, or would they have settled on a date for sometime in the last six months and already be enjoying wedded bliss? They'd never even talked about children, but she'd wanted them eventually.

Acid burned in her stomach as she realized she might never get her dream. What respectable guy would want to marry a girl who'd been the reality TV scandal of the year? The possibility of a camera at her side, shooting pictures and extorting the truth, would always linger.

A warm sensation pressed against her forehead, spinning her back toward reality. She was snuggling with the very man who had caused this whole rotten mess. Where was her head? Pushing out of his arms, she looked in his eyes but caught her breath. She wanted to scream at him, beat him with her fists for what he had done to her. But the compassion and sorrow that shone through those eyes made it impossible.

Could Will have really changed?

No. It was all an act, just like the whole show had been.

Pushing back, she scooted to the other end of the couch and brought her knees to her chin, forming a much-needed barrier between them. "It looks like you've made things even worse now."

Will's face hardened, then he blinked and shook his head. "If I did, I'm sorry. I didn't think they would find out I was here."

"Who all did you tell?"

He sat back on the couch, covered his face with his hands and let out a low growl of frustration, then lowered them to cross his arms over his chest. "Only Mom. And she swore she wouldn't tell a soul. And—"

Hanna wasn't sure she wanted to hear the *and* part. "Yes?"

"I was going to tell you eventually, but—"

Hanna pushed up from the couch. "What, did ENC put you up to coming back out? Want to do a reconciliation show or something? It's not happening, Will. I'm not going back on TV. Ever."

Will stood and put a hand on her arm, but she shoved him off. "Don't you dare touch me. I can't believe you thought I would go through with this."

Will's strong, square jaw locked. "It wasn't ENC who asked me to come."

"Then who?"

"Foster and Jones."

Hanna shook her head. "Your company? What do they care?"

Will put a hand through his hair. "Sales dropped."

"And what does that have to do with me? I mean, I'll be honest. I haven't bought Skintell or any F&J makeup in ages, or any of that other stuff. Except for when the show dolled me up, I'm pretty much a lip-gloss-and-go kind of girl. And my lotion and soap are whatever I get on sale. But I doubt my nonpurchases warrant a personal appearance by the CEO."

Will shook his head. "No, but our customers are mostly women. And evidently women weren't too keen on how I handled myself with you either. Our sales took an initial dive after the show finished airing, the exact opposite of what they'd wanted."

Realization blasted her like a gun going off directly into her stomach. "Wait a second. You mean to tell me, the only reason you did the show was to boost sales?"

"Hanna, the only reason any of the executives do the show is to boost sales. It's how they sold my board on it. And the reason my board demanded I do it or risk losing my job. Sometimes I wonder if it's the only reason I was promoted to CEO in the first place."

Yes, she remembered the conversations. A young CEO, appointed in an unprecedented move by a board of directors determined to turn a failing company around after rumors of scandal and fraud by their former president.

She'd known Will was insecure in his job, something he'd shared with her privately, off camera only. In conversations she'd kept hush about even when she really wanted to air every shred of dirty laundry she knew about him.

"So, did you pick me at the direction of your board, too?"

"No." The reply was quick and firm. "*I* picked you, Hanna. That was all my choice."

She noted the absence of the word *love*. "So now what? You think your board set you up? Made you come here then leaked it to the press?"

He walked to look out the front window, his arms folded against his broad chest. "Something like that." He turned to face her again.

"All I know is sales never recovered. We thought the initial dive was a knee-jerk reaction from consumers. But they got worse. This last month threatened to put us in the red for the first time since they ousted Greg Kasinzisky. We have less than two months of the fiscal year left, and we have to bring things back up. Otherwise, I'm out of a job."

Hanna fell back onto the couch and crossed a leg underneath her. "So, what, you come up here, trying to woo me back into your good graces to save your company?"

"No. Sort of. Fine, that's what they hoped. But what I hoped for was—forgiveness, I guess. I didn't expect you to fall into my arms, Hanna. But I've wanted to make this right for months. The board just gave me a little push."

Hanna took one look at him and, against her better judgment, believed him. It would be so easy to assume he was lying yet again. That he'd tipped off the paparazzi just to get the two of them in the news again.

But the look of remorse in his eyes didn't seem like a put-on to her. But, then again, she'd thought him legit before, and look how that turned out.

Hanna wrapped a curl of her hair around her index finger, then unwrapped it, then wrapped it again. Her mother had always lectured her to stop, but at least she didn't chew on the ringlet like she did as a kid. "What's done is done. But what are we going to do about it? Obviously, we can't let them think that—"

Will sat beside her on the couch. "We'll send an e-mail."

Was he completely dense? "Oh, that would be just peachy. I can see the headlines now. 'Will and Hanna send e-mail from romantic hideaway. . .or delivery room?' "

"I just meant to send an e-mail, clarifying your nonpregnant state, and leave it at that. The rest is none of their business."

Hanna uncurled her legs and stood to face him. "You know as well as I do they'll make it their business regardless of our requests or silence. They'll exaggerate this thing as much as they can, and I'll be even more ruined than I was before."

Will stood to meet her, his voice firm. "You aren't ruined, and I'll find a way to fix this. I promise."

"Hanna?" Her father's voice floated down the front steps. "Everything okay down there?"

She pressed a finger to her eye to try and stop the tear that threatened to fall. "I'm fine, Dad. Just getting ready to head up."

His footsteps thumped against the stairs, and a moment later he stood at the entryway to the den, his eyes shooting bullets in Will's direction. "Don't make me ask you to leave in a blizzard. I warned you."

As much as she hated it, she couldn't let him think the worst. "No, it wasn't his fault. Not entirely anyway. The media got ahold of the juicy gossip that Will is stranded up here."

Her dad looped his fingers in the belt loop of his blue flannel robe. "Well, that doesn't seem horrible to me. It's true."

She shook her head. "They also think he's here to witness the birth of our nonexistent child."

He scratched his head and cringed. "That does put a crick in things, doesn't it? Well, you'll just have to set 'em straight."

Like that would really work. Reporters would twist their words and report only what they wanted to hear.

And even worse would be social media.

Memories crowded in—of being glued to the computer, seeing the horrible comments made by people who knew nothing about the situation. Blog after blog after blog talked about her and philosophized every angle possible. Christians wrote how she was making a mockery of the sanctity of marriage. And everyone else wrote about how she was a poster child for why abstinence was so stupid—why couldn't she just have sex and be proud of it? They asked.

Facebook memes with her face and stupid catchy phrases beside her were shared thousands of times. The hashtag #holyhanna even trended on Twitter for a day or two.

Not to mention the onslaught of late-night hosts switching from making fun of her to asking her to come on their shows.

No thanks.

Her dad turned and started back up the front stairs. "You aren't going to figure anything out tonight. We'll discuss it in the morning."

Sleep. Her dad's answer to everything.

Hanna turned to Will. "You do know an e-mail declaring my nonpregnant status won't change anything. They'll still think we're shacking up regardless of our chaperone."

"Then we'll do something else."

The guy had an ego the size of Canada. Did he really think he could fix everything with the snap of his executive fingers? She sat back down. "So tell me, Mr. Smarty-pants, what grand scheme do you have in mind that will magically fix everything?"

Will paced the length of the living room and back. Several times. His hand rubbed his jaw, and she could see the wheels churning in his head.

Then he stopped and looked at her, his eyes sporting a cautious spark that made her heart shiver in trepidation.

She didn't even want to ask but couldn't help herself. "What'd you think of?"

He inhaled, took two steps forward, and dropped to one knee.

"Hanna, will you marry me?"

CHAPTER SEVEN

*H*anna needed a Q-tip. There must be wax in her ears. Or she was having a bad case of déjà vu. The words were the exact same ones Will used that day, surrounded by flowers, with a billion cameras rolling and her heart fluttering so fast she thought it would take flight. "Did you just ask me to marry you again? Are you out of your mind?"

Will remained on his knee, his hand grasping hers in a death grip. "It's the only way to get the press on our good side, Hanna. Think about it."

The man's brain must have frozen more than she'd thought. Brain damage. Not good. "You've got to be kidding." She closed her eyes and took a long, exaggerated breath. "Okay. I've thought about it. The answer is 'in your dreams.'"

Will got up and slid onto the couch next to her. "We won't actually get married. Just engaged. We'll clarify our nonbaby status and that we won't be living together until we're married. Have a 'someday in the future' wedding date. And eventually, we'll be old news. Then we'll have an amicable split up and go our separate ways."

The idea was ludicrous. Stupid. Insane. Ridiculous. Brilliant. Why was she even contemplating this? He was only suggesting it because, like always, he was looking after himself.

Hanna pressed herself against the far end of the couch and crossed her arms. "You just want to do this to save your job."

"I'd be lying if I said it didn't factor into the equation." He shifted in his seat. "But this will help both of us. It'll restore your dignity, make an honest woman of you."

Fury shot through her veins. How dare he even go there? "Excuse me? An honest woman? You're the one—"

He held up a hand and interrupted her. "You know what I meant. In the eyes of the media. We both know nothing happened."

"And never will happen."

Will shifted closer to her, but she was out of room to move away. "Just hear me out. It'll not only help me keep my job, but it'll help right the wrong I did to you. I really am sorry, Hanna, whether you believe me or not."

She didn't know what to believe anymore. He sounded honest, but she still had an overwhelming urge to gouge his eyes out with her nails. That couldn't be a good Christian thing to feel. William Preston brought out the worst in her these days. Could she really fake an engagement with him?

And then there was the whole honesty thing. How would God feel about her lying to a nation? She was probably already on His naughty list for even doing the show in the first place. One more tick on the chart wasn't going to change things.

Oh, good grief. What was she thinking? Was she actually considering such a crazy scheme? "If we did this, what would it look like? How long are we talking?"

Will whipped out his ever-present phone that had more gadgets and apps than the Inspector himself. A few taps on the touch screen and a calendar popped up. "Let's see. I have eleven days left of the two weeks I told them this would take. If we send a press release tomorrow, then spend the next week or so making it look like we are a happily engaged couple, I think that would work. Then I could fly back and. . ."

"And what? We just stay 'engaged' and never see each other, and the paparazzi is miraculously okay with that? We can only feign a long-distance relationship for so long. I'm not working up here, Will. They'll want to know why I'm not moving."

Will looked up from his phone, his brow crinkled in a V shape, the same way it always did when he frowned. "Wait. You aren't teaching anymore? Why not?"

"No one wants their child taught by the lady who was the reality TV scandal of the year."

"They fired you? Because if they did, I'll have my lawyer—"

"Hush, William." Him and his money. The man tried to talk, buy, or sue his way out of everything. The real, non-upper class didn't work that way. "I quit. Parents were asking questions and looking down their noses at me. I couldn't teach like that. I've been doing some subbing and might go back full-time once I'm completely old news. I was hoping by next year they'd forget about all of this, but now. . ."

Now everything would be opened back up like the fresh, gaping wound it was. January was almost over. The next school year would start in eight short months. Granted, the recent season of *The Price of Love* just ended, and Jeff and MaryJane were supposedly enjoying engaged bliss, so maybe something would happen to them to take the spotlight off Will and Hanna.

There was evil Hanna coming out again. How mean could she get? Really, she wished them all the happiness in the world, even though her own happily-ever-after had turned out to be a sour grape of wrath and disappointment.

Will put his other hand on top of hers and squeezed. "We'll figure it out. Maybe you can take a few vacations down to Nashville.

Do some pretend apartment hunting. And I can make a few trips back up here, too."

It all sounded way too complicated. Couldn't she just kick him to the street and let the press get over this newest complication? But it had taken six months to get them to shut up the first time. Baby drama might keep things going even longer.

And Nashville didn't seem a horrible place for a vacation. Cool versus frigid. But cash was almost nonexistent right now, with the farm barely holding its own and Hanna's decrease in income. Frequent vacations weren't a luxury she could afford.

And she would *not* be asking Will to pay. She had a little pride left.

"Hanna? What do you say?"

His voice jammed into the gears of her brain. What should she say? Crazy, that's what it was. Pure and utter craziness. "My dad would never agree to it. He'd probably send you packing in the middle of the blizzard if he even knew you suggested it."

A thump sounded on the stairs, and her dad appeared. "Actually, I don't think it's that bad of an idea. He's got a problem; you've got a problem. Working together sounds like a great solution, aye?"

A fist pump in the air would be completely inappropriate and unprofessional.

But it took every ounce of strength in Will's body not to jump and holler like they used to do when his basketball team in college scored the winning point.

And even scarier was his desire to pick up his pretend fiancée and kiss the breath right out of her.

A scowl that would melt a glacier kept him from that particular urge.

Hanna stomped over to the steps, hands on her hips, looking

ready to do war. "What do you mean? Dad, do you even know what we're talking about?"

Jim took a few more steps to the middle of the stairs where they could see his face. "Course I do. Getting engaged, but not really, to get those reporters off your back. I think it's a fine idea."

"But it's lying, Dad. You always taught me—"

"I don't recall teaching you to go bartering yourself off on national television either, and remember how well you listened to me then? You got yourself into a pickle, and Will here got himself into one, too. Seems to me, you were engaged once. Don't remember you officially calling it quits either. If memory serves me right, you just refused to answer phone calls from the press, ENC, or Will. No reason you can't wait awhile longer to officially call it off."

Will grinned at the man's logic. A little lopsided maybe, but it was the truth. No formal statement was ever given to the press. Or to him either, for that matter.

When he'd called, she'd yelled "JERK" into the phone, and then he'd heard only the monotone hum of the disconnected call.

After a few repeats of that, he got the voice of an operator informing him the number was no longer in service. Hanna had shut out Will and the world.

On his end, the official statement his lawyer put together, in an attempt to save face for the company, was that they were taking some mutually agreed-upon time apart and would appreciate privacy in their personal relationship.

After that, he repeated "No comment" so many times, he started to say it to his assistant when she asked him questions.

Eventually the hype died down, but the blemish to his character remained, as evidenced in last quarter's sales figures.

"He's right, Hanna. We're just continuing where we left off. Sure, we doubt it will go anywhere, but what's the harm in trying?"

Hanna whirled around, her wide eyes shooting virtual snowballs at him. Snowballs filled with ice—and darts—and maybe bullets. "We doubt it will go anywhere? That's a far stretch, and you know it."

The cell phone in Will's pocket vibrated, notifying him of a text message. He pulled it from his pocket and glanced at the message from Emma, his executive assistant.

ENC CALLED. WANTS SCOOP B4 PRESS. REPORTERS CALLING, 2 MANY 2 LIST. WHAT DO U WANT ME 2 TELL THEM?

Will tapped the bottom of the phone with his finger, deciding how to reply. Hanna peeked over his shoulder.

As she read, her shoulders stooped. "Great. It's begun. What are you going to say?"

"It depends. Are we still engaged?"

She turned and walked to look out the window. "Do I have a choice?"

He glanced down at his phone then tapped in his response on the screen.

No COMMENT. FOR NOW.

CHAPTER EIGHT

Snow, snow, go away. Come back again. . .after Will leaves.

The weather refused to listen to Hanna's ranting. The Doppler radar showed more of the wet stuff headed their way after three days of on-and-off blizzard conditions.

Will had been on the phone the first day constantly, or, that is, when he could get a signal. They'd drafted a joint statement then waited anxiously for the entertainment news that evening.

Not a mention.

Even the Internet seemed eerily quiet. Maybe the story the other day had been a fluke. Maybe everyone really was past it and didn't care.

But then, an A-lister had gotten arrested, and another one had eloped. Reality TV drama was the leftovers, brought out when nothing else good was on the table.

The tabloids could be having a heyday, though, and the outcome of that would be seen as early as today.

At least they didn't have to worry about humiliating pictures. They'd had one whole day without snow right after the announcement, but there was no way a reporter would risk their life in this mess just for a picture.

Hanna's greatest hope was that there'd be no mention at all.

They'd see the happy couple update, roll their eyes, and move on to the next, juicier story.

Oh, Lord, let it be so.

After clicking off the television for the night, Hanna tossed the remote onto the old coffee table, creating another little nick in the wood to go with the hundreds it had collected over the years. "I'm off to bed."

Will and her dad were in the middle of an intense game—chess this time. Hanna refused to play anymore because she fought the urge to hurl knights at Will the whole time.

"You sure you don't want to play the winner?" Will winked at her.

She wished he would stop doing that. Her insides rebelled every time and did a little jig without her permission. Traitors. "No thanks. You haven't heard anything more, have you?"

He ignored her as he studied the board.

"Fine, well, let me know if you do."

Will held up a finger. "Wait, hold on a second." He picked up a knight and shifted it into place. "Checkmate."

Her dad scooted back his chair. "Need to learn to respect your elders, son, and let them win a few times."

"Sorry, sir."

He patted Will on the shoulder, a teasing grin on his weathered lips. "Just don't let it happen again. This old man needs to go to bed and lick his wounded pride." He put an arm around Hanna and pressed a kiss to the top of her head. "Night, sugar."

"Night, Dad."

As the older man made his way upstairs, Will cocked his head toward the empty seat. "You sure you don't want a shot at me?"

"Oh, I do. But a hockey stick or baseball bat might do better than a chair."

He pulled out his ever-present phone and ignored her jab. "I got a text during the game but ignored it. Let me see. . ."

Hanna straightened her back and steeled herself for whatever news there might be. "What is it?"

Will studied the screen. And continued to study it. And took way too long for Hanna's comfort. "What's wrong? What does it say?"

He looked up at her, his brown eyes containing an expression she wasn't sure she'd ever seen before. A mixture of remorse, sadness, and almost. . .almost rage. "You don't want to see this. It doesn't matter anyway. They just need time."

It couldn't be that bad, could it? Maybe they still thought she was pregnant. Had edited in a bigger baby bump. Whatever it was, she needed to face it. Not seeing it wasn't an option. "Give me the phone, Will."

"Sit down first."

Dread slugged her in the gut. "Let me see it *now*."

He handed her the phone.

A picture of the front page of a disgusting tabloid made her knees buckle underneath her. As the world tilted and everything fuzzed, strong arms scooped her up.

CHAPTER NINE

Familiar, scratchy fabric pricked at her fingers. Something fuzzy draped across her body. Warmth caressed her cheeks then her forehead. What was going on?

Hanna peeked open an eye, and her breath caught in her throat. Will knelt beside the couch, his hands rubbing her face.

She batted them away. "What do you think you're doing?"

"You fainted."

"And that gives you permission to get all handsy on me?" She couldn't let him know that her face had loved it. . .until she'd come to her senses. "Besides, I don't faint."

"You do now. You scared me."

"Where's Dad?"

"I didn't get him yet. Wanted to give you a second to wake up first before I panicked him."

At least Will could do *something* right. "Well, don't. He'll be hauling me out in this stupid blizzard thinking I need a doctor or something. Which, by the way, I don't."

"You're spunky. Anyone ever tell you that?"

Not spunky enough, given that she'd fainted. Why in the world— Then she remembered the article cover.

She curled into a ball and rolled to face the plaid polyester couch cushion. Their plan had backfired. Royally.

SEX SCANDAL: HANNA the SEX ADDICT is PREGNANT WITH ANOTHER GUY'S BABY—but Will says he's still in love with her anyway.

Worse still, there was a picture. Somehow, a reporter had made their way up here, despite the snow and warnings, and snapped a shot of them outside. The one nonblizzard day, when they'd gone outside to check on the chickens in the barn, someone had gotten a photo.

Right after Will had thrown a snowball at her.

Hanna, dressed in an oversized parka that made her look about six months pregnant or more from the right angle, yelled at him before launching a missile of her own.

And her angry face, along with Will's pleading expression, is what the camera caught. She looked like a maniac.

"This can't be happening, Will. We've made everything worse."

Will rubbed her back in a circular motion. She should make him stop. But everything was just so crazy. And honestly, she liked his hand there. Needed it even.

"I'm sorry, Hanna. But remember, these are the trashy tabloids we're talking about. No one really listens to them anyway. People know they make things up. It's the social media and entertainment news we really care about."

"Yeah, but they are ignoring us. All everyone hears is 'pregnant.'"

"But you're not. And in a few months, it will be quite clear to everyone when there isn't a baby Hanna anywhere."

"They'll probably report that baby Wilanna was abducted by aliens."

"I hope they do. It'd just underline their ridiculousness."

A tame beeping came from his pocket. Who had such a boring ringtone?

As Will answered the call, Hanna made a mental note to change it sometime for him. No fiancé, real or not, could have a yawn-worthy phone. He needed a cool cover, too. Maybe some leopard print. Or better yet, she could get out her old bedazzle kit and decorate it really cute.

Oh, how she could make his life miserable.

Just like he'd made hers.

She turned to see Will pacing the living room while he talked. "Yes, I saw it. Not what we were going for." Pause. "I don't care about that. I want it fixed." Pause. "Do you think someone's feeding them?" Pause. "I'm not an idiot, Sam. I'm well aware of that. But this is just crazy. You and I both know it." Pause. "Fine, we'll fly back the first chance we get."

Hanna threw off the brown furry blanket that covered her and jumped to her feet. "Wait a second. We? Fly?"

Will held up a finger to his lips to shush her then continued to talk into the phone. "It depends on the weather. Their Internet is spotty up here, so I only have the news stations and my phone to rely on. I'm lucky to get data reception at all. Can you look at the forecast for me?"

He was doing it again. Fixing everything without even consulting her. He didn't know everything. And she was not flying *anywhere* with him anytime soon. "Don't shush me, William Preston. I'm not going anywhere."

He gave her a look then spoke into the phone. "Can you hold on a second?"

A second later, he took her hand and yanked her toward him, causing her to crash into his side. His arm wrapped around her waist and pressed her flat against him. "Hanna, you have to trust me. I'm trying to fix this. So unless you want me to kiss you to quiet you down, I suggest you hush. I'm game either way."

Breathing was impossible for Hanna. The memory of their kisses, their magnificent, off-camera kisses that reduced her to a pile of wobbly Jell-O, flitted in her brain. Those kisses had made staying "Holy Hanna" very difficult that weekend.

Maybe just this once. . .

But Will took her silence as agreement and went back to his conversation. "So it clears up after Sunday? Well, go ahead and book us on a flight Monday afternoon. We can always change it if we need to, but that should work well for now. Tell Emma to get a name and number from any reputable outlet that calls, and ask what they have in mind. Other than that, remember—"

He chuckled for a moment and nodded his head. "Exactly. No comment."

The man was going to "no comment" his way to no job if he didn't watch it.

After he slipped the phone back into his pocket, Hanna raised her head in question. "Care to explain?"

"I'd love to. But unless you'd like that kiss, I suggest we sit back down."

Hanna glanced down to where she was still snuggled to his side then jumped away faster than a frog in a frying pan. She plopped onto the couch and hugged a throw pillow to her belly for protection.

Will sat in the brown leather recliner across the room. "If we can't make them believe our press release, then we have to go to them. You said yourself you aren't working right now. So we'll do a couple face-to-face interviews. Show them your nice trim figure, and that'll be that."

"I still have a life, ya know. And I help Dad here on the farm."

"He managed before."

What did he know about how her dad managed? "He had a helper. His helper quit, and he was struggling. It's the middle of winter, a pretty bad one at that."

"From what I've seen, right now the only thing he has to do is feed the chickens and make his own food. Pretty sure he can deal with that on his own, Hanna. Should we ask him in the morning?"

As much as she loved to use her dad as an excuse, that plan had backfired once before. "Fine, so we leave on Monday if the weather permits. Who will be interviewing us?"

"Haven't decided that yet. We'll find out who's offering then make a decision. That fair?"

The whole thing sounded foolish, expensive, and insane. "Well, your travel guru will need my credit card for my ticket. And where will I be staying?"

A throw pillow flew across the room, and Hanna snatched it before it plowed her in the face. "What was that for?"

He leaned forward, elbows on his knees, determination in his dark brown eyes. "If you think for a minute I'm letting you pay a dime of this, you're out of your mind. And you'll be staying at a nice, classy hotel with all the trimmings."

Lovely. Now she sounded like his mistress he was secreting away. "Ooh là là. Careful, I might faint again, Mr. Moneybags."

"Don't give me credit for that. I fully plan on expensing this to the company. They're the ones who got us into this mess in the first place."

She tossed the pillow back at him. "You're the one that signed up for the show and let your macho ego run wild."

"I'll take the blame for the ego thing. Fully my fault. But the show, that was most certainly not me."

"So you really didn't want to do it at all?"

He shook his head. "The producers approached a board member, and they all thought it was a grand idea. Their young, new CEO becoming America's reality heartthrob, or some nonsense like that."

"I guess you were thankful I bailed on you then, huh? Saved you the misery."

His eyes bore into her even from ten feet away. "That day I called you only to be hung up on was the worst day of my life."

Hanna shook her head. She didn't want to sympathize with him. He didn't deserve it. Time to change the subject. "So, we have a weekend of snow to endure. I hope you like checkers and chess a whole stinkin' lot."

"Actually, your dad said if it lets up a little tomorrow, he might take me ice fishing."

Hanna smiled. Oh, how she prayed it would let up long enough. Stiff-shirt Will in the middle of a frozen lake with a pole in the ice. She would give a million dollars to see that.

CHAPTER TEN

*W*ill clutched the armrest of the truck. What crazy person drove on a lake? Frozen or not, there had to be some law against it.

But as far as he could see, little ice houses—if the small shacks could be called houses—sprinkled the snow-covered ice, a little street plowed out in the midst of it all.

"Are you sure this is safe, Jim?"

"Of course I'm sure. Wouldn't take you out here if it wasn't. This lake has been frozen solid since first of December. No one's even fallen in this year."

That would leave the assumption that in past years people *had* fallen in.

Will took a deep breath and let it out. He would not be a pansy about this. He was a man. He could ice fish. At least he'd been a science major, so with a little guidance, he could probably clean a fish. Dissecting he could do.

But ice? He doubted he could even walk on it. In Nashville, if it flurried, schools shut down for a week.

Jim parked in front of a dilapidated shanty and hopped out of the truck. "Hurry up. We're missing the good ones."

Will opened the door, swung his legs to the sideboard, and edged the toe of the boot Jim had loaned him onto the ice as a test.

It slid over the ground.

Test failed.

Sitting in the truck, watching Jim collect gear from the back, Will weighed his options.

(A) he could call for help and look like a ninny asking Jim to hold his hand as they walked on the ice, or (B) he could step out on his own and risk falling on his rear end and looking like an amateur.

He'd take amateur over ninny any day.

Again, he put his foot to the ground and, this time, put his weight on it.

It held firm.

He added his other foot to the ice then stood.

Will wanted to give a good Tarzan yell in celebration but refrained. No use getting overly confident just yet.

Adjusting the large blue parka, another Jim hand-me-down that made him look like a bloated Smurf, he took a few steps to the bed of the truck, holding a hand to the black metal to steady himself.

This wasn't so bad. Ice? No problem. "Hey Jim, can I give you a hand?"

The older man nodded from the other side of the truck. "Sure. Here, take this bag."

Will looked in horror as Jim tossed a duffel across the truck bed. He held his arms up to catch it just as his feet gave way to the ice. The sky shifted, and a moment later his rear end met the ice, followed by his back and head. Pain ricocheted through his entire body.

He lay there, in shock, when Jim's face appeared above him.

"You okay, son?"

Suck it up, Will. He was a man. A little fall wasn't going to kill him. But he didn't trust his voice to speak in a non-high-pitched tone, so he simply nodded his head.

Jim's hand reached for his. "Let me help you up."

Personally, he'd rather stay still until the pulsating throbs subsided a little. Instead, he lifted his hand to accept the help and gasped at the pain as he stood to his feet, sliding all the while. Jim put a hand on his shoulder to steady him.

"Uh, thanks."

"You'll get used to the ice. Just take small, slow steps." Jim thudded Will on the back again, causing Will to grab the side of the truck to prevent himself from falling again.

"Yes, sir."

Jim picked up the duffel bag and handed it to Will then set off toward an ice shanty a few yards away.

Will hobbled after him and gulped as he entered the tiny wooden box. A partially iced-over hole took up the middle of the six-by-six area. Two small fold-out seats sat on either side of the hole, and miscellaneous fishing items hung from the walls, including a picture of Jim and Hanna, each holding a gigantic fish on a string. Another picture showed Hanna at a much younger age, probably in her teens, holding a more modest-sized fish, with both of her parents behind her.

"That was my Kathy. She wasn't thrilled about ice fishing herself but came a few times. Now Hanna, she took to it like a walleye in water. Between you and me, she catches more than I do when I let her come out here."

Will took a seat on the small camping chair and slid it as far away from the open hole has he could. "Let her come? You don't like company, then?"

"Company I don't mind, as long as they don't yap all the time and scare away the fish. But I'm telling you, the girl's good at it. And I have a little pride. She's competitive and rubs it in my nose every time she catches more than me, which is every dad-blamin' time."

Straight-and-narrow Hanna, competitive?

Will filed that bit of information away for future use.

Jim handed him a Styrofoam container and a pole. "You bait up while I clear the ice."

"Uh, you mean live bait?"

Jim eyed him as he used a tool to break up the iced-over hole. "What? You mean you never baited a hook before?"

"My dad's a retired attorney in New York. The closest I've been to a fish is either at an aquarium or a dead one on my plate ready for me to eat."

"A crying shame, that's what that is. Here, watch and learn, son."

Will squirmed as much from the repeated use of the word *son* as the wiggly black creature Jim was threading through his own hook. He was learning not to take *son* too seriously, though. The older man had called the teen at the bait and tackle shop the same thing.

Man up, Will. Baiting a hook shouldn't be that big of a deal. He could do this.

After three fumbling attempts and two lost bait down the watery hole in the ice, Will managed to ensnare the chub with the hook.

The next twenty minutes went by slower than if he had been watching water drip from a leaky faucet. Lines in the water. No talking, since Jim said it would scare off the fish. He found himself eavesdropping on people walking by the ice house just to pass the time.

Silence wasn't something he was used to. He preferred things to be moving. Fast paced, get-it-done. One didn't accomplish goals by sitting on one's cold, and not to mention sore, bum with a pole in the water.

That is, until now. Keeping Hanna's dad on his good side was crucial.

"So Jim, about Hanna. . ."

"I told you to keep quiet. You'll scare the fish away. You probably already filled their bellies with that dropped bait. A fish isn't gonna eat what we got if you give food away for free."

Will shrugged, his business brain kicking in. Freebies worked. A great sales gimmick actually. "Maybe they'll go back and tell their friends about the cool place where they got hook-free food, and there'll be a flood of fish coming our way. They're probably on their way back for more right now, with all their friends."

Jim grunted and shook his head, staring at the still poles in their hands. "Bunch of baloney. You feed 'em, they get full and leave. End of story."

Will shrugged his shoulders. A moment later, both poles jerked toward the water.

~

Alone at last. Doing the dishes wasn't her typical idea of relaxation, but right now, with her hands swallowed up in the warm, bubbly water, she welcomed the contrast to the snow outside and frost in her heart.

Stupid boys.

The thought made her smile a little. It reminded her of her mom.

When Hanna was little, her mom always teased about staying away from those "yucky boys" until she was thirty, then she could marry and give her grandchildren.

She should have listened to her mom's advice after all. Instead, she'd listened to her best friend, and boss at the time, and applied for a reality TV dating show featuring one very yucky boy she'd made the mistake of falling for, head over tennis shoes.

Stupid Hanna. Really, that's what it came down to. Someone needed to hashtag *that*. At this point, it would be more appropriate than "holy."

Hanna washed the last of the dishes then grabbed a dish towel from the drawer to dry.

As she picked up a plate from the drying rack, a knock at the door almost made her drop it.

Her stomach constricted into a ball of rocks. What if it was the reporter? Would they be that bold to just knock on the door? Had they seen the men leave and assumed she was a sitting duck?

Grabbing the first heavy thing she could find, a cast-iron skillet, she made for the door, fully intending to show whoever dared cross her what kind of stock Minnesota girls were made of.

She fisted the skillet and opened the door.

The business end of a rifle greeted her.

Her best friend—a.k.a. horrible advice giver—stood holding the weapon and sporting a pair of snow shoes. "Where is he?"

"Who?"

"Mr. Skunk himself. How dare he?" Carly elbowed her way into the room and stalked around, wielding the gun as she yelled. "Come out and show your face, you lowdown piece of dirt."

Oh, how Hanna was glad Will was gone at that moment, yet, at the same time, regretted it, too. He would have probably wet his pants seeing sweet Carly aim for him. "He's not here. Gone fishing with Dad."

Her friend and former boss lowered the gun and gaped at her. "Your dad made friends with that reprobate? You cannot be serious."

"Dad seems to think I need to forgive him. Biblical and all."

Carly set the gun against the wall and plopped down on the couch with a huff. "I'll give you biblical. Look up all those verses in

Psalms about David praying for God to smite the enemy and those who hurt God's people. No one hurts the good Lord's people without paying dearly."

Hanna wanted nothing more than to say a hearty "Amen!" but the huge flaws in her friend's theology forced her to shrug her shoulders instead. "He's here. He has apologized. And, well. . ." She paused, unsure how to break the news to her friend.

"Well, what?"

Hanna bit her bottom lip. "We're kinda, sorta, maybe, a little bit. . .engaged?"

Carly shot up and grabbed her gun again. "What lake are they at? I came in here with this thing unloaded, but I'll go find me some bullets if I have to. No one is brainwashing my best friend."

"Oh yes, and the school board would love that. First, a teacher in the tabloids. Then a principal on prime-time news for murdering a CEO. Just lovely."

Carly glared at her. "I won't kill him. Just hurt him a little."

Her friend wouldn't do anything of the sort. She wouldn't even go hunting for fear of hurting an animal. Probably borrowed the gun from her dad. Still, Hanna grabbed the rifle from her and held it for safekeeping. Just in case. "It isn't for real. It was his idea to get the press off our backs for a bit. Fake an engagement, live separately for a while, then call it off quietly. Difference of opinions. Amicable split. Clean and drama free."

Her friend's down-turned face and incredulous eyes told her feelings on the matter. "Sex addict, Hanna? Not so clean, don't you think?"

"You saw that already?"

"Internet. I'd seen the news but figured it was just tabloid crud. My best friend would have called me if something *that* momentous had happened. But no, I have to see my Facebook feed lit up with pictures of my friend the sex addict and her lover. Guess I was wrong."

Hanna sank down beside her, rifle in her lap, and covered her face with her hands. "I was going to tell you. This just all got out of hand so fast."

Carly put an arm around her and gave her a sideways hug. "I'm just glad I live close so I could come knock some sense into you."

The reminder hurt more than helped. Because of Hanna's blunder, Carly's job had been in jeopardy as well. She'd allowed Hanna to take leave to be on the show, in fact, had been the one to encourage it. When all headed south for the winter, the school board had taken the principal to task.

Instead of fighting, Carly had taken a job at a school closer to home. At least she lived in her own house, even though it was a trailer on her parents' property that used to belong to her grandparents. She had plans to buy her own house closer to the school after the winter was over, though.

Still, as much as she owed Carly, Hanna knew what she had to do. "I'm flying to Nashville with him on Monday."

Carly dropped her arm. "And that's supposed to stop the rumors how?"

"We're going to date. Casually. I'm only going for a week or two. Will's gonna set up some in-person interviews from reputable sources to tell the real story."

"Real? I thought you were faking the engagement. That doesn't sound real to me."

Hanna stuffed down the twinge of guilt into her mental box and sat on the lid to keep it tightly shut. "It's more real than what they're printing in those stupid magazines. And it's real for now."

Carly stared at her for a minute. A super uncomfortable sixty seconds. Hanna tried not to squirm but failed.

Then Carly raised her eyebrows. "You're still in love with him, aren't you?"

Hanna gasped even as her heart raced. "No, of course not. I can't stand him. I'm trying very hard not to hate him."

"I think my best friend protests too much."

"You're out of your mind."

"It makes sense. Pretend to be engaged. Snap a few fun pictures. Travel to Nashville. Hope that he falls in love with you all over again and actually isn't an imbecile this time."

Hanna hopped up faster than if she'd been sitting on hot coals and stomped across the room, propping the rifle up against the wall. It wasn't safe in her arms when she was this angry, loaded or not. "You have no idea what you're talking about. Will means nothing to me. I buried my feelings for him at the bottom of the lake seven months ago. And that lake, for your information, is frozen solid."

"What if he dives in there, swims to the bottom, and tries to mess with your feelings again? Then what, Hanna? Your dad's even being nice and drilling the hole through the ice for him."

"William doing that is about as likely as him walking through that door with a fish bigger than the one I caught in '09."

As she finished speaking, the front door opened, and in walked Will and her father, each carrying two modest-sized Northerns.

Jim's face shone like it was Christmas all over again. "You should have seen it. Amazing. Boy-howdy, just downright amazing."

Hanna stood and took the fish from the men. She'd never seen her dad so animated since. . .since the winter of '09 when she blew out his record for largest catch. "Did you catch a big one, Dad?"

"Me? Oh, heavens no. Take a look for yourself. Will, show her a picture I took on that fancy phone of yours."

Carly stood beside her and implanted an elbow into her side.

Hanna shot her a dirty look. Surely, it couldn't be—

She grabbed the outstretched phone from Will's hand and looked at the picture.

Will stood—wet from the knees down, a huge stupid grin on his face—next to the largest fish she'd ever seen in her life.

CHAPTER ELEVEN

*Y*ou're lucky this car still runs." Hanna stared out the passenger-side window of the black Lexus sedan Will and her dad had finally freed from the ditch the day before, ruining all her well-laid plans.

Her dad had agreed to drive them to the airport since they assumed the car would be out of commission for a while. This would have at least put a firm barrier between her and Will until they were out of Minnesota. But low and behold, the two men, emboldened by their fishing triumph, had taken a portable car heater, shovels, sand, and chains out Sunday afternoon, and four hours later, they drove up the gravel drive in separate vehicles.

All the car had needed to start up once they got it out of its wintry jail was a little heat on the engine and a jump.

The resulting high five from the two macho men, way too proud of themselves, had made Hanna stomp back into the house disgusted. She might actually like the stuffed-shirt, doesn't-get-his-hands-dirty Will better than this new version her dad had inspired.

Will had even grown a beard. The stubble made him look even more handsome, which was highly irritating.

Now she was riding all the way to Duluth with her rugged "fiancé" by herself.

Common sense said she needed to get used to it sooner rather than later. But common sense had no part in Hanna's life lately. It had long since flown the Knight's coop and rested in the minds of people like Carly, who declared that Hanna had lost every last one of her marbles and a few checker pieces, too. She'd threatened to kidnap Hanna until Will gave up and flew home.

Hanna almost wished her friend had made good on the threat.

Will flicked the radio button and turned it to a rock station. "I'm just glad we were able to save your dad a trip."

Leave it to Will to make her feel bad about brooding. Why did the man have such an innate ability to make her feel guilty when it all was 100 percent his fault?

And what was with this awful music? She changed the station to country. "He wouldn't have minded. It does him good to get outside of Embarrass once in a while."

"I think he has a pretty good life there. He enjoys it, and that's what matters. Country? Really? I assumed you were a rock kind of girl." He flipped the channel back to some woman screeching about how everything she did was wrong, and how she didn't really care because it was her life and she could mess it up if she wanted to.

"Do you even hear what they are singing about? It's awful." She turned the knob over a few clicks to the familiar twang.

"You've got to be kidding. Like it's any worse than this 'honey done me wrong, so I'm gonna go drink my sorrows away and shack up with some random girl for kicks' kinda song? Real holy there, Hanna."

The dig using the made-up nickname she'd been dubbed with was like a slap in the face. If he weren't driving, she'd return the favor. "Don't be a jerk. And that is *not* what he's singing about."

"Isn't it?"

In truth, she had never really paid attention. The music was just catchy. She clicked the radio off. "There, we'll just drive in silence. Better?"

"No."

She leaned against the side of the door, as far away as she could get, and glared back at him. "You're from Nashville, and you don't like country? Really? That's an oxymoron if I've ever heard one."

"I'm not from Nashville. I just live there. And I like it just fine, actually."

"So your problem with it today?" She narrowed her eyes when she saw his smirk.

"Would you be mad if I said I just wanted to see you all riled up?"

Cross out *oxy* and what do you get? *Moron.* That fit just as well. "It depends. Would you be mad if I said I wanted to fix this whole mess by saying you forced me into bed against my will that weekend and have been stalking me ever since?"

He slammed on the brakes, causing the driver behind them to swerve and honk their horn, and pulled to the side of Highway 53. His eyes were almost black with anger. "You wouldn't dare."

She wouldn't. She'd been mostly kidding, but seeing him this mad made her rethink things a minute. "How do you know? You only knew me for, what, six weeks? Maybe I'm really some girl who likes to extort CEOs for their money."

His glare turned into a smirk, and he reached over and tweaked her on the nose. "No. You're not that kind of girl. Even I know that, Hanna. Now, revenge, maybe. But extortion? That's out of your league."

She twisted so he couldn't read her face and stared out the window. "You have no idea who I really am."

"No? Let me give it a whirl. You're a Christian. A goody-goody. You try not to do wrong but mess up every once in a while, like going on a TV show that brings your morals into question. You love your family and would do anything for them. You take your reputation seriously, which is the only reason you've agreed to continue our engagement and come to Nashville with me. You are sweet, and loving, and. . .competitive."

Hanna turned full in her seat to see him sitting there, a triumphant look on his face. "What? I am not competitive."

"That's what I thought at first when your dad told me. But then I saw your eyes when you saw the picture of me with that fish."

Hanna didn't want to remember the fish. She hadn't been pleased about her record being broken. But it was the sign Carly took it to mean that bothered her the most. "I was surprised, that's all."

"I'll bet the moment you get back to Minnesota you'll be out on that lake trying to outdo me."

The thought of being back in Embarrass and done with this whole mess made hope swim in her chest. "Of course I'll beat you. That's a given, William Preston."

"You sound like my mother when you say my whole name."

"I'm sure she added your middle name, too."

While he talked, Will shifted in his seat and looked over his shoulder at oncoming traffic. "Only when she was really mad."

"How often was that?"

He flashed a boyishly handsome smile back at her. "Too often for her liking."

A second later, before Hanna could get a thought in to stop him, Will leaned over the console, put his hand behind her neck, and pressed his lips to hers.

CHAPTER TWELVE

*S*he really should push him away, and she would.

But the kiss brought back memories. Sweet silly ones, when they knew cameras were rolling yet kissed anyway. When Will would look at the camera guy and say, "If you didn't get a good shot, I'd be glad to do a retake," then wink at her. She'd felt shy and delighted at the same time.

This time, no cameras were rolling.

She was just kissing Will.

Kissing. . .the enemy.

Realization splashed her in the face like a bucket full of icy cold water from Lake Superior. Hanna jerked back and would have slapped him if he hadn't caught her hand in time and pinned it in her lap. "Cameras, Hanna. Pulled over a few lengths behind us."

Both hurt and relief swirled in her belly. So the kiss hadn't been real. Just like all the other ones.

She started to turn her head to look, but a squeeze to her hand stopped her.

Will tilted his head toward the windshield. "Rearview mirror."

A glance confirmed a suspicious pickup truck in the distance parked on the side of the road as well.

At least the sleazeball knew to get a decent vehicle instead of a swanky sedan like Will.

Ignoring the pounding thud of her heart, she squeezed her eyes shut to block out the feelings she did not want to be having. "You had no right to kiss me."

"Had to. Otherwise, who knows what kind of story they'd come up with about us fighting on the side of the road?"

For a CEO, the man had the brains of a rat. "So you'd rather us be making out on the side of the road? That's better?"

"Given my options, yes."

Hanna's lips ached from the kiss. She could still feel his mouth against hers and caught the long-forgotten woodsy scent of his aftershave tickling her nose. She'd always teased him that he smelled handsome. And doggone it if he still did, maybe even more so if that was possible.

No need to let him know all those tidbits, though. It was purely a natural physical reaction. Nothing deeper. She reclaimed her hand, turned in her seat, and adjusted her sweater. "Warn me next time, okay?"

"Would you have let me?"

"In your dreams."

He winked. "My point exactly."

"Just don't do it again."

Will inched the car forward, the wheels sliding in the snowy shoulder before he could merge back into traffic. Finally catching traction, the sedan made it onto the road.

Hanna peeked in her side mirror. The truck pulled out as well.

Will turned the radio back on, country this time. "You'll have to act like you don't hate me in public, you know. Think you can handle it?"

No. That was the part she was dreading the most. Acting all lovey-dovey like nothing was up. Like they were a happily engaged couple living on their hopes and dreams of a future of happily-ever-after bliss.

All the while, Hanna's hopes of a future with anyone might as well be swirling around a flushed porcelain commode. She was destined to work on Dad's hay farm the rest of her life. Joy, joy.

"I understand what's expected of me, Will. I have as much invested in this as you do."

Will laughed. Not a ha-ha laugh, but a haughty, unbelieving chuckle. "I doubt that, Hanna. Unless you stand to lose a six-figure annual salary, bonus, and millions of dollars in stocks, that is."

The man and his money. Is that all he ever thought about? "You can pick up and start again. We're talking about my whole life here. What decent man is going to want a wife who will risk putting him and their kids into the tabloids at any moment? My teaching career is over for now, maybe forever. I thought I could go back, but now, I'm not so sure anymore."

Not to mention her faith. But she didn't want to go there. Her relationship with God was complicated at the moment and not something she cared to dwell on. She'd figure out what wasn't right later.

Will didn't reply to her. Instead, he just drove a little faster. A clear male sign that he disagreed with her but didn't want to get into it.

And avoiding a deep discussion was perfectly fine with her.

⁓

Whoever the snitch was, they had access to their itinerary in advance.

"So what do you think about dates?" Will spoke a little louder than he normally would have in the first-class compartment, but the man catty-corner behind them with a large newspaper spread out in front of him spurred the increase in volume. He wanted to be sure the snoop heard every word. If the tabloids were going to print something, hopefully Will and Hanna could maneuver it to their advantage.

Hanna scrunched up her cute little nose. "Dates? What are you talking— Ouch!"

Will released the small piece of skin on her arm that he'd pinched as gently but accurately as possible. "For the wedding, sweetie. The day you'll make me the happiest, luckiest man alive."

The look she shot him suggested that he'd be lucky to even be alive after this flight.

Still, he kept on. "If it were up to me, we'd be off to Vegas. But I know you want something big, and anything my snookums wants, my snookums gets." He accentuated his speech with a hand patting her cheek gently.

This fake engagement could be really fun.

And given the kiss earlier in the day on the way to the airport, dangerous as well. He'd forgotten her effect on him.

Physical, he reminded himself. It was all a purely physical attraction, nothing more. Any man would be attracted to a beautiful woman like Hanna. Blond, petite, perfect curves, a bit of an attitude but sweet. Not to mention her amazing, kissable, pink lips.

He had to get his mind off those lips.

A sharp pain in his ankle accomplished that. "Did you just kick—"

Hanna snuggled up to his side and patted a hand against his chest, cutting off his words. "Oh lover bug, I'm so happy you've agreed to a big wedding. I can see it now. Fountains and ice sculptures and diamonds and flowers galore. And the biggest, fanciest, most expensive wedding dress we can find. That's what I want us to do first when we get to Nashville. Dress shop!"

Will clenched his jaw. They had interviews to do. He had work to do. Shopping did not factor into this equation. "Remember, dear,

I do need to get back to work. And we have a few appointments to schedule, too. We probably want to figure out a date and a place before we do much shopping."

Hanna laughed so loud a businessman on the other side of the aisle glared at them and cleared his throat. "Oh, darling, surely you know that a wedding dress is the single most important purchase a girl makes. I want to look like a princess for you, and what better way than to shop together. I'm not one of those girls who are superstitious about the groom seeing the dress before the wedding. Your opinion matters to me."

The evil woman beside him obviously recalled the conversation they'd had on camera during one of his dates about his hatred for shopping of any kind and his penchant for online purchases to get out of the mundane task.

Two could play at that game. "Whatever you want, dear. Your wish is my command. Oh, I forgot to mention, I've made reservations for dinner tomorrow night. I hope you don't mind."

She flashed a genuine-looking smile his way. "Not at all. Where to?"

"Oh, just a Thai place downtown. I remembered how you said that you've grown to love Asian food lately. Amazing how taste buds change."

If he wasn't mistaken, her cheeks flushed a strange hue of green. "But I don't like—"

He squeezed her closer to him. "To spend too much money on food. I know, love, but you're worth every cent."

Will sucked in a breath as an elbow caught him in the side. He'd need to ice his bruises when he got home.

Hanna leaned back in her chair, closing her eyes. "I'm glad you feel that way. Because even more important than dress shopping is ring shopping. I totally love that you didn't give me one yet so we could pick out the perfect cut together. In fact, we should do that the moment we land in Nashville. I don't want to go another minute without your love displayed on my finger." She popped open an eyelid and raised her eyebrow. "I'm thinking, what, two karats at the least?"

Will groaned and closed his eyes as well. At the rate this was going, he wouldn't have two pennies to rub together when she was through with him.

But he'd have a job, so he could always make more. That's what mattered in the long run.

CHAPTER THIRTEEN

I think that one is pretty, don't you?" Hanna bit the side of her cheek to keep from laughing as she pointed at the gaudy princess cut diamond solitaire that had to be over three karats, not including the smaller diamonds that lined the white gold engagement and wedding band.

Will squirmed at her side. "It's...interesting. Maybe we shouldn't decide on one today, though. Don't you think we should look a few different places? Make sure you're getting the perfect one?"

She knew he was only speaking with her in such a forced, patient tone because he'd seen the sales associates whisper excitedly as they entered the shop. The price of that monstrosity of a wedding band was the only thing that would make him suggest more shopping, too.

At least they'd had a moment on the drive from the airport to discuss the matter in private. As much as it pained his wallet, an engagement ring was a necessity if they wanted to look official. And unless he wanted to look cheap, he would need to pony up some cash for a decent one at that.

They'd driven directly to the jewelry store, wanting to get her finger blinged-up before too many more pictures were taken.

The saleswoman pulled the ring dripping with dollar signs out of the display case. "This is a beautiful and rare piece, Miss—" She raised her eyebrows as if to verify her last name.

Hanna was sure she already knew. "Knight. But please, call me Hanna."

The older woman—midforties maybe, dressed in a manicured suit—looked out of place with the giddy laugh that came over her. Whether it was because of who her customer was or at the thought of making such a high sale, Hanna wasn't sure. "Yes, yes of course. Hanna. Would you like to try it on?"

Hanna took the ring, made a display of examining it closely, then slipped it on her finger. The rock was so heavy she was afraid her finger would bruise, so she took it back off and held it up to the light. "It's stunning. Not that it matters, because Will's already told me I could get whatever I choose, but what is the price of this one?"

"Well, it's a great deal, as we have a sale going on today. And let me tell you, this particular piece is fourteen karat white gold with a princess cut diamond solitaire. It has a D for color and a VS2 for clarity. A fabulous choice."

Will cleared his throat. "And the price?"

The woman, a Mrs. Bellman according to her name tag, fidgeted with the ring holder in her hand. "It is also over four karats in the solitaire. You'll be the envy of all the other wives."

Hanna twirled the ring around. There would be no envious wives. Because she wouldn't be a wife anytime soon. If ever. She forced cheer she didn't feel into the smile on her face. "I'm sure I will. And the price?"

Mrs. Bellman's throat dipped in a swallow. "It's regularly $145,000, but we have 10 percent off today only, so you'd get it for a steal at only $130,500. Actually, I'll make an executive decision and let it out the door for $130,000 flat. Can't beat that!"

Hanna sucked in a breath as she tried to wrap her brain around the obscene number. She was holding $130,000 in her hand.

Forcing her fingers not to shake, she placed the ring on the counter, but her fingers fumbled. Six-figures of diamond spiraled downward and hit the carpet then rolled under the counter.

Hanna screamed.

Mrs. Bellman shrieked.

Will pulled Hanna back and dropped to his knees as if he were called on to do CPR to save someone's life. A second later, he yelled, "Got it!"

To Hanna, he might as well have said, "I found a pulse!"

He righted himself and placed the ring back on the glass counter. "No harm done."

She looked at Will and noted his face was void of color. She probably looked no better. "I think we'll choose something different. Maybe less—scary."

Mrs. Bellman looked crestfallen as Hanna walked farther down the counter to the less auspicious selection.

Time to get serious and get out of here. But how did one pick a pretend engagement ring? She'd had one already, the one Will had presented her at the end of *The Price of Love*. It had been nice but not what she would have picked herself.

She'd mailed it back to the producers without blinking an eye the day after her humiliation aired.

Now she'd accept another temporary engagement ring. She wanted to choose the ugliest dumpy one they had to match the aching of her heart, but she and Will did have an image to create.

She walked down the ring case, her hand trailing on the smooth glass, not really looking.

A sparkle caught her eye, and she gasped.

Will caught up with her and put a hand on her waist. Oddly, the warmth and possessiveness of it calmed her. "Do you see something you like?"

Hanna blinked away tears. There, in the case, was a ring that looked exactly like her mother's. The one she'd slipped into the casket at the funeral three years ago at the insistence of her father.

Mom had been adamant during those last days when the cancer began to win that they not bury her with it. She was convinced the funeral home or grave diggers would steal it.

But Dad insisted it was not her but the cancer talking and had given it to Hanna right before they closed the casket, and asked her to slip it into Kathy's hand, out of sight from everyone. She was still his wife, he'd told her later, and even though her body was empty, it made him feel better that she was buried clasping the symbol of their love.

Hanna had understood, but she privately mourned not being able to keep it for sentimental value. She'd always loved Mom's ring. It was simple yet sweet. The solitaire was round and small, but the band was curved on both sides, lined with tiny diamonds. Mom had told her only the round diamond was real, but it didn't matter. The ring was beautiful.

The ring before her was so similar, Hanna wondered if someone had dug up the grave and stolen it after all. She pointed to it for the saleswoman. "That one right there, in the middle. May I see it?"

The woman frowned. "Of course, but there are so many with better clarity and color you may want to view. In fact, we could have this one set with a larger—"

Hanna shook her head. "Just let me see that one, please."

Mrs. Bellman unlocked the cabinet and pulled out the case the ring rested in then handed it over without saying a word.

Up close, Hanna could see a few differences. The diamonds on the band were definitely real instead of the dingy look that Mom's had taken over the years. And the diamond in the middle was definitely bigger.

She slipped it on her finger.

An unbelievable perfect fit. "How many karats?"

The reply was one of dejected sales loss. "One-half."

"And how much does this one cost?"

"Well, only the rings over ten thousand are on sale."

Will took the ring from her and looked at it closely, as well, then lifted an eye to the woman and spoke in a firm tone that demanded no argument. "How much?"

The woman lifted her chin in defiance. "Six thousand."

He handed it back to her and pulled out his wallet. "We'll take it for five. And just wrap up the box. My bride will wear it as we leave."

Will pressed the IGNITION button on his Audi. All he wanted was to get Hanna checked into the hotel, safe and sound, and get back to his townhouse to clear his thoughts. He had a date with his laptop and spreadsheets. His analytical brain needed a good dose of problem-solving techniques. Maybe a pro versus con analysis or something.

A call to his parents was in order as well. They wouldn't be pleased he hadn't notified them of his new "engagement" before the press release went out, but a phone call would redeem him a little. He'd put it off long enough.

He glanced at Hanna, expecting her to fasten her seat belt so they could get going.

Instead, she sat there, absently twirling the ring on her finger.

He resisted the urge to run a hand down her gorgeous blond hair. She wore it straight today, with little barrettes on each side to hold it out of her face.

No one was watching, though. He had no good excuse except

being male and attracted to her. And the latter he needed to work on curbing. Another item to add to his problem-solving list. "Hanna? You okay?"

She sighed and pulled off the ring. "We need to talk, Will."

No part of him wanted to go back into that wretched store, especially to return an overpriced ring. The lady ought to be thankful he'd paid the exorbitant amount he did. He was thankful, though, for a halfway modest price compared to the others Hanna had looked at.

One look at her face when she gazed at it had made it impossible for him to sway her. He might have even bought it had it been the hundred-grand one. "What? Isn't that the ring you wanted?"

Hanna shook her head. "No, it's not that. In fact, the ring is perfect. I think that's the problem."

Women were so confusing. "We could always go to a pawn shop and get a cheap, gaudy one for a hundred bucks. Would that do?"

One side of her mouth curled up an inch. "People would love that."

Will took her hand and tugged her to face him. "What's going on, Hanna? You're still in this with me, right?"

She sighed and nodded. "Yes, yes I am. I guess I'm just tired and overwhelmed. And the ring. Really, it's perfect, Will. Thank you. And when we're done with this charade, you can take it to that pawn shop you mentioned, maybe get a little of your money back."

His little thrifty fake fiancée. Most women would be joking if they said that, intent on squeezing every last dime they could out of him. But he knew Hanna well enough to know she was drop-dead serious. He squeezed her hand. "Is the cost what's bothering you? Let's just say, I'm thankful you chose this over the other choice. It suits you. And it's yours to keep when we're through. Think of it as a souvenir."

She drew her hand back and turned to face the window. "Let's just go."

"Hey, I have an idea." He pulled out his phone and clicked on the Instagram app and changed the camera direction toward them. "Let's take a selfie of us with your new ring."

Her lips tipped into a smirk. "A selfie?"

"Why not? All the big-time celebrities do it."

He stretched his arm out until they were both in view then leaned toward her. "Okay, I'll do a smug, proud face; you do an 'OMG, look what I've got' face, okay?"

She laughed and obeyed, her eyes wide and mouth in the shape of a perfect O, her fingers splayed in front of her, showing off her bling. He put on his best smug expression and clicked the button.

A few clicks and it was posted, going to his Twitter, Facebook, and Instagram at the same time. "There. We're officially introduced to social media as a couple."

"Good, because"—she pointed her finger toward a group of pedestrians crossing at an intersection not far from them—"I think there's a guy over there who took a picture of us a minute ago, too."

"Well, buckle up. Let's get you to the hotel."

He pulled out of the space and hit the gas harder than he normally would, hoping no one would follow him. Not that it really mattered. If someone wanted to figure out what hotel she was staying at, it would be pretty easy. And maybe that would clarify their non-living-together status. Once on the highway, he relaxed a little. "I've been meaning to talk to you about my parents."

"How are they doing with all this?"

After the picture he just posted, they were probably both pretty livid at the moment for him not calling. The more he thought about it, the more he determined to put that conversation off as long as possible. "They actually haven't technically been informed yet, although

I'm sure they've heard it from other sources by now."

A small fist caught him in the shoulder.

"Hey, what was that for?"

"That's on behalf of your mother since she isn't here in person to do it herself. I can't believe you didn't call them."

Will rubbed the spot she'd nailed. "I don't want to tell them it's fake."

"You're going to lie?"

"More like not tell them the truth."

Hanna narrowed her gaze. "It's the same thing, Will. My dad knows. I don't know why we couldn't tell your folks, too."

She didn't understand. His parents about ordered his head served on a platter when they saw what he'd done. They both loved Hanna and thought her the best thing that happened to their family since smartphones were invented. Since his dad was a retired corporate attorney and his mom did social media consulting for a billion-dollar company, that was no small distinction.

Perhaps he could get back in his parents' good graces as well. Make family get-togethers not quite as tense. Christmas would have been more comfortable if he were having acupuncture—while walking on hot coals—in the middle of winter—in Alaska—naked.

His mother had given him a wedding cake topper as his gift. She'd told him she'd purchased it as a gift for the two of them and couldn't return it, so he could do whatever he wanted with it. He was quite certain she'd purchased it with spite in mind only.

His father gave him an empty box. Told him his gift was to be a honeymoon in Hawaii. But since Will now wasn't getting married, he and Mom were going this summer instead.

When his parents wanted to make a point, they pulled out all the stops.

He drove in silence the short distance to the four-star hotel he'd booked a room at. Hanna shifted in her seat several times, but he really didn't want to talk about it right now. She would just have to get over it.

After pulling into the hotel's valet lane, he shifted the car into PARK.

Hanna took that to mean talk time. "You need to tell them, Will."

Instead of answering, he opened the door, popped the trunk, and tossed the keys to the attendant.

Hanna met him at the back of the car. "Ignoring me won't help, William Henry Preston. Are you going to tell them, or shall I?"

Aware of the valet's frown, Will abandoned the bag he'd started to pick up, put an arm around her, and pulled her flush to him, ignoring her gasp. He pressed a quick kiss against her lips then put his forehead against hers. "I will be glad to tell them how happily in love and engaged we are, my sweet. Don't you worry."

Hanna's eyebrows furrowed into an unpleased U shape. A second later, her forehead smoothed like melting butter, and she sent him a lopsided smile. A product of the staring valet and approaching bellman, no doubt. "That sounds just great, Willie-poo. I do so love your parents."

The awful nicknames were going to have to stop. He handed the valet a sizable tip, handed Hanna's lone bag to the bellman, then wrapped an arm behind Hanna, resting a hand on her waist, and ushered her toward the revolving front door. "Oh, Hanna-banana. They'll just want to eat you to pieces when they see you. But let's not worry about that right now. We need to get you settled in."

When they entered the hotel, Will scanned the ornate luxury lobby and steered Hanna toward the reception desk. A moment later, he stopped short.

Leaning against the marble counter, making a receptionist blush and flutter, was Doug Perry. The man who'd been the burr in Will's saddle that had spurred him to climb the corporate ladder and achieve C-level in record time.

The man who hated Will's guts because he'd stolen Doug's future job.

CHAPTER FOURTEEN

Hanna looked from her fake fiancé to the stranger with a too-suave smile on his face.

Will extended a hand. "Doug. I didn't expect to see you here."

The man shook Will's hand then immediately withdrew. "Business doesn't stall while you're off sweeping lovely women off their feet." Doug glanced Hanna's direction and winked in an attempt to—charm her?

William's fingers clenched in a ball. "My business is not—"

A strange protective urge pushed Hanna closer to Will. She snuggled to his side then extended her left hand, ringside up. "We went to go pick out this."

Doug took her hand to inspect the rock then raised his eyebrows. "Nice. Would have thought you'd spring for something a little bigger, though."

She shook her head and pulled her hand back from his cool, too-smooth hands. What'd he do, soak them in baby oil? "Nope, it's just perfect. Exactly what I had in mind. Too big and it's just gaudy and pretentious, you know?" She made a point to stare at his giant gold wedding ring on his left hand that probably weighed a ton and cost even more than her diamond.

He folded his arms and looked down at her as if she were a

teenager being reprimanded. "Remember, Hanna. You aren't in backwoods Minnesota anymore. Will's an important man. He has an image to protect, and you're part of that now."

She had an image all right. One of her with Dad's hunting rifle and Mr. Doug screaming like a girl, running the other direction. The man was clearly a rich pansy in a suit who didn't care about people, just what people thought of him.

Hanna took a step away from Will, nonchalantly disengaging his arm from her waist. It was a fantastic reminder that despite Will's charm, he was no better than Mr. Full-of-Himself Doug here.

Will's lips lowered in disappointment, but she was thankful he didn't pull her back. Instead, he adjusted his focus to Doug. "Hanna's going to be a fantastic wife just as she is, and her ring is perfect. It suits her. Now, it must be important for you to meet us here. What's going on?"

"I talked to Steve this afternoon. Just wanted to give you a heads-up."

"And?"

Doug cleared his throat. "You don't have much time, Will. I'm not sure if your, uh, efforts will help." He slanted his head slightly toward Hanna.

Will grabbed Hanna's arm a little firmer than necessary and all but pushed her toward the counter. "We can talk about this at the office tomorrow."

"What, don't want your delicate little flower to hear about your potential financial crisis?"

Hanna couldn't decide if the troll knew the engagement was a fake, or if he was trying to out Will in front of Hanna to get her to break up with him. Either way, this was not good. "I really am tired, boys. I'd love to get up to my room and have a little nap."

If it hadn't been totally inappropriate for the tense moment, she'd have giggled at the pompous sound of her words. Next she'd be powdering her nose or freshening up a bit. Hanna wasn't quite sure she even knew *how* to powder her nose. Pink tinted lip gloss was as fancy as she got.

Doug called after them. "I'll bet. You and Will have a nice time, now."

Will swirled around, Hanna with him. "Hanna will be staying here alone, Doug. I'll escort her to her door, and that's it."

"No need to get testy, Will. Your personal business is between the two of you." He angled his body toward Hanna and held out his hand. "It was lovely meeting you, Hanna."

She fought to find her nice voice versus the "eat dirt, pig" one she knew was threatening to escape. "Likewise."

For propriety's sake only, she pulled her arm from Will's grasp and shook his offered hand. At first, the pasty fingers were as limp as a cooked walleye. But then he tightened his grip and pulled her to him in a rough hug. It took her a moment to register the sound of a camera click in the distance.

CHAPTER FIFTEEN

*W*ill moved his body between the pair and the camera then pulled Hanna to him. Through gritted teeth, he hissed at Doug. "What are you doing? Are you crazy? Just leave before you make everything worse."

To his credit, Doug looked baffled, his eyes wide. "I had no idea there were cameras, Will. I was just trying to—"

"Save it and get lost, okay? We'll talk later."

The man must have no brains left, which was not great since he was Foster and Jones' CFO. They were trying to improve sales to save their hide, not send them tanking with an added scandal.

He left Doug behind and escorted Hanna to the counter. "Reservation under Knight, please."

The woman in a coiffed uniform nodded. "Right away, sir. And"—her eyes glanced in the direction of the man who'd clicked the camera then walked away to lean against a wall—"I've already called security as well. They should be here momentarily to escort the gentleman off the premises."

Will took the key card from her. "Thank you. I appreciate it."

"Also, I took the liberty of having her bag delivered to her room while you were, uh, in conversation. I hope that is agreeable to you?"

"Yes, fine, thank you." Will put a hand on Hanna's back and

maneuvered her toward the elevator.

She turned to him when he pushed the UP button. "You can't come up, Will. Everyone will talk, even if you do come right back down. They'll assume the worst, just like Doug."

Managing people's perception of his morals didn't come naturally. In the past, going up to a woman's hotel room would have earned him points on his man card. "If I don't come up, you'll have to kiss me again here."

Hanna's eyebrows arched high. "I'm sure a hug good-bye would be good enough."

Half of him agreed, but he knew onlookers would suspect something if they parted with such a tepid good-bye. Plus, the other half of him wanted to back her up against the wall and kiss the breath out of her. "They are expecting a happily engaged, in-love couple who kiss good-bye from time to time. Especially before our first departure since our reunion."

Her eyes flitted to the man arguing with a security guard then back to Will. Without a word, she stepped up to him, put a hand to his cheek, and brushed her lips to his.

It was the briefest, lightest kiss he'd ever received.

Meaningless. Just acting.

But as she slipped into the elevator and disappeared behind the closing door, he couldn't help but feel like his traitor heart was riding up with her.

CHAPTER SIXTEEN

*P*assing Emma's desk, William wordlessly motioned her to follow him.

His large corner office was bathed in the late-afternoon sunlight, looking the same as he'd left it. Folders and papers littered his over-sized mahogany desk, and new product samples dotted the round table in the corner. The only thing organized was the small sitting area where the black leather couch and chair sat.

Normally, his office was meticulous if he was leaving for more than twenty-four hours, but he hadn't had time to clean up before his hasty trip to the frozen tundra of Minnesota.

Knowing he'd left such a mess was the only thing that brought him here instead of his condo in downtown Nashville.

That, and the fact that he couldn't shake the feeling that something was amiss after the encounter with Doug.

A knock sounded on the doorjamb behind him, and he turned to see Emma stick her head in. "Welcome back, boss. Did you need something?"

He waved her in. She was the best executive assistant he'd ever known. All his previous ones had been adept at getting him coffee and that was about it.

But Emma—he got his own coffee because she was too valuable

to waste on menial things like that. She could put together a board presentation better than anyone he'd ever seen, and he genuinely valued her opinion.

She was finishing her MBA by taking night classes at the University of Tennessee. When she was done, he had big plans for her future at Foster and Jones.

"How'd the trip go?"

He fell into his leather office chair and leaned his head back, eyes closed. "I'm engaged."

"So you said. Your choice?"

William opened an eye. "What do you think?"

The tall redhead relaxed into the chair opposite his desk and crossed her long legs that were covered in thick black tights. She smoothed the lap of her knee-length red shift dress. "I think you're in love with her but won't admit it."

Maybe she wasn't as smart as he gave her credit for. Wanting to kiss a girl wasn't the same as being in love with her. Although he was sure many women would disagree with him. "It's business, Emma. That's it."

"Whatever you say. I have that list of news and talk shows who've called requesting interviews."

He sat up and nodded toward the desk. "Just leave them on top. I'll let you know which I need you to call back."

"You gonna do these in person or video in? They'll want to know."

His brain ached with all the decisions that needed to be made. "Let me think about it. I'll let you know in the morning."

She nodded and headed toward the door. "Sure thing." Just before she reached the door, she paused and turned back. "By the way, Doug was in here earlier."

William frowned as he reached for a file on top of the stack. "What did he want?"

Her red dress bobbed with her shrug. "Didn't seem like much. Just rustled through the folders. He did open the Costco file and glance at a few things but put it right back."

At least that made a little more sense. The pending bulk-product deal was all but finalized and should be a nice addition to sales starting next quarter. He was probably just double-checking a detail. But he had his own file. What did he need from Will's? "Thanks. You need to get home. It's getting late, and don't you have classes?"

She waved off his concern. "Most of mine are online this semester, so I'm flexible. But I'm heading out in a few. See you in the morning."

After she exited, he cleared the space in front of him and picked up the stack of notes.

The Today Show. Maybe pile.

Jerry Springer. Not-a-chance stack.

A slew of local news shows. Probably not enough impact to be worth it, so he tossed them on top of *Jerry.*

ALIVE with Kate and Mike. Extreme possibility. With a reputation for more fun interviews and a younger audience that would mirror the audience for *The Price of Love,* it might be a good fit.

He flipped through the rest, but none held the possibility that *ALIVE* did.

Granted, it was filmed in New York, and they didn't have a remote interview option.

Going to New York with Hanna would be dangerous on many levels, the least being the even more overwhelming presence of the paparazzi.

But the thing he worried about most was that it would obligate them to visit two people who had him on their bad list. Whom he hoped to avoid until this all blew over but, considering the three voice mails he'd not yet listened to on his phone, wasn't going to be a possibility.

His parents.

～

Room service was the greatest thing ever invented.

Especially when someone else was footing the hotel bill.

Hanna adjusted the pillows against her back and flicked the TV on with the remote control then dug into the scrambled eggs on the tray in front of her.

She could get used to this life.

Even as she thought it, she shook her head. No. She probably couldn't. This all had been super cool for a night. Sleeping in late, bubble bath in her in-room whirlpool tub, room service. Will had even had a laptop delivered for her to use, as well as the biggest bouquet of flowers she'd ever seen.

But if she was locked away in this room one more day, she would go crazy.

And probably gain about fifty pounds. The dessert menu here was to die for.

Will had texted her earlier to let her know he needed to catch up at work today but would take her to dinner tonight, and that a rental car was waiting with the valet for her use whenever she needed.

She had no idea how to get around Nashville, but she'd figure something out. She needed more daylight than the sun that shone through the large windowed wall on one side of her room. She'd have to give Will a hard time for not springing for a room with a balcony.

Her cell jingled beside her. She clicked off the morning talk show she'd been half watching and smiled as she saw Dad's number on the caller ID.

"Hey, Pop."

"Just checking up on my girl. Everything going okay?"

She moved the tray to the floor beside her and snuggled down in the bed. "Yeah, I guess. Will's busy at work today, and we still need to decide which interviews to do. I'm having dinner with him tonight, so we'll make final plans then, I think." Or, at least, she hoped they would. They really needed to get this figured out. The sooner they finished acting like the love-struck couple they were not, the sooner they could break up.

"Sounds good. Carly's been keeping an eye on the Internet for me and says nothing too bad has come up. What's this about you hugging some strange guy, though?"

Hanna rolled her eyes. That had barely gotten a mention on some obscure blog, so Will had said not to worry about it. "It was nothing. An exec at Will's company is just a hugger, I guess. Not my choice."

"You tell him about my twelve-gauge I'd be happy to acquaint him with?"

Hanna grinned. Her daddy was a gun man. Had always kept it out and visible when boys came to pick her up for a date. She'd never been out past curfew. Her date's choice, not hers. "I'll be sure to let him know if it happens again."

"Well, I best be seeing to the chickens. Just wanted to make sure they were taking care of you. You say the word, and I'll buy you a ticket on the first plane back to Duluth."

An odd, foreign lilt of emotion laced her dad's words. "Daddy, are you having second thoughts about telling me to come?"

He cleared his throat and hemmed and hawed a bit. "Well, I just—I just want to see you happy, girl. You know that. You deserve the world, and even though I thought you were off your rocker for doing that TV show, you were dealt a pretty bad hand after that. If I could fix it, I would in a second. And, well, I miss ya, Hanna. Old Pete down the road just isn't a challenge at checkers anymore."

Hanna blinked away a tear. "I'll be back before you know it. Take care of yourself, 'kay? And don't forget your medicine." She'd worried about that since they'd left. He promised he'd take his heart meds, but he had a tendency to get busy and need reminding.

"Oh, stop worrying about me. I'm fine and fit as a fiddle. Tell me what you decide about the interview, all right?"

She agreed, and they hung up.

Goodness, she missed that man. She'd been so excited to "leave" on an adventure when she'd signed up for *The Price of Love*, she hadn't given her dad a second thought. He was an adult and could handle himself. Besides, she hadn't lived with him since college, but she'd always been within an hour's drive.

It never occurred to her that he'd be lonely.

Even more guilt to heap on her shoulders.

But she didn't have time for that today. She had a city to explore and sun to reintroduce to her vitamin D–starved skin.

Finished with her breakfast, she padded to the door in her robe and slippers and set the tray outside.

Click.

She whirled around and came face-to-face with a closed door.

Her hands immediately patted her hips where her pockets should have been.

Only her thin robe and equally threadbare nightgown underneath met her probing fingers.

This was like a scene out of a very bad cliché movie where a naked guy gets locked out of his hotel room.

At least she was covered.

Mostly.

Surely there was a housekeeper somewhere on the floor? She'd hung the Do Not Disturb sign, as there'd been plenty of towels to last her and she could make her own bed. But she'd heard the vacuum in adjoining rooms about an hour ago.

With quick steps, she walked down the hall, but no one was in sight. Turning around, she gasped when she ran into a man.

For a moment, she feared it was Will.

But when she looked up, she would have given anything for her fiancé to be standing there with her.

CHAPTER SEVENTEEN

*H*anna grimaced at the tight hold he had on her arms. "Doug. What are you doing here?"

His fingers relaxed and slid up and down her arms. He probably meant to calm her, but instead, it made her nerves tighten even more and gave her an overwhelming urge to let his cheek meet the sting of her hand across it. "The question is, what are you doing out here in next to nothing? I could have easily been a guy with a camera. Or even another guest with a camera phone."

She'd almost have preferred either of those options. "But you aren't. I was just setting out my tray and got locked out."

His mouth tipped up in a crooked style, and he pulled a piece of plastic from his coat. "Well, then it's your lucky day. I have a spare."

Alarm shocked through her. "How'd you get a key to my room?"

He winked. "Connections, my dear. The room is being paid for by Foster and Jones. I have every right to have a key to make sure our interests are protected."

Fine. She'd just move into a cheap rat motel, one *she* could afford. She'd prefer that over having to worry about someone slipping into her room at any hour. Did Will have a key, too?

Probably.

Oh, that man was in *so* much trouble.

She grabbed the card from his hand and marched back to her room. She turned to hand the key back to him, but he pushed her into the room and let the door close behind them.

She swung around, fists clenched, ready to swing. "Just what do you think you're doing?"

He turned and put his eye to the peephole. "The elevator was opening. I didn't want anyone to see us and get the wrong idea."

Hanna tightened the robe around her. "And barging into my hotel room helped how?"

Ignoring her, he glanced around and nodded toward her suitcase. "Get dressed. You can leave first, and I'll follow in a few minutes after you're gone. If it was someone who mattered, they'll follow you and won't even know I was here."

The man must think she was completely naive. Just because she knew Jesus, didn't make her stupid. In fact, she'd argue that it should give her a boost up in the intelligence department, but given her current situation, that probably wasn't a great debate to start. "There is no way I'm getting dressed with you in here. Get out. Now." She marched to the door to open it, not caring about the consequences.

Doug stepped in her way. "It's called a bathroom, Hanna. With a lock. I'm not looking to ravage you. I have plenty of women who are willing, including my own wife. I don't need to force myself on one. And I'm looking to help save our company, not add to the scandal. Despite what William might have told you, our goal is one in the same."

He had a point. His job was on the line, too, if he got caught up in this.

And she'd googled Foster and Jones last night. She hadn't realized all the details behind William's original promotion. He'd gotten the job at the shock of pretty much everyone in the business community after the previous CEO, Greg, was ousted by the board due to some accounting irregularities that pointed straight to him.

She had to wonder how that sat with Doug since articles leading up to the announcement had noted Doug was the presumed replacement.

Regardless, the CFO obviously needed to steer clear of all this if he wanted to save his own hide.

The knowledge made her feel a little better. "Fine. But I'm keeping the spare key, and you will *not* come here again for any reason." She grabbed her hefty suitcase and headed for the bathroom. No way would she pull out clean underwear in front of him. Before she closed the bathroom door, she turned. "Speaking of. Why did you come up here in the first place?"

He stuffed his hands in his pockets and shrugged. "Will mentioned he'd been busy and hadn't been able to see you, and I wanted to check on things. Make sure our get-out-of-jail-free card hadn't gone all crazy on us, sitting up here by herself."

Something smelled fishy, but Hanna ignored the stench and shut the door. Dressing in record time, she slapped some water on her face, put on a pair of earrings so she didn't look too drab, and glided some gloss on her lips.

She brushed her rod-straight blond hair and fastened the top portion of it into a large barrette to keep it out of her face.

The proper look of the style made her seem. . .professional.

Yup. She was a corporate beauty queen in the making. Ha.

As she turned to open the door, her phone, which she'd set on the counter, vibrated. She looked at it and saw a text from Will.

How's it going, fiancée?

If he only knew. Just peachy. I have a man in my room.

The moment she hit Send, she regretted it. He'd think she was joking, but should she tell him the truth?

Um, should I be worried. . .or come and rescue you?

Hanna put the lid down on the toilet and sat. Yes. Long story. Doug is here. Not my choice or fault. Don't call tho, he'll hear me talk.

It only took two seconds for the reply to come. On my way.

That's what she was afraid of. No. That'd make it worse. I have it handled. Will tell u more 2night.

U sure?

The man obviously thought she couldn't handle problems on her own. Mr. Fix-it assumed he was the only one who could solve problems. Yes. Don't worry. Gotta go.

Opening the door, she bit her lip to control her temper and not throw the shoe that lay on the floor directly at the man of her recent nightmares.

Doug sat propped up on her bed, feet crossed, watching TV. He clicked it off and smiled. "Ready, princess?"

Her fingers itched for the shoe. "I am not a princess, and get off my bed."

He complied. "Now, I'll stand out of sight as you leave and will follow in about ten minutes. You have plans for today?"

Her stomach churned at the thought of him in her hotel room for even a minute by himself, much less ten. But she had no other choice. She grabbed her hotel card and purse. "Sightseeing, if you must know. And maybe a little shopping."

"Good, you need to spruce up that wardrobe of yours. You look like a little country bumpkin."

Her modest, purple cotton shirt and jeans looked fine to her. "My goal isn't to revolutionize the fashion world. And besides, I'd rather look like a country mouse than an uptight, overstarched shirt."

With that, she flung open the door and let it shut behind her.

Thankfully, the hallway and elevator foyer were clear.

On the way down to the first floor she fingered the purple shirt she and Carly had gushed over at Target just weeks before. She'd actually picked it because it was the most fashionable item of clothing she owned.

In Embarrass, she wasn't judged by her clothing. More than likely, she'd be laughed at if she was all high-and-mighty. She'd already donated the flashy clothes she'd gotten to wear when she was on *The Price of Love*. She was ashamed to admit it, but they all showed too much cleavage or clung too tight to her body than she'd ever been comfortable with. Yet, on the show, she'd felt—sexy. For the first time in her life. To see men, Will specifically, eye her curves with a glint in their eyes had been exhilarating.

She sighed as the elevator dinged, signaling her arrival back in the real world.

Maybe she did need a shopping trip.

Regardless of his staunch support of tighter gun control, William would give anything for a nice semiautomatic at the moment. In fact, this was the exact reason people shouldn't own guns. Because as mad as he was right now, he could easily do some serious damage.

He'd tried to work for the last hour since getting Hanna's text, but his anger at his CFO made it impossible.

He pounded a fist on his desk and yelled for Emma. He should have used the phone, but he needed to yell, and it was a good excuse.

She poked her head in the door. "Everything okay, boss?"

"No." He motioned her to sit. "I still have a hundred things to address today and that meeting this afternoon, but I have to go see Hanna."

"Well, let me know how I can help. Did she find the mall okay?"

Will's head shot up. "Mall?"

"She called me awhile ago and was lost. I gave her directions to Opry Mills. Hope that's okay?"

He tapped his pen on the desk. The mall was good. But— "Did she recognize your voice?"

Emma shook her head. "Not that I could tell. Would it matter if she did?"

"I'm not sure. But I'd rather not go there just yet." No one except the ENC executives and the board knew that Emma had posed as a member of the show's crew while he was there. She was his inside connection to the women, making sure he didn't pick someone who would have disastrous effects on the business.

In the end, it hadn't mattered. Hanna had been his choice, and Emma had wholeheartedly approved.

But if Hanna was already a ball of nerves and mad at him— If she thought he hadn't really picked her—

No. Best she not know who Emma was.

Glancing at his watch, he calculated the time it would take to get to the mall, shop with Hanna a bit, eat a quick lunch, and get back here. "I think I'll go to lunch a bit early and meet up with her there."

"Will you be back in time for the staff meeting this afternoon?"

A throat cleared at the doorway. He glanced up to see Doug leaning against the doorjamb, a cocky smile pricking his lips. "No need to go check up on your prize possession, Will. I already did that this morning."

Fury slammed into William's gut. How dare he— "Emma, I'll be back in time. That'll be all."

She gathered her notebook and made a wide berth around Doug to exit.

Doug walked to the vacated seat with his trademark arrogant stride. "Hanna seemed well. Relaxed."

William tightened a fist on the desk. "You could have ruined everything, going there like that."

"She could have ruined everything, prancing around the hall in her nightgown that didn't hide a thing. By the way, you have very nice taste in females."

Confusion swirled in William's usually clear head. "The hall in her nightgown? What are you talking about?"

"I went there on my way to work, just to make sure that she didn't need anything. Made sure no one saw me, but when I got to her floor, she was prancing around the hall in her nightie. You really do need to talk to her about that. Anyone could have seen her."

"Then why did you go into her room?"

He shrugged. "The elevator was opening. I didn't think you'd want me seen with your half-dressed fiancée, so I grabbed her and put her back in her room where she belonged."

Hanna was going to have a long lecture ahead of her. Yet— "She's not an object or asset that we own, Doug. She's a woman with a mind of her own. She belongs to no one. But I am going to have lunch with her, so I'll talk to her about it. In the meantime—" He stood and grabbed his jacket. "Leave her alone, Doug. She's my responsibility, not yours, so you don't need to be checking in on her. Got it?"

Doug stood and squared his shoulders. "What I get, William, is that you're on thin ice. You need to control your trashy reality TV bimbo before she sends us all packing to the poorhouse. I care about this company, and I won't see you put the final nail in its coffin." He turned around, his steps heavy on the ground as he left.

William walked out of the office after him, but slower.

There was only one thing that thin ice reminded him of. Driving that pickup onto the lake with Jim.

How appropriate to how he was feeling.

His company was a big 4x4 Dodge Ram, and Hanna was the waif thin ice that it was all riding on.

Hanna would have kissed the tiled mall floor if not for the fact that people were already looking at her oddly, and they probably all had cameras on their phones.

The concierge had given her directions, but the interstate system was beyond confusing. She'd taken so many wrong exits that she had absolutely no fear that she'd been followed. They would have gotten dizzy just trying to keep up with her.

But she'd made it after she'd called William's sweet assistant, who'd given her much better directions to what she claimed to be a much better and closer place to shop.

Now that she was here, though, she had no clue what to do. She'd always shopped with Carly before because it wasn't her favorite thing to do, especially alone.

Checking out the first store, her enthusiasm crashed even further.

All the price tags were laughable when compared to her meager bank account balance.

And each one was a reminder of the insane amount of money she'd spent a year prior when preparing for the show. Almost her entire savings.

What had she been thinking?

Oh, yeah. Adventure. Romance. Breaking the bondage of small-town living. Realizing the potential her best friend insisted she had.

"You're more than a small-town kindergarten teacher, Hanna. You need to stop doing what everyone expects of you and do something daring, something spectacular, something fun."

Oh, it had been spectacular all right.

And for those three months—wow. It had felt good.

She'd convinced herself it was God's will for her life, too. That was the real element of hilarity. She'd been able to keep her "Christian witness" and remain chaste and let the world know that Jesus was her Lord.

But then she'd shamed Him. Royally.

According to a handful of letters from some particularly zealous watchers, she was now destined for hell because of the bad name she'd brought to God.

She walked by a skin cream vendor and shook her head, turning down an offer of a sample. That'd be really nice, sampling Will's competition.

Stopping at a little couch probably reserved for men to sit on while their women shopped, she watched the other shoppers walking past.

Maybe she had brought God a bad name. But in her heart, she knew that God had done that on His own. The people He'd created had been cursing and disgracing Him since, well, the beginning of time. That the *world* hated Him was not this new, Hanna-induced phenomenon.

"Penny for your thoughts."

She started at the familiar voice then scooted over as Will lowered himself beside her. "How did you know I was here?"

"Emma. Once I got here, it was pretty easy to follow the whispers and points of various people."

Nice. She'd been so involved in her thoughts she hadn't even noticed. "They can point on. I don't even care anymore." Almost true. She didn't *want* to care anymore.

"I heard about your escapade this morning."

"Doug?"

He nodded. "You really need to be more careful. Being out of your room, uh, dressed like that isn't a good idea. It's probably a good thing Doug came along."

Hanna sat up straight and turned to him. "Excuse me?"

He grabbed her arm, pulled her to him, and muttered in a hushed tone. "Don't cause a scene. All I'm saying is if you're going to be out in the hall, make sure you're properly clothed. That's all. I've told Doug to stay away from the hotel."

She shrugged off his hand. "I don't know what Doug told you, but I wasn't out there nak—"

He cut off her words when he tugged her to him and planted a chaste kiss on her lips. He looked into her eyes with a look that held pretend warmth and real warning. His breath tickled her cheek as he whispered, "People around, Hanna. Remember that."

How could she forget?

He released her and then stood, offering her a hand up. "I came to have lunch with you and help you shop a bit. That all right with you?"

Thirty minutes ago, she would have welcomed company that wasn't threatening to take her picture. But now. . . "Fine."

William tucked a stray hair behind her ear. "I love you, Hanna." He said it loud enough for bystanders to hear.

I'm trying not to hate you, William. She hooked her arm into the outstretched crook of his elbow. "Love you, too, sweetums."

CHAPTER EIGHTEEN

*H*anna closed her eyes, relishing the distinct smell of all things beef that came along with a visit to a steakhouse. She allowed herself a moment to imagine what thrill she'd receive by taking the glass of wine that sat in front of her fake fiancé and flinging its contents in his face. It would be a fantastic shot for all the people with camera phones and would satisfy the urge that had been building all day. It had started during their shopping trip when Will insisted on buying her three over-the-top expensive outfits at Saks Fifth Avenue, and blossomed to full bloom a moment ago when Will laid out his plan.

"Hanna? Did you hear me?"

She brought her own glass of water to her mouth and took a sip to keep her hands occupied and out of danger. "Yes. You expect me to fly to New York City and do some crazy talk-show interview and subject myself to even more humiliation. Yup, I definitely heard."

Will's frown was slight enough that she was probably the only one who would notice it. "I thought you'd like the idea."

For being a CEO, the man was as clueless as a fishing pole with no hook. "Of jetting off with you to yet another big city where I feel totally uncomfortable? Yeah, not so much." She could just imagine it. Being shut-up in another unfamiliar hotel. Will spending all his time on his laptop or stupid iPhone. Interviewing with some daytime talk-show duo who were known for their silly antics, then being on a late-night talk show that had featured her as the butt of the comedy intro on more than one occasion.

Not that she'd ever watched it. Carly had informed her but spared her the details.

"I suppose you'd prefer Jerry Springer?"

Ha. Ha. Ha. "I'd prefer just to sit down with ENC right here from Nashville and do a quick interview then call it a day."

Will jabbed a piece of steak with his fork. "They'd see right through that. No one would believe it, and you know it."

Hanna bit her lip. No, it would work. It had to. She just wanted to do the interview and go wee wee wee all the way home, just like the little piggy. Fitting given the french dip on the plate in front of her. She'd trade the middle roast beef–eating piggy for the pinky-toe piggy any day of the week.

"Go, Hanna."

She wiggled in her seat and stared at her sandwich. God had been totally silent for the last year. Why did He choose now to speak up?

It was probably just in her head. She'd also thought she heard God tell her to go on *The Price of Love*, too, but obviously that had been the devil in disguise, because everyone knew how well *that* turned out.

Maybe this was that same voice.

Go to New York City? Fly somewhere else other than home? No. She couldn't. No. No. No.

"Go, Hanna."

Maybe—maybe God was telling her to go *home*. Yes, that was it. She'd shake her boots off as she left Nashville and head home. Hide away for a couple of years until this all really had blown over.

She could maybe find a babysitting job. Continue doing substitute teaching until she felt like she could start teaching again full-time. Maybe find some nice logger or farmer to marry. . .

"Hanna, don't push your luck. Go. And you know exactly where I'm talking about."

She shoved her sandwich in her mouth and bit off a huge chunk. Yes, she knew exactly what He was saying. Why did God always have to talk to her with a bit of an attitude? She'd prefer the *thees* and *thous* and *begottens.*

Right now, she'd begotten herself a nice, raging headache.

"Hanna? Have you heard a word I've been saying?"

Her head snapped up. Will was staring at her, his lips tipped into a worried frown.

She hadn't even known he was still talking.

Swallowing the chunk of beef in her mouth, she started to respond to him a moment too soon.

The food shifted the wrong direction.

Her lungs inhaled sharply, only to be met by resistance and no air.

The restaurant surroundings swirled as she heard shouting and was jerked up from her seat.

Arms wrapped around her and the most painful pressure she'd ever felt thrust into her stomach, like someone punching her repeatedly.

Just as the world was spiraling into black, her airway shifted and released its captive.

After taking a deep, much-needed breath, she realized Will had sat down, her in his lap.

As the world stopped swirling, she looked up and nodded, her throat eking out the words she knew God was forcing His hand in making her say.

"I'll go."

CHAPTER NINETEEN

Hanna stretched her arms and legs out wide and tried to suppress the heat blazing on her cheeks.

Only she could be dumb enough to pick the "no X-ray" mandatory pat-down line at the airport. While she had agreed to this trip for fear of a lightning bolt from God, she still hadn't let Will off the hook. She'd picked a line on the opposite side just to get a few minutes away from him before she was stuck by his side during yet another flight.

As the TSA agent patted a more personal area, she caught the eye of a smirking Will leaning against the far wall with his rolling carry-on.

After the humiliation was over, she could only hope that some camera hadn't caught that fun event. She could see the captions now.

Hanna goes wild with the TSA...

At this point, she almost didn't care. After having to spend the rest of the week in Nashville before they could get scheduled on the shows Will had picked, and being unsuccessful at ignoring the fascinating pictures of Will performing the Heimlich that popped up when googling her name, she was just ready to get all this over with.

Will pushed off the wall and sauntered over to her as she reclaimed her bag and purse. "You have a thing against X-rays?"

She shot him a frosty glare she hoped would freeze his eyebrows. "Shut up. They're bad for your health." That was her story, and by golly, she would stick to it until the day she died. Or the return flight home, whichever came first.

"You know, it's not nice to tell someone to shut up. Didn't your momma ever teach you that?"

Hurt thumped her heart. Her momma had taught her a lot of things she'd pushed aside lately.

Ignoring the pain and the man who'd inflicted it, she glanced at the gate number on her boarding pass. "We're down this way. Think we have time to grab coffee?"

A hand on her elbow halted her. "Hanna, forgive me. I wasn't thinking when I said that."

Hot tears threatened to escape, but she shook her head and blinked them back. "Really, it's fine. She's been gone a few years, and I probably needed the reminder. I just need to get this done and over with."

Thankfully, he let go of her arm and didn't push her further. Instead, he led the way to the nearest airport coffee stand and ordered himself a tall black coffee and her a grande mocha latte.

That he knew her drink order without even asking would have been sweet under normal circumstances.

But nothing about the past two weeks had been sweet or even close to resembling normal.

She accepted the cup without a word.

They sat down in seats not far from the gate. It was still close to a half hour until boarding. Despite the mix-up in lines, security had gone much faster than they'd anticipated.

A year ago, all this flying would have left Hanna awestruck. *The Price of Love* had changed that. She'd flown to various parts of the earth on different dates and "location" episodes, so this was just a frustrating déjà vu, with William at her side instead of a bunch of overly giggly and, more often than not, drunk women.

A nudge to her arm snapped her to attention. "Yes?"

"Thank you."

She widened her eyes in surprise. "For what?"

"Agreeing to this. And for not dying in the restaurant."

She shrugged and sipped her latte. "Hey, that's what a fiancée is for, aye? Although you do realize me taking the big ride to the sky would probably solve all your problems."

Will reached for her hand and squeezed it. "That's not even funny, and you know it."

Her hand scorched at his touch, but withdrawing would look awkward to those watching.

She definitely didn't keep it there because she liked the warm feeling of his strong hand engulfing hers, his thumb rubbing circles on her skin.

Hanna, this is pretend, and he is a jerk. Don't forget that.

Oh crud, now was that God or her?

Probably her. But regardless the source of the thought, it was right.

And she needed to remind her heart of that more often.

"So, what did you think of Nashville?"

That he didn't know already when she'd been there for almost a week was more than a little humorous. She sent him an overly chipper smile. "It was a blast. Note sarcasm."

"What? You didn't have a riveting time? I put you up in a pretty swanky hotel, you know."

"That was fantastic for the first two days, and the little sightseeing I did was fun." Kinda. Will had been busy, and sightseeing on her own was kinda boring. "By then I'd seen enough soap operas and game shows to last me the rest of my life. And I think I took so many whirlpool baths that my skin is probably prematurely wrinkled." She used the opportunity to pull her hand free and pretend to examine her smooth skin for the nonexistent raisin-like crinkles. Her hand had gotten a little too comfortable.

"Your skin is gorgeous, and you know it."

Despite her resolve to make sure he knew this was not a fun trip for her, she let herself laugh. It was either that or blush profusely. She held up her hand to display it in all its majesty. "What can I say, it is pretty amazing."

Will slunk back into his seat and brought his foot up to rest on his knee. "That's a sign of a secure person, you know. That you can laugh at yourself."

She lifted her coffee cup in a mock cheer. "You know me. All grounded in reality." The untruth of that bit at her.

"I think these interviews will be fun."

Fun didn't quite ring true to her. They would be going on *ALIVE* in the morning, then on a late-night show with some guy she'd only heard of in commercials and from Carly. She was always in bed before it came on.

What really pricked at her was that this was almost a mirror schedule of what they should have been doing the day after the final show of *The Price of Love* aired.

If Will hadn't put his foot in his mouth.

If Hanna hadn't called the producer and, in one of the most un-Christian/un-Hanna moves she'd ever made, told him in explicit language where he could shove the contract she'd signed. Complete moral deprivation was not in the cards, and they could sue her if they wanted, but she wouldn't be a part of a show that had completely ruined her reputation so single-handedly.

By some miracle of God, ENC hadn't pressed charges. In fact, every month or two, they'd call and ask for an update and if there were changes.

They were currently salivating over the engagement. Probably hoped it would boost the ratings of the next show.

Ratings could get flushed down the toilet for all she cared.

Getting her life back was all that mattered.

Hanna glanced at William, who'd leaned his head back and closed his eyes, evidently not expecting a response to the whole *fun* comment.

Good grief, the man was handsome.

Not that it mattered. Looks weren't everything, just like her momma always used to tell her. It was the heart that counted.

Unfortunately, William had fooled her on that, too.

Still, she couldn't help but take the opportunity to study his square, tanned jaw, the perfect line of the trademark Preston nose, his lips. . .oh, good night. Those lips.

The squeak of the intercom jerked her to reality as William's eyes popped open to meet her gaze.

"Flight 2904 departing for New York is beginning to board. All passengers requiring extra assistance and those in our first class are welcome to board at this time."

William winked one of his hazel-green eyes. "Guess it's time to go."

Her voice stuck as if thick cotton lined her throat. She settled for nodding and stood to get her bag.

From behind her, she heard someone gasp, followed by a rush of whispers. "Is that who I think it is? That skank from *The Price of Love?*"

Hanna felt Will stiffen next to her, but she pushed him on. Now was not the time to make a scene.

"It is! That's Will, too! He's way too good for that stuck-up prude anyway. Are they like back together or something? Too bad. She's probably horrible in bed anyway. Can't you just see Holy Hanna wearing like a turtleneck during sex or something? I could totally give him—"

Hot fury coursed through Will at the vile words the women spoke. Did they think he and Hanna were deaf?

Unable to ignore it anymore, he whirled around and pointed Hanna toward the ticket counter. "Go. I'll take care of this."

Hanna tugged his arm. "Come on. They aren't worth it."

He shrugged her off.

If this is what Hanna had dealt with these last months, he was more of an idiot than he'd thought. Magazine articles and stupid letters were bad enough. He'd received his fair share, too, but he'd decided not to mention that to Hanna. He was a big boy and could handle hate mail.

She shouldn't have to.

Striding toward the two women, he took a second to assess the situation.

No men with them. Probably midthirties. One blond and one brunette. Both looked like they'd had one too many trips to the tanning booth and had probably auditioned for every reality TV show out there. Most likely bitter for not being chosen.

Will's voice raised louder than he'd planned. "Excuse me, but I do not appreciate the way you're talking about my fiancée." He pointed a finger back toward Hanna while glaring at the trash in front of him. "I expect you to apologize. Now."

The women glanced at each other and rolled their eyes. The brunette, the larger of the two, stood up and crossed her arms. "What are you going to do about it? Tell all the newspapers you had sex with me, too?"

"Now boarding passengers in zone one for New York flight 2904."

Before Will could respond, Hanna stepped forward and put her arm around his waist. "Honey, come on. We don't want to miss the plane."

Honey? His *woman* was doing a fabulous job at acting. And she was right. This would only cause a scene, and knowing his luck, someone would shoot a video or something.

He started to turn toward the gate when a strong arm clamped his shoulder.

When William looked back, all he saw was a large fist plunging toward his face.

CHAPTER TWENTY

*S*ir, do you need some more ice?"

William fingered the plastic bag of half-melted ice he held against his throbbing eye. "No. It's fine."

The perky flight attendant finally walked off. It was humiliating enough to be laid out in the middle of an airport terminal in front of Hanna and all the world to see—and given the number of phones that were aimed his direction, he was sure the whole world *would* see very soon—but he didn't need the woman stopping every two seconds and drawing even more attention to him.

How was he to have known that Millie, the brunette, had a heavy-weight champion for a boyfriend who had walked up to only hear her "sex with me" comment?

It was not his finest moment. He hadn't even gotten a chance to defend himself.

And their interview on *ALIVE* was scheduled in the morning.

Beside him, Hanna returned the in-flight magazine to the back of the seat cushion in front of her and shifted to face him. "That's going to leave quite a bruise."

"Any chance it'll be gone by tomorrow, you think?"

She shook her head. "None whatsoever. Might be able to cover it with makeup, though."

He'd look like a clown if he put on enough makeup to cover this up. "I'm thinking of postponing the interview."

Hanna stilled, her pink, glossy lips pursing into a frown. "Postponing? How long? It could take a week or more for that to go away. What would we do in the meantime?"

The one thing he had hoped not to have time to do. "Visit my parents."

"You ever tell them the truth?"

"No, and I don't plan to." He glanced at the window, catching a glimpse of his reflection in the tiny plane window. His eye blazed in all its darkening glory. No way would he do an interview looking like this.

"You know, a black eye can be kinda handsome on a man. Shows you're willing to fight for your girl. Maybe if America sees you like that, it'll help our cause."

Humiliation bubbled to the surface yet again. "I'd agree with you, if the other guy sported one just as bad if not worse."

Unfortunately, Will had blacked out for a moment, and in the commotion, he hadn't been able to retaliate. That might be a good thing though, since security led the jealous boyfriend away in handcuffs.

Will in handcuffs. Now *that* would have gone viral.

Hanna patted his arm then sat back and closed her eyes. "Thank you for standing up for me, though."

He studied her perfect face, complete with an adorable sloped nose, petite lips covered with a thin film of lip gloss, all framed with her blond hair. Curly today, instead of her usual straight. What kind of idiot had he been *not* to stand up for her just six months before?

But that made it even more important for their farce engagement to appear real. It was the only way he could redeem himself.

And keep his job.

Hanna fidgeted with her hands in her lap. "I think we should still do it. Everyone will know about the airport incident anyway. You know it's probably all over Facebook now."

Was Holy Hanna nervous about the thought of spending a week with him and his parents? The thought suddenly held a glimpse of promise. In Nashville, he'd been so busy at work they'd barely seen each other except for a few keep-up-the-act dinner dates and the one mall date where they'd picked out a few outfits for interviews.

But at his parents' place in Jersey, there would be no escaping each other.

"No, we'll go spend a week with Mom and Dad. My eye should be faded enough that camera makeup will cover it by then."

Hanna shook her head, sending her bright curls bouncing. "William, no. . ."

He patted her knee and squeezed. "Think of it this way. If we do the interview now, all of America will assume you gave me this shiner, regardless of what we try to say otherwise."

She gasped. "No. They wouldn't."

"And let me tell you. The only thing worse for *me* than being laid flat out by some guy in an airport would be for people to think that I was beaten up by a girl."

An evil grin came over Hanna's face. "Payback is oh-so-wonderful."

He clicked the button to recline his seat and lowered his eyelids. "That's okay, then. We'll do the interview tomorrow. I'll just tell them that on top of being sex crazed, you also have a penchant for violent behavior in bed."

He heard her gasp beside him. "You wouldn't."

"I just talked to Mom last night. She said the snow is beautiful up there right now."

She shifted, and given the rustle of paper, he guessed she'd grabbed the magazine again. "Fine. But if they don't own snowmobiles, you're buying a pair for us to use. If I have to be stuck up there for another week, I might as well make it feel like home."

Will smiled. "Done." The purchase part anyway, since he knew his dad owned a couple. Actually riding one of those death-mobiles? Someplace very hot would have to freeze over first.

Hanna held tight to the door handle as the rental car dipped into a hole in the gravel driveway. By the condition of the drive, she wasn't sure if she should expect more of a rundown shack than the Land of Oz she'd had in her imagination.

Will maneuvered around a curve, and the trees they'd come through broke free into a massive homestead. The cutest house she'd ever seen stood in the middle of the snow-covered lawn.

Hanna bit the side of her cheek to keep the "awwwww" she wanted to say inside.

Will nudged her with his elbow. "Well, this is it. What do you think?"

Her dreams for a future caught in her chest and didn't allow her to reply, so she just shrugged her shoulders.

If she'd been asked to describe her dream home, this would be exactly what she'd picture.

A covered porch lined the light blue-gray Cape Cod, sporting more rocking chairs than she could count. The porch extended over to a separate building to the side she assumed was the garage but couldn't be sure from this angle. At the far end of the property sat a modest-size barn and storage building.

It was—perfect. She'd never have guessed Mr. Proper's parents, who both seemed pretty high-end when she'd met them last year in Bermuda, would live in such a cozy country house.

It felt like home.

Well, to be fair, the farmhouse she and Dad lived in had seen better days. Dad patched the roof every year, and more than a few floorboards squeaked no matter what they did to try and fix them.

This home was definitely about one hundred notches up, but still, she'd expected a cold mansion like she'd lived in while on *The Price of Love*, not a place that made her want to settle in and stay for a few years.

If she closed her eyes, she could almost imagine living with Will in a house like this, kids running around, playing in the yard, maybe a few horses in a field nearby.

Almost.

Will the CEO, the self-absorbed businessman who put his job and reputation before everyone else, seemed to stand out like a handsome sore thumb in her picture.

If she could just take Will's body and transplant his personality with someone else's, everything would be peachy.

She glanced over to see him staring at her with curiosity in his gaze and a black ring around his eye.

The poor guy looked pitiful. "It's nice. Very nice."

He nodded, parked in front of the house, and unbuckled. "Well, let's get this over with."

His reticence confused her. "What do you mean, get this over with? Coming here was your idea, buddy."

Will's jaw worked for a moment before he nodded. "You're right. It'll be fine. But. . .I don't want to tell them."

Not a chance. She was already lying to half the world. The only reason she finally relented to coming here was the chance to let down her guard and be herself. Playing the doting fiancée was exhausting. "We've talked about this. I can't lie to them."

He leaned over and tweaked her nose in a way that made her want to add a crooked nose to his facial ailments. "Let's go." With that, he escaped the car before she could argue.

She flung the car door open and stomped out, a protest on her lips, but his mother was running out the door, dishrag over her shoulder, a squeal that could rival a five-year-old's escaping from her lips.

"William Henry Preston, you get over here and hug me this instant." Before he could take a step, the older woman reached him and smothered the red-hued executive in a bear hug. She held him at arm's length and gasped when she looked at his face. "What'd you do to yourself? Have you been fighting again? I thought you quit that after high school."

"It's good to see you, too, Mom. You remember Hanna?"

The man was a pro at ignoring and diverting the conversation. Hanna smiled and took a step toward mother and son. "It's nice to see you again, Mrs. Preston."

A second later she found herself in a massive hug as well. "Oh, it's Lilith to you, sweetie. You have no idea how thrilled Harrison and I were when we heard that you'd agreed to forgive our William for his stupidity."

"Mom."

She scowled at Will. "Don't *Mom* me. It was stupid, and you know it." Looking back at Hanna, she gave her one more quick squeeze. "But don't you worry. He's mended his ways, and if he tries anything else, I'll have no issue taking the paddle to him again."

Hanna glanced at Will, who had puppy dog–pleading eyes fixed on her. Telling the truth had seemed like such a good idea a few moments ago. But bursting this sweet woman's bubble? She wasn't sure she could do it, either. "Well, he's been a perfect gentleman since, but hold on to the paddle for later, just in case."

Will stepped closer and put a hand around her waist. "Thanks for letting us stay here for a few days, Mom."

She waved off his thanks. "I would've been crushed if you hadn't.

136

Now, Hanna, come with me so I can show you around. Will, you can bring the bags up."

Hanna followed, thankful to get away from Will's constant habit of touching her. They were just little things—hands on her waist or shoulders, or a hug. It was all for show, and thankfully, there had been no more "for-the-camera kisses" in a while.

She hoped they could avoid that completely from now on.

Each time, it was like a knife to her heart, reminding her of times when those kisses were the most glorious thing on earth. Reminding her of what she might never have again.

No, she needed to find a way to keep up this charade and minimize hands-on activity.

They entered the house, and again, Hanna got chills. Everything was tastefully decorated, dark mahogany wood accents with varying cozy tones of paint. She inhaled the aroma of vanilla and lavender, then her eyes caught the flickering glow of candles on the fireplace hearth.

What she'd give for a nice, thick book and a fire. And maybe a good snowstorm outside.

Lilith walked ahead of her, motioning to the breakfast and kitchen area. "Help yourself while you're here, Hanna. You're family now, so you're welcome to anything."

The memory of Will's midnight raid of her refrigerator made her bite her tongue to keep from giggling. He was always so proper and professional, he had to have been starved to resort to that.

They walked up the stairs, and Lilith pointed out the various rooms. Down the hall, she opened a door then fumbled with a button on her sweater. "This, uh, is where William usually sleeps. I'd planned to put you in the bonus room over the garage. . . ."

The implication was clear. Would they be sleeping together?

Hanna was a lot of things, and blunt was definitely one of them.

No way did she want Will's parents thinking the worst. "Lilith, I decided a long time ago to not sleep with a man until we were married. Will's a fantastic guy, and I—" she almost said loved him. Should say love him, to help cement their little act, but the words meant too much. She'd thrown them around before and had them thrown back in her face. "I think the world of him, but we'll sleep in separate rooms until we're married. The bonus room sounds great."

Guilt filled her veins as if someone had hooked her up to an IV full of it.

But no. She hadn't lied. Everything she said was true. Lilith just didn't realize that the "married" part was never going to happen.

The door downstairs shut and voices filtered up the stairs. Lilith took her arm and guided her back to the steps. "Before you see Harrison again, I just want to explain to you. He was not too pleased with William about this whole thing. He always held his son to a high standard, so—just know that things aren't always so tense around here."

As they neared the stairs, Hanna's defenses shot up.

Below, voices ping-ponged back and forth in a game of who could yell the loudest.

Hanna followed behind Lilith, wanting to run to wherever the bonus room was that would be her haven for the week and hide. She didn't do well with yelling. Her dad barely ever raised his voice, apart from the moment she'd told him about her getting accepted as a contestant on *The Price of Love*.

And even then it was more disappointment than anything.

She'd have preferred him to just yell.

But Will's dad obviously had yelling down to a science.

His voice thundered through the house, sending a chill up Hanna's back.

"You think you can just fix all this with money and smooth

words, don't you? It isn't that easy, William. You screwed up, son. In all your philandering, I've yet to hear you take responsibility for your actions like a man."

The man had a point. Will liked to fix problems, not take responsibility for them. It was a fine line, but there was a definite difference.

Will's voice, low and full of emotion, volleyed back. "No one's perfect, Dad. I'm sorry I don't meet your standards, but Hanna has forgiven me, and we're good now. It's in the past, and there's no use rehashing it."

Score one for the son. The past is best left where it is sometimes, in the past.

She heard a loud boom, and both she and Lilith jumped. A fist against the wall maybe? Hopefully, it wouldn't leave a mark. "William, I thought I raised you better than that. The past may be in the past, but if you don't learn from it and deal with it, you'll be haunted by it forever." A heavy sigh escaped his lips, and the decibel lowered a degree. "I just want the best for you. And a hasty marriage with this girl is not going to solve all your problems."

"We're taking our time. It's not like we're eloping tonight."

Hanna straightened. Eloping? Ha. In his dreams. Even if she were going to marry him, which she wasn't, she'd make him spring for the biggest, most extravagant wedding he'd ever seen, no expense spared.

And since it would all be for spite, it was a good reason why they *shouldn't* get married.

"What if it'd been Claire? What if some guy had dragged her name through the mud in front of the whole world and ruined her reputation? Would you expect her to just forgive and forget? Would you even allow it?"

"I'd have killed the guy, and you know it."

Lilith turned toward her, having stopped outside the living room with her, knowing they were both listening but apparently not wanting to interrupt either. Her eyes conveyed her apology, and with a jerk of her head, she motioned Hanna to follow her into the room.

But it did nothing to satisfy the insane curiosity that brewed in Hanna.

Who was Claire?

CHAPTER TWENTY-ONE

William tiptoed down the stairs, taking care not to step on the empty basket of "take upstairs" items his mom left on the second step. Years ago, it had been full of misplaced socks and toys from Will and Claire. They'd been required to take up anything that was in the basket at the end of the day.

His mom was super organized like that.

These days it was mostly empty when he came to visit. Tonight was no exception.

Reaching the other side of the kitchen, he debated as he glanced at the time on the microwave.

A quarter after midnight.

Should he tap on the downstairs door that led to the bonus room?

Doing so could wake up his parents, and while he was a grown man and CEO of a publicly traded company, he still felt like a ten-year-old sneaking around at night, trying not to be caught so he wouldn't get in trouble.

But walking on up would invade Hanna's privacy. Surely she was already in her pj's and in bed at this time of night.

It was the only time he could talk to her in private, though. His parents had been a constant annoyance all evening, not giving them a moment alone. He was fairly certain his dad intended to keep it that way.

Will knew Hanna had heard most of their disagreement downstairs but wasn't sure how much. It had started off with an edict that there would be no "hanky-panky" in the house as long as there was no marriage license, and if they didn't like it, they could turn around and leave.

While Will agreed, the way it had been said and the insinuation hit a nerve.

Feeling like a prisoner in his childhood home, he tossed propriety to the wind, opened the door, and with the moves of a not-so-stealth spy, slid into the stairwell and silently shut the door behind him.

As quietly as he could, he slipped up the stairs. When he caught sight of Hanna's form under the blankets, the stupidity of his mission hit him.

What if she wasn't decent?

Somehow he pictured her wearing footed pj's that zipped up to the neck to bed, but it hit him that the thought was just as dumb as the two women in the airport.

While Hanna was innocent, she was equally as passionate. He could only imagine…

Will shook his head of the rogue thoughts that flooded his mind.

He needed to leave. Fast.

Turning on his heel, his foot came into contact with something hard and sharp, and a muffled gasp escaped his lips despite his attempt to stay silent.

"Will?"

Pain seared his big toe. He twisted around and saw her silhouette sitting up in bed. The moon shone through the single window behind her, accentuating every perfect line of her.

She wasn't in footed pajamas either. A spaghetti strap from her nightgown hung off her shoulder, but he forced his eyes to remain on her face. "I wanted to talk."

Her head shook as if she were ridding her brain of the sleepy fog. "Um, did you knock?"

"I didn't want to wake Mom or Dad."

Hanna scooted up in bed, tucking the covers around her modestly. "Okay. What do you need?"

What did he need? Great question. "I—I just wanted to make sure you were okay. I know you heard Dad and I—"

"I kinda wanted to know the same about you. He was pretty mad."

Will used the moonlight to pick his way around the room to the overstuffed chair near the bed. "I deserved it." And it was true. His dad's words had hit their mark like they always did. William had been so bent on fixing the problems he caused that he hadn't really dealt with the initial incident that started the whole thing.

A half laugh escaped her lips. "True."

He could get used to that laugh. "I really am sorry, Hanna. What I said in that interview was wrong and stupid, and there's no excuse."

She stared at him for a moment, then she shifted to her side and slid down in bed, legs curled behind her, and stuffed her pillow under head. "Will, who's Claire?"

Settling back into the cushion, he closed his eyes, letting the sweet, smiling memory flood. "My sister."

"Where is she?"

He swallowed the lump that formed in his throat. Most days he tried to forget. To put the memory out of his brain. Except on her birthday, and the anniversary of her death. "She died when I was fifteen. She was only twelve."

Hanna slipped her arm out from under the covers and reached over to press a hand on his knee. "I'm so sorry, Will."

"It's been a long time. She was born with a heart defect. It was miraculous she made it to that age. She defied a lot of odds."

His parents had always said that it was God Himself who allowed her to beat the statistics and hold out for so long. That God had blessed them with twelve wonderful years, and they were so thankful for that.

Will had a different perspective. What kind of God would kill a precious twelve-year-old like Claire? She had the sweetest soul, never hurt a fly or said a mean word to anyone. Most brothers and sisters fought, but not them. He'd taken on the role of her protector from the moment she was born. He'd been just shy of four years old but still remembered seeing her for the first time in that hospital bed, hooked up to all those cords and tubes and such. His dad had whispered in his ear how important it would be that he took good care of his little sister. That's what men do, he'd advised.

William had done his best and prayed his heart out but, in the end, had failed.

There was no justice in a sweet girl like Claire dying. No purpose or divine reason that would ever make sense.

And what he'd said to his father tonight was true. If Claire had lived, and some guy had treated her like he'd treated Hanna, Will would be in jail for murder and wouldn't regret it a bit. Well, okay, maybe not murder. But the guy sure would be sporting a black eye worse than his.

That's why it was so important to fix this. Nothing he might do could erase his actions, but he'd pay as much penance as he could.

For Hanna. And for Claire.

What *should* happen is that God would punish him with a nice dose of wrath. He deserved it.

But God hadn't paid attention to anything in this world for a long time.

Hanna's finger rubbed a spot on his knee. "I'm sorry for your loss, Will. She sounds like she was a fighter."

He smiled. "She was."

"You should probably go before your parents catch you up here."

"You're right, I probably should."

"They seem nice, by the way."

He sat up, resting his elbows on his knees. No use getting too comfortable. "When they aren't yelling at me, you mean."

"Well, your mom never yelled. And your dad was nice to *me* anyway."

"They like you. Have from the moment the show started."

She withdrew her hand from his knee and propped up on her elbow. "Really?"

"I'd get weekly calls while the show aired. . .'You better have picked Hanna!' They were pretty adamant about it."

Even in the moon-brushed room, he could still spot her deep blush.

"Well, they're pretty sweet as well. I remember thinking that when we met them in Bermuda. I could do much worse in the in-law department."

"Your dad seems like a solid guy as well."

She settled back down, her head snuggling into the pillow, causing Will to have to sit back in the chair again to create distance. She had no idea how adorable she was, how appealing a picture she created.

It made him realize all over again just what he'd lost with his stupid mistake.

Hanna sighed. "I wish you could have met my mom."

"I saw her pictures at your house. She was beautiful." Just like her daughter.

"Yes, she was. My dad always joked that he'd definitely

married 'up.' I love my dad, but he's right. Mom was something else. I miss her."

No longer able to take it, he stood up and took a step toward the bed.

Her breath caught as she shifted toward the wall a hair. Any other woman and he'd have guessed she was making room for him on the bed. But with Hanna, it was probably her attempt to flee.

He leaned over, a hand on either side of her. "You're a wonderful woman, Hanna."

Her throat dipped in a gulp, and her chest clothed only in the thin, cotton nightgown heaved up and down. Then he noticed a tear inching its way down her milky skin. He bent down and captured it with his lips, pressing a kiss firmly to her cheek. "Good night."

Retreating quickly, his only thought to get away from the temptation before him, he completely forgot about the mystery object in the middle of the floor.

Until his other foot collided into it with the force of the *Titanic*.

CHAPTER TWENTY-TWO

WILD WILLIAM BEAT UP BY A GIRL—
details and pictures of the brawl inside!

*H*anna tried her best not to collapse on the floor laughing when she took the magazine from Lilith.

Will seemed like he was in a good mood at breakfast since his eye was finally looking a bit better, a big change over the last two days when he'd been a grouch and a half, so he obviously hadn't seen the tabloid.

She was surprised that it had hit the press this soon. They must have needed a big story and inserted it at the last minute. His picture had already made the rounds on social media, but they had determined just to ignore it at this point.

But this. Oh goodness. Will was going to be ticked off big-time. Maybe she could just hide it. . . .

"Have you shown this to Will yet?"

Lilith's sheepish grin smelled of guilt. "No. I thought since you're engaged to him, you could do the honors."

Hanna let out a hefty breath. "Thanks a lot." Although Hanna's vote was that giving birth to him was the higher honor at the moment and much more deserving of such a task.

But before she could protest, Lilith skittered off, muttering about some chores in the barn she was late for.

Hanna had seen that barn in the tour yesterday. They had a small handful of laying chickens and one very old horse. The chores were definitely not dire.

"What do you have there?"

She whirled around at the sound of William's voice. He stood in the entryway of the kitchen, his shoulder resting on the doorjamb.

"I, um, just a magazine. What are you up to today? I haven't seen you since breakfast."

"Helped Dad fix a fence. You know, macho stuff like that."

"Wow, I didn't realize CEOs were so handy."

He winked at her, and her heart rebelled with its gleeful skipping. "There's a lot of things you don't know about me."

She knew much more lately, actually. The few nights they'd been there, he'd taken up the habit of sneaking upstairs after everyone was asleep. At first, it scared the crazy out of her. But except for that one moment the first night, he'd been super respectful and kept his distance. Even pulled the chair a little farther from the bed.

And she'd taken to wearing a T-shirt and shorts to bed instead of her normal nightgowns.

As much as she loved being here, she felt a little cornered during the day. Harrison or Lilith were always with them or taking them somewhere. There had been no time to discuss a plan for the interview or anything.

Not that they'd talked about all that in their midnight chats. Oddly, they'd discussed Hanna's mom and Claire mostly. Even talked a little about God.

Which scared Hanna the most.

Will's feelings ran deep on the subject, much past her own theological IQ. While she missed her mom and had prayed for her recovery, she knew where her mom was. And as much as it hurt, her mom had made it clear she was at peace with God taking her home, and that made Hanna at peace, too. Most days anyway.

But she had no idea how to combat Will's anger at God.

And it scared her more than a little that she'd almost married a guy who hated God.

She'd known he wasn't where she was spiritually, but on the show, they'd talked about it very little. He'd grown up in church. He knew there was a God. It just seemed natural that he was a believer as well.

The blame rested on her shoulders for that, though. Deep down, she'd known. She just hadn't wanted to accept it.

And marrying a guy who didn't love Jesus was not an option.

She'd already done enough to catch God's ire. She'd had the oxen and yoke analogy buried into her brain in Sunday school for as long as she could remember.

Yet here she was, engaged to a guy who thought God was evil.

Lovely.

Will cleared his throat. "Hello! Hanna? What world did you escape to?"

She snapped her gaze up to his, his eyes crinkled at each corner in a smile. A smile that wouldn't last very long. "I'm sorry. My thoughts ran away with me."

"I asked what was so interesting about the magazine that you had a death grip on it."

Hanna took a deep breath. Best get it over with. "You might want to sit down."

Smile: gone. Frown: returned. "What's it say?"

She pointed to the couch in the living room behind him. "Seriously. Sit."

He snatched the magazine from her fingers before she could readjust her grip. His eyes scanned the page, widening the longer he scanned. "You've got to be kidding me." He flipped to the detailed pages like a madman on a mission.

She hadn't even gotten that far. Was afraid to look.

After a minute of reading, he shoved the magazine back into her hands and pounded into the living room to stand in front of the fireplace, a hand on the mantel and his face turned downward.

"Will. . ."

He turned and looked at her, eyes narrowed. "You don't even seem upset. Finally glad to have the tables turned, right?"

Guilt nipped at her heels as she remembered her moment of humor when she'd first seen it. But it was a wee bit of a vindication. In all past articles, she'd taken the brunt of the ire from the media. It was nice not to be the one on the front page.

But she felt bad for him. This was a pretty low blow to his male ego. "I'm sorry, Will. I really am. I guess—maybe I'm getting used to brushing it off or something."

As she said it, the truth of the statement hit her.

The crazy stories still stung, but not as much as they had. She was beginning to roll her eyes and recognize it as the trash it was.

She just hoped others reading it would do the same.

"Well, we knew they'd run something. I just didn't expect this."

"Me either. What do you want to do?"

He turned around and took a breath, his body a little more relaxed. "Actually, I just got off the phone with Emma. They've rescheduled the *ALIVE* interview for Monday. My eye should be close to normal by then. We're going to skip the late-night one though, if that's okay with you. They couldn't reschedule until next Wednesday, and I need to get back to Nashville."

"So we've got the weekend here, right?"

"Yup."

Her eyes met his, and she tried to read his thoughts. A futile effort. "What then, Will?"

"What do you mean?"

She sank onto the couch and curled her legs underneath her. At some point, she'd started acting like this was home and not caring about things like putting her feet on the couch. That was so not like her. "I mean, what do we do after the interview? Do we go back to Nashville? Do I go home to Dad? What do we tell them? We've only really talked about it far enough to announce our engagement and explain ourselves to the media. I've put my life on hold for this, Will."

He settled next to her in his typical in-charge, elbows-on-knees stance. "I know. We're doing this to help each other, remember?"

The man was a master at spinning things to look "good." Hanna was a master at seeing things at face value. "No, we're doing this to help ourselves. It will help clear my name and help keep your job. This is a lot of things, but selfless and benevolent aren't any of them."

"You don't think I'd do this if my job wasn't on the line?"

"Not a chance on earth."

He sat back and stared at her for a moment. Unable to handle the scrutiny, Hanna reached for her bracelet, a gift from Carly, and twirled it around her wrist.

Will reached over and grabbed her hand, and the silver bracelet fell off to the hardwood floor with a clatter. "I would, Hanna. I know you don't believe me now, and maybe it wasn't always true. But right now, I'd give up my job in a heartbeat if I thought it'd help you."

He sounded so sincere. So honest. Contrite.

But the only problem was. . .

She didn't believe him farther than she could throw a hundred-dollar bill.

CHAPTER TWENTY-THREE

*D*ress nice,*"* Will had said.

What in the world did that mean? Nice as in slacks or evening wear?

She didn't own anything formal, so she hoped that wasn't what he expected.

Instead, she threw on what hopefully would be tolerable in either case. A knee-length, black skirt that had the potential for a fantastic twirl and a ruffled blouse to go with it. It was one of two options she had for Monday, so this would leave her with only one. But the other outfit included dress slacks, which would probably be best for the interview anyway. It would avoid the worry about making sure her legs were crossed just right.

Their "deep" discussion in the past and the tabloid thrown out in the trash, Will had resumed his midnight excursion to the bonus room last night like nothing was amiss.

Hanna had decided that, for now, it was best to let the sleeping monsters get their rest. No need waking them until absolutely necessary.

He'd announced that they were going out tonight, and she was to look her beautiful self.

His words, not hers.

She assumed he wanted to face the cameras head-on, show that they were still together and that Wild Will was intact and in one piece, not almost hospitalized by a girl who beat him up.

Was it horrible that she could barely squelch a giggle every time she thought about it? Probably.

After dotting on a minimal amount of makeup so it didn't look like she was trying too hard, she slipped on her dreaded heels and headed downstairs.

She'd give her last rifle to wear a pair of tennis shoes tonight.

Will sat in the living room, like he had come courting and was waiting to whisk her away on a date. It almost felt like she was back on the set of *The Price of Love*, except instead of a handful of other women seething with jealousy, she had Will's parents smiling like they'd just won the daughter-in-law lottery.

Not that she was "lottery" status. But knowing their thoughts made this ruse even more difficult.

She was betraying two very kind, loving people. And the fact that it didn't even seem to faze Will was just confirmation that their relationship would never have lasted.

She couldn't stand liars.

Now she was one of them.

And wow. One look at Will made her need to sit down.

While she was used to him in a suit, he was usually clean shaven and all proper looking.

She hadn't realized how scruffy he'd gotten the last few days. But in his sports coat and slim black tie with a dark black shadow on his face...

He had gone from professional handsome to rugged sexy.

Her palms suddenly felt sweaty, and her heart tripled its pace. Since when did Will have that effect on her? Maybe she should turn and run back upstairs.

Before she could, Will spotted her and stood, and in a move that made blood rush to her already flushed cheeks, he let out a low whistle. "You look fantastic."

Yeah right. She looked like a frumpy schoolgirl compared to him. "Thanks. I wasn't sure where we were going so—"

He took two strides and held out his elbow for her, ever the gentleman, and looked her in the eyes, the heat in his gaze melting her. "You are gorgeous."

Hanna lectured her heart to slow down to at least a trot instead of its current full-on gallop. The man was putting on a fine show for his parents. That was all. And she'd do best to remember that. "Thanks. You ready to go?"

He escorted her to the rental car, and twenty minutes later they pulled into the parking lot of a swanky looking restaurant, the kind that has high, even numbers for prices instead of $9.99 specials.

Instead of parking, William pulled to the curb where a man in a suit opened her door. "Welcome, ma'am."

Oh, this was rich. Literally.

Determined not to be rude, she took the valet's offered hand and stepped from the car. "Thank you."

Will tossed the keys to him and, in a possessive hold, put a hand on the opposite side of her waist and pulled her flush to his side. He leaned down to her ear, his warm breath tickling her skin. "Gawkers at ten o'clock."

Reality filtered into her rattled head. Yes. Right. Cameras.

Flipping into actress mode, she laid her head on his shoulder as they walked, and wrapped an arm around his back as well. She could see the picture now. They would make a cozy pair.

Inside the restaurant, the scents of flame-grilled meat mixed with the tart smell of seafood, both of which made her put a hand on her belly, hoping it wouldn't give a starved growl. She'd only had half a sandwich for lunch earlier to make sure she saved room.

Will gave their name, and they were immediately seated at a private booth in the back of the dining area.

She was fairly certain she'd seen him wet the palm of the hostess's hand with a few green bills.

"Today's special is smoked salmon with pea soup. May I start you off with a bottle of wine?"

Will eyed her.

Hanna smiled at the waitress and shook her head. "I'm fine with water, thank you."

"Same for me."

The waitress nodded and left, and Hanna took her napkin and spread it over her skirt. "You could have had wine if you wanted."

He just shrugged. "Water sounded good."

She didn't buy that for a second. He'd told her a long time ago that he was a bit of a wine connoisseur, but still, it was sweet that he tried to make her at ease, even though she had no problem if he had a drink. It just wasn't her thing.

Picking up the one-page menu, Hanna glanced over the options.

This wasn't just a "no cents" establishment.

Half of the items displayed "Market Price" next to them. Maybe that was better. She would be blissfully unaware of the amount of money she was putting into her mouth.

Will put down his menu. "So what sounds good?"

Hanna peered over the sheet of paper. "Do you recommend anything?"

"The sushi is to die for."

She tried not to snort when she laughed. "I think if I ate sushi, I might actually die for real. I was thinking about the filet, actually."

"Good choice."

After their orders were taken, Will slid a red envelope across the table, her name printed in boxy, decidedly male handwriting.

"What's this?"

He smiled and nodded. "Happy Valentine's Day. Open it."

Happy what?

A moment later it dawned on her.

Today was February fourteenth.

They'd been rather secluded the past few days, so it hadn't even occurred to her.

Their little date made more sense now.

Fingering the card, she glanced up. "I forgot. I don't have a card for you."

"I didn't expect you to. Now open it."

She slid a nail under the paper flap, pulled out the card, and suppressed a grin.

The cover sported Mickey and Minnie Mouse looking like they were flirting, with hearts dotted above their heads.

Inside was a corny little verse she didn't even read.

Her eyes skipped to the handwritten note below. *Will you be my valentine? –Will."*

Not able to keep the smile from her lips, she glanced up at him and the small square box he held in his hand. "Will, you didn't have to."

"You have to say yes in order to get the present." His eyebrows wiggled as he teased her with the petite velvet package.

Cameras, cameras, cameras. It was just for the cameras. She had to remember that. Turning on the charm, she accessed her inner drama queen and laid it on thick, complete with a hand clap of glee and a mini squeal. "Oh, I'd be happy to be your valentine, my sweet."

He winked and slid it across the table.

Opening the gift, she sucked in her gasp. A pair of shiny, dangly diamond earrings stared back at her.

Like, real diamonds. Not the fake stuff for $19.99 she usually splurged on.

She hoped he didn't expect them back when this thing was over.

As if he could read her thoughts, he reached across the table and squeezed her hands. "They're yours, Hanna. To keep forever. A token of how thankful I am for you."

She swallowed the lump that was preventing her reply and nodded. "I—I don't know what to say. They're beautiful."

He withdrew his hand and took a sip of water. "Now, if you behave the rest of the night, I might have one more surprise for you back at the house."

She couldn't imagine anything more surprising than this.

The flash from a camera phone a few tables over where two women were whispering barely registered in her brain.

Yeah. Nothing surprised her anymore.

CHAPTER TWENTY-FOUR

Hanna gripped Will's arm to keep from falling in shock as they walked toward the house.

There, in a rocking chair on the front porch beside Harrison and Lilith, sat Carly.

Will beamed from ear to handsome ear. "Surprised?"

She could only nod. He leaned down and whispered for her ears only. "Carly is going to be sharing your room for the weekend, so I guess this means no more midnight chats."

Oddly, the thought made her sad.

But only for a moment because she found herself squeezed in a hug by her best friend.

"Carly! What in the world are you doing here?"

Her friend punched Will in the arm playfully. "Your man here flew me in to surprise you. Thought you'd like to see a familiar face before the big day."

The big day?

As in—wedding day?

Confused, Hanna looked from beaming Carly to proud Will and narrowed her eyes. "The big day?"

Will rubbed a hand up her arm. "Yeah, you know, the interview Monday? The whole reason we're here?"

Oh, yeah. That big day. Duh.

She really needed to get "wedding" off her mind.

Hanna moved from Will's side and linked arms with Carly. "Have they shown you around yet?"

"Yeah, I put my bags in the bonus room with you. It's okay if we bunk together?"

"I'd be mad if we didn't. I'm in desperate need of girl talk."

They started toward the house, and Will cleared his throat.

Hanna turned back, remembering his presence.

Disengaging from Carly, she ran back to him and flung herself into his arms, squeezing him around the waist in the first real, heartfelt hug since he'd come back into her life. "Thank you, Will. I needed this."

He smoothed a hand over her hair and kissed the top of her head. "I know."

Will shut the door to his room, shrugged out of his suit coat, and yanked off his tie.

After pulling on some sweats and an old Nashville Cowboys T-shirt, he grabbed his laptop and settled onto his old bed.

The room was still covered in memorabilia from years gone by. Yankees pennants and little league trophies mingled with certificates from his geeky chess and math league days. He'd been a jack-of-all-trades and never really fit in with any specific crowd.

Given that he was alone on Valentine's Day night and didn't really have anyone he'd call a close "friend," things hadn't really changed that much.

He blamed it on being obsessed with his job.

Same reason he'd stayed out of the serious dating scene for so long.

But he didn't want to analyze his love life, or lack thereof, tonight.

The list of things at Foster and Jones that needed his attention was growing by the minute, and he was determined to stay up all night if needed in order to catch up. He'd been taking care of only urgent things for the last week, and there had been a rash of those. He'd spent most of the week on the phone handling as much as possible while nature took its course on his eye.

Logging into the company's virtual network, he clicked on his e-mail and browsed the list.

Methodically, he scanned each subject title and sender, tagging each e-mail as to importance and deleting the junk mail that hadn't already been filtered.

Then he sorted by importance, the "red" flagged e-mails showing at top.

The e-mail that rose highest was from his ever-faithful assistant. Since she usually tried to take care of everything she could, anything she needed to address with him had to be fairly important.

Will,
Attached are scanned copies of some sales forecasts for next
month Doug put on your desk. Call me when you get this,
doesn't matter the time. I'm probably working late anyway.
                                                    –Emma

He glanced at his watch. 11:15 p.m., which was 10:15 in Nashville. Surely she wasn't still at the office.

Then he glanced at the time stamp on the e-mail.

Only twenty minutes ago.

He grabbed his phone and pressed the button. "Call Emma."

A moment later, the night owl answered. "I was wondering how long it'd be before you called."

"What are you still doing there? It's late."

"I'm worried, Will."

Something about her voice, not to mention her words, made Will sit up straighter. "What's going on?"

"Did you look at the report I sent you?"

The attachment. He'd almost forgotten about it. "Hadn't gotten a chance. Saw your note and wanted to catch you before you left. Hold on, let me get it up here."

He double-clicked the file and scanned the numbers included.

Something must be wrong. A typo. The last projections he'd seen, they were starting to trend upward. Not by much, but any improvement was better than the alternative. They'd gotten a big order from one of the major big-box stores, one that hadn't ordered in way too long due to the drastic dip in sales.

"What's going on, Em? This can't be right."

He saw the projected numbers again and just shook his head.

"I asked Doug about it, too. He said something about having to discount more than normal."

He took a deep breath. It would be fine. Maybe just a fluke. They still had another month before the end of the fiscal year. They could make it up.

Hopefully.

Because if not, no crazy interviews or fake engagements would be able to save his hide then.

"All right. I'll e-mail you a list of reports I want so I can double-check this. Something just doesn't feel right about it. Can you have those to me by the end of day tomorrow?"

"I'll try my best."

Wait. What was he thinking? Tomorrow was Sunday. "Never mind. You can do it on Monday. I forgot it's the weekend."

"I planned to come in for a little while in the afternoon, anyway. I'll get you what I can."

He could hear the sigh in her voice. "You're doing great, Emma. I'll make it worth your while in the long run, I promise."

"You keep saying that. I'm going to take you up on the offer when I'm out of school once and for all."

William smiled. That's the spunky assistant he knew. "I had no doubt you would. We should be flying back home on Tuesday. Thanks again for holding down the fort."

Hanging up the phone, he no longer had the brain for the rest of the work he needed to do.

How ironic would it be to go through all this and still lose everything?

Although, if what he'd said to Hanna was true, he'd have done it regardless.

He would have—right? He hoped so anyway. She didn't deserve what she'd been given.

Out of all the girls who'd played the TV game, she was one of the few he'd actually contemplate giving up everything to make sure she didn't get hurt.

Hanna was different. She was classy and honest. Something about her eyes just said, "You can trust me."

And he had.

And then like the idiot he was, he'd messed it all up.

Tossing the laptop to the side, William stood and stretched. If he was going to reawaken his brain to get any work done, he needed a kick start.

He padded down the steps to the kitchen, but as he rounded the corner, a soft body slammed into his chest, and a loud thump sounded on the floor.

CHAPTER TWENTY-FIVE

*W*ill circled the small, familiar waist in front of him and lifted Hanna to sit on the counter, away from the mess that was on the floor. And because it seemed appropriate in the déjà vu moment.

Something smooth and wet soaked through his socks, but he ignored the mushy feeling. "We have to stop meeting like this, Hanna."

A fist clipped his shoulder. "You're the one that scared the catfish out of me."

"Catfish?"

In the sliver of moonlight, he could make out her slight shrug. "Dad never liked it when I said 'crap.' "

Will tried not to laugh. His parents would have been thrilled if he'd used such a delicate term. "Catfish it is, then."

"Sorry about the mess."

He wiggled his foot and frowned. "What is that squishing between my toes?"

"Yogurt. Your mom said to help myself, and I couldn't sleep."

"Carly?"

"Already asleep."

A cloud must have shifted outside the back window, because the moonlight chose that moment to shine into the kitchen and illuminate the room and Hanna with it.

She wore a fitted T-shirt with shorts shorter than he'd ever seen her in—definitely reserved for sleeping.

And her face. Her lips were tipped into an adorable frown, and her hair was in a high ponytail, making blond hair spill all around her head.

Why women ever dressed up was beyond him. This look was enough to bring a man to his knees.

There were no cameras.

No onlookers to fake out.

But he couldn't help himself. His hands reached for her face and brought her mouth toward him. When she didn't pull back, he covered her frown with his hungry lips.

Her sharp intake of breath almost caused him to stop, until she scooted closer and wrapped her arms around his neck and kissed him back.

His brain went crazy as her lips matched his hunger, inch for inch.

This kiss was different than any other. They'd had some great ones on the show, but they had almost all been filled with a bit of theatrics with cameras rolling, and even when not, there'd been a hesitance in Hanna that screamed of innocence.

And since then, all kisses had been for the sake of keeping up the ruse. Well, most of them. There were a few he'd done just to irk her.

But this.

There was nothing innocent about this kiss.

He slid his hands down her body to her hips and pulled her toward him.

That she didn't resist thrilled him. Instead, her fingers ran through his hair and gripped the back of his head with a passion he hadn't known she possessed.

His brain on autopilot, he let his hands shift back up her body, savoring every soft curve they met, until he heard Hanna's gasp. Her arms shoved him away like he was a shark ready to devour her.

Which wasn't too far from the truth.

Her breath came in shallow puffs, and her arms crossed over her chest as if trying to protect herself from him. "What do you think you're doing?"

Good question. What had he been doing? He blinked, the heady passion melting away, replaced by an awareness of what had almost just happened.

What had *they* been doing? Guilt settled like a rock in his stomach, stomping out the other carnal feelings of moments ago. "I just—"

"I didn't ask you to kiss me."

He jerked his head back as if he'd been slapped. "You didn't seem to object very much either."

Even in the dim moonlight, he could see fire spewing from her eyes. "I didn't give you permission to grope me."

He hadn't—okay. Maybe he'd been really close to it. "You certainly didn't turn it down, either. Listen, we both got caught up there. It was a mistake."

"I'm not that kind of girl, Will."

"So what? I'm that kind of guy?"

Her eyes turned to cold stone. "You said it, not me."

Anger replaced the raging hormones of just moments ago. He took a step toward her and, ignoring her objection, put his hands around her, lifted her off the counter, and set her on the ground, not caring about the yogurt that still covered the ceramic. "I'm sorry to break the news, Miss Virtue, but you kissed me back and were just as much a party to what we were doing as me. I wasn't forcing you to do anything. I know my morals might not be as nice and holy as yours, but I don't take what a woman doesn't want to give."

Her chin stuck out. "Well, let me just go on record as saying that I don't want to give you anything. I want to tell our fake story and go back home, and that's it."

"Fine. We'll keep the pretend kisses to a minimum and the real kisses to zero. Happy?"

She tossed her spunky ponytail and took a wide step around the mess on the floor then turned back. "You'll keep your hands to yourself, too."

He'd give anything to toss a nice big glob of strawberry yogurt at her right about now. "Yes, your moral highness."

As she disappeared, he grabbed the carton of yogurt and threw it with every ounce of frustrated muscle he had in him. It thudded on the kitchen wall beside the bonus room stairs, sending more streaks of yogurt everywhere.

Just great. He should have stayed upstairs in the first place. He'd come down here to gain some energy to conquer the mess that was Foster and Jones, and now he'd added two more messes to the pot.

The only good news was—he was no longer tired.

———

Hanna ignored the thud that sounded on the other side of the wall as she climbed the stairs.

Men were a bunch of sex-crazed idiots.

Hanna forced herself not to stomp as she walked, but only because she really didn't feel like facing Carly right now. She couldn't explain the crazy jitters playing ice hockey in her stomach to herself, much less to anyone else.

Slipping into her side of the bed, she tried not to pull on the covers too much and just draped them over her waist.

What had she been thinking to let Will kiss her? This was supposed to be platonic. A game to get the media off their back.

Midnight kisses were not part of the equation.

And late-night hand roaming was *definitely* against the rules.

No man had ever. . .

She squeezed her eyes shut to block out the thought. She should have expected it from him. She'd watched the tapes of the show. Watched him being all chummy and more "handy" with the other girls than he'd been with her.

He'd always respected her. And until that final episode had aired, she'd eased her mind by convincing herself that he saw something different in her. Something innocent and worth protecting. Something worth loving. That's why he'd chosen her above the others, right?

But tonight had just confirmed what she'd already found out so many months ago.

Maybe this was a good thing. She'd gotten sloppy. Her heart was more involved than she realized, and this was the wake-up call she needed—

Her head yanked back as a piece of her hair was given a gentle tug.

She turned to see Carly staring at her, eyebrows raised, lit only by the same moonlight that had touched Will's features just minutes ago downstairs. "I didn't realize you were still awake."

"Kinda hard to sleep when your roomie sneaks out at ungodly hours of the night. What was all that racket downstairs? I almost came down to check on you."

If Carly had walked in on them. . .oh goodness. Hanna was thankful for the darkness because her cheeks were probably lit up like a Christmas tree. "I was hungry and just dropped some yogurt. No biggie."

Carly sat up and propped her head on her elbow. "Let me

rephrase that. I *did* come down to check on you but saw you, uh, involved, so I came back up."

This could not be happening. Hanna tugged the pillow out from under her head and smothered her face with it. There went the option of burying it deep into the recesses of her memory so she never had to think of it again, and never mentioning the humiliating experience to a living soul.

The pillow tugged out of her grasp, and her best friend and former boss sat up, legs crossed, with that "teacherly" look on her face. "Do you still love him?"

Stealing the pillow back, Hanna sat up against the headboard and hugged it to her chest. "Ew, no. Of course not. I just. . .he just kissed me. I wasn't expecting it and let him."

"Bull."

"Excuse me?"

"You heard me. Baloney. I saw more than you think I did. And what I saw was *you* kissing *him*."

She started to retrace the moment in her mind but shook her head. She didn't want to remember. "No, that's not what happened. He made me kiss him then—"

"Yeah, saw that, too."

Oh, this was bad. Very bad. "It wasn't my fault. He—"

"Someone needs to get off her moral high horse and face the horse manure. He kissed you. You liked it and kissed him back. Things got carried away and you let him—"

"Stop. I didn't let him do anything. That was totally his unauthorized hand movements."

"Honey, you authorized those hands, and you know it."

Hanna shoved the guilt that threatened to bubble up back into its little white box where it belonged. "I didn't authorize anything. I'm not that kind of girl."

"Hanna, we're all that kind of girl. I've been married before, remember?"

Her friend's short marriage and subsequent divorce wasn't something they talked about much. "It's late, and I'm tired. And I don't need the birds and the bees speech. I'm a grown woman." She twisted to turn over, but the thud of a pillow landing on her head stopped her. "Did you just hit me with a pillow?"

"It's not about the birds and the bees, Hanna. If you needed that at this stage in the game, I'd just buy you a book or something. Ugh. You act like it's awful that he kissed you and that it's awful that you liked it."

"It *is* awful. I can't stand the guy, much less want him kissing me."

"He didn't just kiss you. You, my friend, kissed him back."

Hanna shook her head so fast it made her dizzy. "Did not."

"Did to."

"Fine. Maybe a little."

"I'm not saying what I saw was right. You know your boundaries, and what y'all did down there was dangerously tightroping on those lines. But don't fool yourself into thinking it was all his fault. And definitely don't go around believing you didn't like it. Because I saw you scoot close to him, not the other way around. I couldn't have fit a sheet of paper between you if I tried."

"But—"

Carly snatched back her pillow and laid down, pulling the covers up over her shoulders. "You may act all holy and righteous, Hanna. But even the holiest people have sex and like it. Just make sure you have two rings on your finger first. And word of advice. If you don't want him sampling, you might not want to advertise."

Hanna could no longer keep the little box in her head closed. The memories of those moments, filled with more passion than she'd ever felt before, filled her brain.

She had wanted it. A lot. Like, more than she'd ever thought a pure Christian woman would.

But advertise? No. That she hadn't done. "I might have gone a little too far. And yeah, so I liked it. But I did not put my goods out on display."

Carly shifted to her other side, her back now to Hanna. "All I'm saying is next time you go for a midnight snack, you might want to throw some sweats on and a bra."

Pressing her hand to her fitted T-shirt, her palm probed for what she already knew wasn't there.

How could she have been so dumb not to realize just how unpresentable she'd been? What must Will have thought?

As she lay down, back to Carly, she stared at the stairs William had used for the last week to come and "visit" her.

Yeah, she knew exactly what he'd thought.

And knew exactly what she'd been tempted with herself.

A sick churning of guilt gripped her middle.

Hanna didn't feel quite so holy anymore.

CHAPTER TWENTY-SIX

*C*offee.

Must. Have. Coffee.

Hanna gripped the stair rail as she attempted not to stumble down the steps. After her humiliating midnight rendezvous with Will, she'd barely been able to sleep the rest of the night. She'd even resorted to picturing sheep flying over the bed and counting them.

She'd finally fallen asleep somewhere between three and five hundred. . .or was it thousand? There'd be no complaint from her if she never saw another sheep in her life.

The fantastic aroma of rich, dark brew caressed her nose and beckoned her into the kitchen, warring against her instinct to run back upstairs and hide.

At least she'd remembered to put decent clothes on and strap in the "girls" this time.

"There you are, sleepyhead. I have some ultra-caff ready for you." Carly set the mug on the table and put a bottle of creamer beside it. "Lord knows you need it."

"I didn't keep you up, did I?"

"Who, you? Of course not. Your baaing in your sleep didn't wake me up at all."

Her what? A second later it clicked. Baa. Sheep. Oh crud. "I did not baa in my sleep. You're making that up."

Carly wiggled her phone in its bejeweled case. "Wish I could. I even caught the moment on my iPhone in all its wooly glory."

Hanna grabbed for the phone, but her dead-meat friend snatched it back and held it to her chest. "No way. This is some fabulous blackmail right here."

"You didn't show Will, did you?"

A low sound rumbled behind her, a cross between a sheep and a horse in pain. Hanna turned to see William standing in the doorway, looking way too fantastic for the sounds coming from his mouth. This could not be happening.

Without a second thought, she lunged at her friend and the phone she held.

Carly squealed and dropped to the floor in a ball to protect her phone, and large hands encased Hanna's waist, pulling her back.

"Easy, little lamb. No one showed me anything."

On the floor, Carly laughed so hard tears were streaming down her face. "Girl, do you really think I'd video something like that?"

Hanna shoved Will away and stood, looking between the two. "So you didn't show him?"

Her friend held her hands up in surrender. "While you did do some great livestock impressions somewhere around 4:00 a.m., the only thing I'm guilty of is confessing the reason I got up early and couldn't get back to sleep."

Hands on her hips, she couldn't decide if Carly was telling the truth or trying to preserve the health of her expensive phone. "Promise?"

"Check for yourself." She laid the phone beside the coffee mug then gave Hanna a sideways squeeze. "And believe me, I was really, really tempted to. You should be proud of me."

A quick click through the camera roll showed innocuous pictures of the ranch, the silly picture they'd taken together last night to commemorate the trip, and some shots from the airplane.

Breathing a sigh of relief, Hanna sank into the kitchen chair as Carly took the phone back. "I'm going upstairs to get dressed. Drink. We have stuff to do today, girl!"

Carly disappeared upstairs as Hanna poured a generous helping of creamer into her mug and sipped the caramel-colored goodness. *Aaahh, perfect.*

Will settled down beside her with a cup of his own. "Need a little coffee with that cream?"

She shot him a look. "You're already in enough trouble this morning. No need to add offending my coffee to the list."

"Think your coffee will forgive me?"

Was that a double-edged question? "It depends."

"On what?"

"On if you're really sorry for what you did—I mean, said to my coffee, or if you are just apologizing because you don't want me to be mad at you again."

He slid his hand to her cup and took it from her. His gaze was serious as he stared at the light brown liquid inside. "I'm sorry that I offended you. You are a fabulous cup of coffee and deserve all the respect in the world. Sometimes stupid guys get carried away and do things—er—say things they shouldn't. Do you forgive me?"

Hanna rescued her cup from his grip and took another sip, willing herself to sound natural when she could really use a good cry. "Yes."

"Hmm?"

She elbowed him in the arm. "The coffee says yes. It forgives you."

He put his own cup to his lips. "The coffee is very beautiful this morning."

Despite her vow from the night before, her heart rebelled and sighed with pleasure. "It now lectures that flattery will get you nothing."

Will set his cup down and swiveled to look at her. "I'm serious. Both on the 'I'm sorry' and the 'you're beautiful' part. I shouldn't have gotten carried away. There was no excuse."

She swallowed the bitter pill of guilt in the form of now luke-warm coffee. The "right" thing to do would be to accept her portion of responsibility. But what did it really matter? He went too far, regardless of whether she'd allowed him to or led him on. She was only faking an engagement to get her reputation as a good Christian girl back, so obviously what almost happened last night was beyond inappropriate. He should know better.

Scooting back the chair, she stood up and walked to the sink to dump the rest of her coffee down the drain. "It's in the past, and it won't happen again. Now, what's on the agenda today?"

Lilith chose that moment to walk into the kitchen, a soft pink robe hugging her small frame and slippers on her feet. "I can answer that. I thought it'd be nice for us all to go to church together."

Hanna turned to look at William just as the mouthful of coffee he'd taken came spewing from his mouth, most of it landing in his cup. As he coughed and recovered, Lilith smiled. "You haven't been home on a Sunday in ages, William, and I know Hanna and Carly are churchgoers, so I thought it'd be perfect."

Will stood, objection written on every tense muscle in his body. "Mom, I don't think that's a good idea."

His mom flapped her hand in his direction, dismissing his opinion. "Oh, it'll be fine. Going to church is like being with family, sweetie. Right, Hanna?"

Even though she was supposed to be the "spiritual" one of the bunch, even Hanna wasn't digging this suggestion. Church? Considering she was in the middle of a lie the size of Texas and had almost gone to second base with her fake fiancé last night, church did not sound like the most comfortable place to be right now. "Will might actually be right on this one. It's been a long week. Maybe we should just—"

"We're all going to church, and that's final."

Hanna looked to where Will's father stood in the doorway, already dressed in classic khakis and a dark blue dress shirt.

She opened her mouth to protest, but one look at Will's angry expression and she could already see the storm brewing if they didn't comply. Stepping to Will, she put a hand on his arm and smiled. "Of course, we'd be happy to go to church with you."

That was if happy meant that feeling one got when you went to the dentist and had a root canal or two, minus the anesthesia.

⁓

William stepped into the sanctuary and inhaled. The older church smelled exactly as he'd remembered it. A mixture of lemon-scented wax used on the wood pews and old dust that came from the hymnals they refused to replace, even though Mom had said they rarely use them anymore, opting for the more modern method of posting the words to the newer-style praise and worship music on an overhead screen.

It had been a compromise, a way to keep the older generation that refused to accept change and the newer generation that liked the modern style both happy.

Will didn't give a rip about either. He just wanted the service to hurry and start so it could hurry and end and he could escape without speaking to anyone.

"Well, wouldn't you know it? Is that little Willy Preston I see?"

His bad dream just morphed into a nightmare as he turned and found Lena Wallis, his old second-grade Sunday school teacher. Not that she was mean or anything. She just had a difficult time understanding the difference between polite conversation and sticking her nose in everyone else's business. Thankfully, Hanna and Carly had already excused themselves to the restroom, so hopefully he could make this short and sweet, get to a seat, and be done with it. "Mrs. Wallis. It's good to see you again."

"I know your mom said you moved to Nashville awhile back and all, but that doesn't mean you have to stop visiting here every once in a while."

He smiled and humored her. "It's been over ten years since I moved down South. That'd be a long way to come up for church." No need to mention that he'd timed his visits to his parents' house so that Sunday was a travel day.

"Then you've found a good church down there in Tennessee, have you?"

"Well—"

"Don't tell me you're skipping church now. Your mother said something to me about that, and I told her there was just no way my Willy would do such a thing. I was there when he prayed to ask Jesus into his heart when he was just seven years old right in my Sunday school classroom. No siree. No way at all."

William gritted his teeth. He didn't need to explain his nonexistent church attendance or his revised view of God. A man couldn't live his life based on some flippant prayer he made in elementary school. Claire had just had a "miracle" happen when she'd almost died after a heart procedure. Everyone had been so busy praising God for her miraculous turnaround that the Sunday school lesson about God healing our spiritual hearts had hit home, prodding Will to take the step he'd always heard about but hadn't been sure of.

And he'd stuck by his decision until the day Claire died. The day God had turned His back, shrugged His shoulders, and decided He didn't care about the Preston family anymore.

Will came to church today for his parents' sake only. And he'd choose not to make a scene based on that fact as well.

Blessedly, Hanna and Carly chose that moment to walk into the sanctuary.

He motioned them over to where he stood. "Excuse me, Mrs. Wallis, but I want to introduce you to my fiancée, Hanna, and her best friend, Carly. They are visiting us from Minnesota." A pinprick of guilt stabbed him for lying in church, but he brushed it away as easily as he did all the other pricks he felt on a daily basis.

The older woman gave him a look with those squinted eyes, wrinkles hinting at the wisdom held within, that said she knew exactly what he was up to. But then she turned to Hanna and Carly and gave them both generous hugs. "It's so good to meet you both. I've never been to Minnesota. What's it like up there?"

Hanna glanced at him for a moment, her knowing look seeing right through him, but then smiled at Mrs. Wallis. "Honestly, we have only two seasons in Minnesota. Winter and Mosquito-Mud season. But it is also beautiful, and we wouldn't trade it for anything in the world. It's home."

Carly leaned toward Mrs. Wallis and pretended to whisper. "Except maybe Hawaii. I might trade it for that, but don't tell Hanna."

Mrs. Wallis giggled, but the band began to warm up, so William grabbed the opportunity to usher the women to their seats.

Much had changed in the ten years since he'd last been forced to visit church. There was still a piano, but the organ was replaced with drums, a keyboard, and a guitar. The worship team began to sing a song that wasn't even remotely familiar but had a decent beat to it at least.

And unless Will was imagining things, a few of the musicians were old friends of his from high school who'd had a garage grunge band back in the day. He'd smoked a few cigarettes with them that they'd stolen from one of the guy's dad's stash. He'd coughed for hours after that then was grounded for a month when he came home reeking of smoke. That had been the year after Claire died.

Odd that his former partners in crime who'd persuaded him to get into trouble were now leading worship to God. And he, the goody-goody they'd had to push into it, didn't want to be anywhere near a church.

The song changed to an upbeat version of an old hymn he remembered, so he mouthed the words to at least give a semblance of participation.

Then to his right, a sweet voice trickled to his ears.

A sweet, very off-key voice. One that really shouldn't sing in public. Ever.

He bit the side of his cheek to keep from laughing. That his "fiancée" couldn't hold a tune if her life depended on it was a great tidbit of information. He wondered if she knew the degree of horribleness she possessed or if everyone had always lied to be nice to her.

The way she belted out that high note, he'd bet his bank account on the latter.

Yet another song started. Great. Had things changed so much that there was no longer a sermon? They just sang the whole time?

On one hand, sitting down anytime this millennium would be nice. But not having to sit through a long, drawn-out sermon expounding on the details of hell and the fact that he was headed straight there sounded great, too.

The feminine screech of a high note rang next to him again.

If he were a praying man, he'd opt for asking for the sermon to start immediately. To save both his ears and Hanna's, uh, reputation.

Hanna closed her eyes and sang with all her heart, letting the music wash over her like a waterfall.

Goodness, how she'd missed church.

The whole car ride this morning she'd dreaded it. Her life these days wasn't exactly God glorifying. Her prayers seemed to fall on deaf ears, and that was the few times she'd made herself pray.

But the moment the music began and the band started singing praises to Jesus, the bricks she'd been piling up in her heart came crashing down faster than the walls of Jericho. The louder she sang, the clearer her vision became.

God was still there.

She was the one who had nicely stuck her index fingers in her ears and sung "la-la-la-la" at the top of her proverbial lungs, drowning out God's voice.

Her mom had always told her God inhabits our joyful songs of praise to Him. And that's what today's service had done for her. For the first time since starting that crazy reality TV show, she felt close to God again. Like He was there, basking in the praises.

She didn't care if they even got to the sermon. They could just sing for the next hour and she'd be good.

Will took a step closer to her, enclosing an arm around her and pressing her to his side. Warmth curled in her belly, and despite her best intentions to remain focused on God, she rested her head on his shoulder. His responding squeeze of her body sent shivers of pleasure straight to her toes.

For just a moment, she allowed herself to stop singing, close her eyes, and dream.

William and Hanna Preston—in church, side by side, maybe a little blond-haired boy between them, a baby girl with a polka-dotted bow in her hair snuggled in Hanna's arms. A family. Worshipping

God together on Sunday. No reporters. No lies. No putting arms around her just for show.

For the first time since the big lie, she didn't despise Will.

Oh, he still had his issues.

But she fit him. And he fit her. Maybe it was the kiss that almost went too far that changed her perspective. Or maybe it was just being in church and yearning for what wasn't. But the dream was oh-so-clear right now.

Except when she glanced up at his face. His stony, hard expression staring into space reminded her that their relationships with God were very different. Hanna was struggling, yes, but all Christians went through seasons of struggling, right?

William was rejecting God, though. He had done more than just stick a few cotton balls in his ears; he'd slammed the door and walked away.

The scene in her daydream changed at that moment to Will sitting in a recliner, watching football on Sunday morning while Hanna left for church, two kids in tow, by herself.

That wasn't nearly so dreamy.

Neither was the next moment, when she noticed, three aisles behind them, a man with a phone pointed at them, not-so-discreetly trying to take a picture.

Couldn't they leave them alone in church, at least? Was nothing sacred anymore?

A moment later, the preacher took the pulpit and invited everyone to sit down.

As the sermon began, Hanna took solace in the fact that at least the picture taker was in church. She hoped the preacher had prepared a good Bible thumping for today. It would serve the man right.

CHAPTER TWENTY-SEVEN

After church, the Preston family and guests headed for Red Lobster, an old family tradition according to William's mom.

Once seated and a seafood appetizer in front of them, Lilith got down to business. "So, Hanna, what did you think of Faith Community Church?"

"I really enjoyed it. Reminded me a lot of my church back home, but about ten times larger." It had overwhelmed her at first. Her church at home counted it a miracle of God if they hit fifty in attendance on any given Sunday. The five-hundred-plus-member church had taken some getting used to, but the worship time had been completely worth it.

As did the benediction and altar call at the end, when she'd been pleased to see the camera phone–toting man haul tail down to the front, red-faced and teary-eyed.

The sermon had been nothing but perfect. While no Bible thumping had occurred, the message was about God's grace, not just hiding sins from view but *removing* them. About the power over sin that the Holy Spirit gives us. And how we needed to lift others up instead of tearing them down. It was exactly what she'd needed to hear.

Harrison jabbed a few shrimp and put them on his plate. "What about you, William? Changed a little since you were last there, hasn't it?"

"Yeah, it has. How anyone convinced them to put in an overhead projector and drum set is beyond me."

"Numbers were slipping, and we were going to have to start cutting staff if it kept up. A few of the young guys suggested modernizing the worship a little, and it's helping. Pastor Wrightsville wasn't pleased though, but he was about five years past ready to retire. Did you like the new pastor?"

Hanna noticed William shift in his seat but couldn't think of a gentle way to change topics for him.

"He seemed nice." His cell phone started to jingle, and he looked almost gleeful as he rose from the table. "Sorry, I need to take this."

It didn't escape anyone's notice that he hadn't even looked to see who was calling. Hanna wouldn't put it past him to have a long conversation with a telemarketer about sales strategies until lunch arrived just to stall.

Lilith took the conversation ball, though, and rolled with it. "Hanna, I thought I'd take you and Carly on a little shopping expedition this afternoon. Maybe pick out an outfit for the interview tomorrow? My treat, of course."

While that sounded super sweet, Hanna forced herself not to look down at her outfit. Was she that frumpy? She thought she looked fairly nice today, although she was going to have to reuse an outfit for the interview tomorrow. Not that she cared, but William and his mother might.

But still, shopping was expected, whether she liked it or not. "That'd be great, Mrs. Preston."

"It's Lilith, remember. Or Mom would do as well. You're almost family, you know. Speaking of, after we find your interview outfit, I say we stop by a bridal shop or two. I know it's too early to decide on a dress, but it's fun to start browsing and get an idea of the style you like."

Hanna was still stuck on "Mom." This sweet woman viewed herself as a mother figure to her, wanted to go wedding dress shopping with her. She blinked away the tears that threatened to fall. She hadn't missed her mom more than at this very moment. Yes, it was a fake engagement. She wouldn't *really* be buying a wedding dress.

But going through the motions was still a reminder of what she was missing.

And lying to her fake future "mom" didn't help.

Maybe she should just tell them the truth. Her conscience would thank her.

She opened her mouth to do just that when Will slid back into his seat, a scowl on his face. "Something has come up at work. We'll have to head out tomorrow right after the interview."

His dad wore a matching frown. "Why is work calling on a Sunday anyway?"

"They scheduled an emergency board meeting for tomorrow afternoon. Long story." He glanced at Hanna, and the worry in his eyes made her shudder. Something wasn't right. But then he put on his game face, smiled, and picked up a menu. "You haven't ordered yet, have you?"

Hanna smoothed a hand over his arm, partially as an act but deep down, to reassure him. Why she felt the need to do that she wasn't sure. "No, we were waiting for you and talking about shopping this afternoon."

His mom smiled and clicked her long, manicured nails on the table. "Yes, you and Dad can do whatever you'd like. Us girls are going wedding dress shopping."

William looked down at his menu, his throat bobbing from the deep gulp he took. "I'm in the mood for lobster. Anyone else?"

Yes, the man had perfected the art of changing the subject. Must be in the job description of CEO or something.

～～

No crying allowed.

This isn't real, Hanna. Pretend only. Like when she was four and Momma got her a "play" wedding dress for Christmas. It had fake flowers along the waist and probably cost less than five dollars at the thrift store, but she'd worn that thing out dressing up in it so many times.

Today was no different. Except that the white dress had an almost five-digit price tag on it and represented just how impossible her childhood dreams were now.

Hanna twirled around in front of the mirror, not able to take her eyes from her reflection.

Big mistake. Her heart took flight with delight. The ball gown style dress, with its full tulle bottom, flowed in a circle, so very princess-esque. What girl didn't want to feel like a princess on her wedding day? And to have a twirling dress. Oh, she might just swoon right there in the overpriced bridal salon.

And the top of the dress.

It was nothing she would have picked off the rack for herself. The saleswoman had decided the wife-to-be of a CEO and reality TV star should at least try on something with a bit of glitz.

Hanna was usually more a fan of simple. She'd tried on a nice, tasteful—both in price and modesty—A-line that she'd liked, as well as a mermaid dress per Carly's suggestion that, after trying on, had made Hanna laugh so hard she thought her sides would burst. She wasn't fat, but God had blessed her with hips. And she had no plans to show off their magnitude on her wedding day, be it fake or not.

But this dress. Wow. Simple was out the door and glamour rocked the salon. Literally. The strapless bodice was smothered in rhinestone embroidery, with a thin silk band around her waist. She could totally picture herself walking down the aisle in this dress.

It was everything she never wanted, but only because she hadn't allowed herself to dream *that* big.

And oddly, the image of Will at the altar beside the pastor wasn't nearly as yucky as it had been just a short month ago.

What was happening here? Was she actually falling for him again? Like, more than "oh my gosh he's a good kisser" falling? Maybe it was just his charm getting to her. The man could charm the parka off an Eskimo. He had that air about him that just said, "Hey, I'm not perfect, but I'm a good guy." He opened doors for her when she wasn't too quick to open them first. He made jokes that really weren't funny but made her laugh anyway. He looked too adorable with that black-and-blue eye that was finally, mostly, gone.

Ack. This was not good. She *was* falling for him again.

She put a hand to her stomach, the feeling of three very different textures meeting her skin. Jewels, silk, and tulle. All meshed together to make something more beautiful than she could imagine.

Was that how she and Will could be? Different, yet together something wonderful?

Oh, what was she thinking? Will didn't want this just as much as she didn't. It was a ploy to save face, secure his career, and maybe, a little bit, make retribution to her. That was all. She needed to remember that, needed to remind her heart of that.

He'd hurt her. He could do it again just as easily, if not more so now.

The Hanna and Will mixture was more likely to cause indigestion than to be delectable.

But that reality didn't change the fact that with this dress on, sound reason threatened to escape through her fingers like sand scattering in the wind.

Carly stepped up beside her and put an arm around her waist. "Whadya think?"

Hanna took a breath, trying to blink away tears, not able to take her eyes off the dress. "It's perfect." Except that it was fake.

The saleswoman, who'd introduced herself as Anita, looked prouder than Hanna's dad holding a prize-winning walleye. "We're having a ten percent off sale this weekend, just so you know."

Smile and nod, Hanna. She did just that. No need explaining this was for dream purposes only. Instead, she twirled again, allowing herself to experience the giddy princess feel one last time. "Actually, we haven't set a date yet, so I don't think I'm ready to buy a dress today, but—wow. If I were getting one right now, I'd definitely be saying yes to this dress."

The saleswoman was not to be denied. "You never know if you'll be able to find this one again, though. The spring-season dresses will be coming out soon, so this isn't going to be available much longer."

Her pretend future mother-in-law came up behind her, arms crossed, a finger tapping her chin. "You know, I think she's right, Hanna. This is the perfect dress for you. It fits your personality and William's, and it's not every dress that makes a bride tear up. I think you should get it."

Panic rammed into Hanna, threatening to send her falling to the floor, expensive dress and all. Buy the dress? She couldn't think of a worse idea. "No, I need to, uh..."

Anita came and put an arm around her. "I know it's a big decision, dear. But the more dresses you look at, the more confused you'll be. When you find the right one, you need to snatch it up. Trust me. I've been in this business for over twenty years."

Hanna eyed Carly, who shrugged her shoulders. "The dress *is* gorgeous, Hanna."

Never had she wanted to backhand her best friend as much as she did at that moment. Did she not read the *"get me out of this"* message she'd sent with her eyes?

Lilith pulled out her checkbook. "It's settled, then. And if I wasn't clear before, the dress is your wedding present from Harrison and I. We've already discussed it, and it's well below our price limit. So don't you worry about the cost."

Anita looked like she'd just landed in commission heaven. She fluttered over to Lilith, so giddy she might as well be the one getting married. "Come right this way, and we'll get it all settled." As an afterthought, she turned back to Hanna. "Your friend can help you get changed. Oh, you're going to be just the most beautiful bride."

Stuck, Hanna just stood there, not sure what to say. She commanded her mouth to move, to call out and tell them to stop. That she hated the dress and wanted to keep looking. That was the sensible, right thing to do. But her voice jammed in her throat, and no words came out. Not to mention Carly was squealing like a ten-year-old and pushing her toward the dressing room and saying something about picking out veils.

She went through the motions of taking off the cursed, amazing dress and getting back into her jeans and sweater. The dress hung from the wall in all its tulle-covered glory.

This was just fantastic. On top of a fake fiancé and a fake wedding ring, she was now the proud owner of a fake wedding dress that cost almost ten grand.

William was going to have a cow. No, take that back. A cow was much too mild. It would be more like a bull. A raging, angry bull.

CHAPTER TWENTY-EIGHT

*W*illiam put the last shirt his mom had washed for him onto the top of the stack of clothes and zipped up the black Samsonite suitcase. The only good part of this day was that he hadn't been made to go shopping with the women.

A thought of Hanna decked out in some fabulous all-white number made the hairs on the back of his neck stand at attention. She'd probably pick something simple, high-cut neckline, very few embellishments. But simple fit her. She'd look stunning, he knew.

At least she wasn't purchasing one. Not yet, anyway. They had to finish this charade so she could go on to someone who deserved her first.

Guilt plunged into his gut.

That was the crux of his issues lately, wasn't it? As hard as he'd worked, as important as his job was to him, the fact that he didn't deserve an amazing woman like Hanna was about to kill him.

Heaving the baggage from his bed, he set it by the door and looked around at his childhood bedroom. He'd hung his outfit for the interview tomorrow in the closet. He wore old sweats and a T-shirt around the house tonight so he could just stuff them in the side pocket of his bag tomorrow. Everything was planned. It would go perfectly, just as he liked it.

Except he had no clue yet what to do about Hanna after the interview. He should probably just put her back on a plane to Minnesota. That was the intelligent thing to do.

But the impromptu board meeting tomorrow night was not a good sign. They were either saying his efforts were too little, too late, or giving him an ultimatum.

There was no logical reason for Hanna not to go home for a while. They'd made their statement. They'd been seen in public together plenty of times. And besides a few sleazy magazines, most of the press from anything reputable seemed encouraging. He'd even had a message this afternoon from a writer at *People* about doing a feature story on them.

But he'd told them he'd get back with them next week. No use committing to something before he knew if he was still employed or not. Then again, they were offering a hefty sum for a feature photo op and inside story. That could be useful for an unemployed Hanna.

Nothing could be decided until after tomorrow night, though.

Which probably meant that Hanna should come back with him.

Not because he needed her there for moral support. He flopped onto his bed as he'd done so many times as a kid. No. He didn't need blond-haired, blue-eyed, sweet-as-sugar Hanna to support him. It was *his* job to support *her*.

He shifted to his side and stared at Claire's picture on his bedside table, taken a year before she died. She'd been eleven. He was in the picture, too, making some crazy face that was giving her the giggles. It had been his favorite thing to do. Making his sister smile. She had so many moments of not smiling in her life, it had felt like the one thing he could do to make things better.

That, and he prayed. His mom had called him their personal prayer warrior. For a kid of fourteen, he'd been on fire for God, believing that miracles happened and that he lived daily with one of those miracles who was walking and smiling and breathing.

A year later, God turned His back and stole their miracle away.

William reached out and picked up the picture, blinking away the highly unmanly tears that weren't allowed to fall. Duped. That's how he felt. Like God had made them think everything was going to be fine, made them trust Him, then just pulled life out from underneath them.

Claire's life.

And sometimes it felt like He'd stolen Will's life, too.

His parents seemed unscathed though. They'd mourned for a while, but look at them now. Active in church. Praising a God who had abandoned them. The ultimate naïveté.

It was why he hated coming home. Seeing them all smiles-for-Jesus made him sick to his stomach.

A knock sounded on the bedroom door, and he shoved the picture under his pillow and stood up as the door opened to reveal his dad. "Will? Thought you might want to go for a ride with me with the girls all gone. Get out the snowmobiles and make some tracks?"

Hanna would be jealous. But no part of Will wanted *fun* right now. "I'm all packed, actually. Not really dressed for the cold."

"Oh, come on. You can borrow something of mine."

What part of no didn't his old man understand? "I'm surprised you're still snowmobiling."

"What, you mean because I'm such an old guy now? Don't think I can handle it?"

Will shrugged. "You said it, not me."

"I'll have you know your mom and I go out once a week when there's enough snow. You aren't putting us in the grave just yet, son."

The thought of losing his parents almost made him want to sit down again. But he didn't dare show weakness in front of his father. "How about we go down and get something to eat? It's almost dinnertime, and who knows how long it'll take them to shop?"

His father begrudgingly agreed, and they made their way downstairs. With a feast consisting of popcorn, salami sandwiches, and soda, they broke Mom's rule and settled into the living room.

Concern prodded at Will. His dad was a stickler for house rules. There were probably a few scars on Will's rear end from the paddle for eating candy in the living room to prove it. Either his dad had seriously mellowed in his old age, something he'd yet to see a sign of since he'd been home, or he wanted to talk about something unpleasant.

Kinda like the time Dad sat him down to have the sex and puberty talk. That had resulted in ice cream and brownies for dinner.

But so far, Harrison just clicked the TV to ESPN and tossed a few kernels of popcorn in his mouth.

It was about ten minutes later when the food was gone that the older man cleared his throat. "William, I wanted to talk to you."

Will settled back in the recliner, feet up, trying to look relaxed. "I already know how babies are made. We had that discussion awhile ago, remember?"

His dad didn't even crack a smile. "It's about Hanna."

He'd figured as much. "Okay."

"And Claire."

Pushing in the footrest, William stood up. "Think I'll go up to bed."

His dad stood to meet him, his voice low instead of his usual booming demands. "We should have talked about this a long time ago, William. I'm sorry for that."

Will clenched his hand into a fist, really wanting to punch something right now. "For what? For not talking about it, or for forgetting about your daughter?"

"I never forgot about her, and you know it. I love you and Claire more than life itself." His loud drumlike voice was back. "Now sit down so we can have an adult conversation about it. You're a man now, William. It's time to act like it."

"What kind of man turns his back on his daughter? I'm sick and tired of seeing you all happy-go-lucky and 'God' this and 'God' that. If your God was worth anything, He would've actually *answered* our prayers, and you know it. Claire was the sweetest girl who ever lived and loved Jesus more than anyone I've ever known. God killing her was just wrong. How can you sit there and be okay with that? Especially as her dad?"

William took a step forward, looking directly into the eyes of the father he'd always feared and used to respect. "I hope I never become a father, because if it makes me anything like you, I don't think I could live with myself."

He stomped off and started back up the stairs.

"William, wait."

He looked down at his father from over the banister and saw tears in the older man's eyes for the second time in his life. "What?"

"I love you, William. It doesn't matter what you say to me. I know you're hurt, but I won't ever stop loving you. Neither will God. I'm praying for you, son, whether you like it or not."

CHAPTER TWENTY-NINE

*H*anna stood at Will's bedroom door, fiddling with a button on the lime-green cardigan sweater Lilith had insisted on buying for her. She'd said it was classy but hip.

But what wasn't so classy and hip was that it was time to tell her faux fiancé about the fake wedding dress that now hung in his parents' closet.

The man was going to be mad enough to steam a fish.

If she didn't tell him now, though, Lilith would say something later, and William might blow their cover.

As much as that had sounded good a few hours ago, she couldn't fess up now that a ten-thousand-dollar dress had been purchased. This enagement plot was going to have to die a slow death, but regardless, it wouldn't heal her guilt.

Lord, give me courage.

Yes, this was great. Praying for God to help her continue a lie to billions of people. She sure was quality Christian material today.

Raising her hand to knock on the dark, wood-grained door, she jumped when it opened before her knuckles even made a sound.

"Hanna? What are you doing here?"

"We, uh. We're back from shopping."

"Yeah, I heard you pull up. Why are you up here though? My parents will see you."

She glanced behind her, heard the voices filtering up from the living room. "They're busy talking. I told them I'd come and get you."

He took a step out of his door and put a hand on her elbow. "Well, let's get on down, then. It's our last night here, you know."

Oh, good night. This was getting harder and harder. "Actually. . ."

He turned and lifted an eyebrow. "What's going on?"

Hanna gulped and tilted her head toward his room. "Can we talk a minute? In private?" Because she hoped four walls and a door would help muffle his reaction. Although he wasn't normally a yeller, just a liar, ten grand of his parents' money could change that.

Pulling at his T-shirt collar—the shirt that was way too hot on him because it hugged his sculpted torso—he looked toward the stairs again and back at her. "You sure you wanna be alone in my room with me?"

She took his hand and pulled him into the room, shutting the door behind him. "No, but it's important."

"Hanna, what's wrong?" Worry lines carved into his forehead.

Trying to ignore the fact that she was in his bedroom that was still decorated like he was sixteen, she pointed to the bed. "You're gonna be mad, so you better sit down."

Instead of obeying her suggestion, he paced the carpet. "What happened? Did you talk to reporters? No one found out, did they?"

That might have been better in the long run. "Quite the opposite, actually."

He stopped in front of her, hands folded at his chest, gaze pummeling hers. "Spit it out, Hanna. What's going on?"

"Your mom bought me a dress."

Will blinked then shook his head. "Uh, okay. I thought that was the point. To pick out an outfit for tomorrow."

She turned and took a few steps toward his dresser and picked up an old basketball trophy. It helped to have something in her hand. And maybe something to defend herself with. "No, Will. She bought me a wedding dress."

Silence.

Then she heard some scuffling, so she turned around and found him sitting on the plaid comforter–covered bed, hands on his knees, his gaze focused on some unknown spot on the carpet. "Will?"

"Okay. We can handle this. I'll just pay her back, and we can return the dress later."

"She said they wanted the dress to be a gift from them."

He took a breath. "Well, they can still take it back once we break up."

She'd thought the same thing until she'd read the receipt on the way home from the bridal shop. "Wedding dresses have a no-return policy."

This brought his gaze up to meet hers. "What kind of scam business are they running? Who doesn't accept returns these days?"

Hanna shrugged her shoulders, still holding tight to the little gold man pretending to shoot a hoop. "They don't want people wearing it for their wedding day then trying to return it, I guess."

He leaned forward, elbows on his knees again. "Then I'll just pay them back after it's all done."

And here comes the thunder. Hanna took a step back so her hip rested on the dresser for support. "It was, uh, kinda expensive."

As he looked up, the side of his mouth quirked upward. "Honey, I have money. I can afford to pay them back for a dress. Don't worry."

Two very unique urges filled her from her toes to the tip of her head.

The desire to kiss that adorable mouth of his.

And the desire to just nod her head and not mention just how much he'd have to pay back.

Unfortunately, she'd regret doing either of those for a very long time.

She took the folded-up paper from her pocket and handed it to him. "This was the, uh, receipt."

He smiled at her, took the paper, and glanced at it.

Then did a double take. He lifted his eyes up to hers, then back down, then up to hers again. "Do you mean to tell me this dress cost almost ten thousand dollars?"

She took a breath and squared her shoulders for the onslaught. "Your mom picked it out. I promise I tried to talk her out of it. I really, really did. But Carly started in on me, too, and before I knew it your mom was scribbling out a check and they were packaging up the dress. It's breathtaking, Will. I know I'll never wear it, but oh my goodness. I've never seen anything like it. I'm sorry. I just didn't know what else to do. I know you want to yell at me and curse and who knows what else, just—we can't back out now. I'd feel horrible if they knew I lied to them and made them waste that much money."

Hanna looked him in the eye, unable to read his thoughts. "Please, Will. I'd give anything not to hurt them more. I'll save my pennies and pay them back myself, I promise."

She turned and put the trophy back in its assigned spot. Blinking back tears, she headed for the door to get the heck out of Dodge.

But William's hand on her shoulder stopped her.

He turned her around and folded her into his arms, her head resting on his shoulder.

The clock on the wall ticked, the only sound in the room, but Hanna just held on. She had no idea what else to do, and this Will—a kind one that would hold her to try and make her feel better—this was not what she'd expected at all.

Will's hand smoothed her hair and pulled her head back, bringing her gaze to his. "Was the dress pretty?"

She allowed her mouth to curve up just a hair. "It was breathtaking, Will."

"Would you have picked it out?"

She closed her eyes and pictured the sleeveless, rhinestone and tulle dress again and sighed. "Never in a million years. But it was perfect."

Hanna gasped when his lips covered hers, tasting and probing for just a moment. Just as quick as it started, the kiss ended, leaving her shivering and breathless.

Then his forehead rested on hers and he winked. "Good." He eased her back and opened the door. "Let's head downstairs. They might send up a search party, complete with buckets full of cold water, if we don't get back down there soon."

Sure enough, as they descended the stairs, Carly stood on the bottom step. "Thought I was going to have to intervene."

Will ruffled Hanna's hair like he would a ten-year-old. "Was just showing her my old basketball trophies, is all."

~~~

Ten. Thousand. Dollars.

The dress better be made of solid gold.

William glanced over at Hanna in the back of the car he'd hired to take them to the studio. She was staring out the window as if she'd never seen a city before.

If they weren't flying out tonight, and if he could have figured out a way to get past his mother, he would have made her model the dress for him. He should at least get that pleasure since he was going to fork out ten grand on a dress that would never be worn again.

But no. His parents and Carly were ever present, and the dress was tucked safely away in his parents' closet.

It was probably for the best. He'd been stupid to kiss Hanna again last night. But she'd just looked so worried, and holding her in his arms had awakened every manly desire in him.

The kissing needed to stop, though.

They wouldn't be getting married. And there had been no cameras in the bedroom to make a show for.

And thank goodness for that.

He reached over and squeezed her hand. "You ready for this?"

She glanced at him with a smile that didn't quite make it to her eyes. "As I'll ever be."

"You're going to do great."

"What's the plan after the interview? I mean, you're flying back to Nashville and Carly's flying home. What's the plan for me?"

He shifted back to her. "I figured you'd come back to Nashville."

"I'm not a fan of living out of hotels. Maybe it's best for me just to go back to Minnesota for now. I can visit again in a month or something."

Will hesitated. "Would it be bad to say that I need you?"

She threw her head back and laughed. "Need me? Mr. Corporate CEO who has the world planned out and in order? You don't need me, Will. I have full confidence in you."

He looked out the window of the black sedan at the tall buildings of Manhattan and the flurry of busy people hustling by. Lately it felt like all his well-thought-out plans were fizzling into a fine dust and being scattered into the air, landing who knows where. Maybe that's why he felt so. . .lost.

He was a grown man, leading a multi-billion-dollar company, and he was more lost than he'd ever been in his whole life.

And the only thing that made him feel even slightly grounded was the woman who sat beside him.

Who loved the God he hated.

Who was pretend-engaged to him.

Who made his blood boil and surge at the same time.

Life made zero sense at the moment. But Hanna was the only thing remotely "right" about it. And she was temporary.

He tugged her across the seat so they sat hip to hip, and he put his arm around her, mindful of the ears and eyes of the driver. "I don't know why, but I just do. Tell you what. You come back to Nashville with me tonight, and I'll have you back in Minnesota by week's end so you can spend some time with your dad. Deal? Then we can play it by ear from there. I'll come visit you one weekend, then you can come visit me. We'll make wedding plans and figure it out as we go. None of my outlined plans that irritate you so much. How about that?"

She laid her head on his shoulder, the warmth of her cuddled up to him sending unwanted spirals of pleasure down his body. "That sounds like a good plan, actually."

He turned his head and pressed his lips against her smooth hair that reminded him of sunshine. Then he took out his phone and started typing a text.

Hanna sat up and tried to peek at his phone.

He held it back from her. Not because she couldn't see what he typed, but just to be ornery. "Hey, Miss Nosy. Do you mind?"

She gave his arm a playful shove. "Stop it. I just wanted to see who you're texting."

"If you must know, I was making sure Emma had gotten my message to book your plane ticket with mine for this afternoon, and telling her to book another one for you to go home on Friday. That okay with you?"

"Must be nice having an assistant."

He shrugged. "It has its perks. And Emma is the best."

"Can I meet her when we get back to Nashville?"

William controlled his breathing, not wanting to act suspicious. He should have anticipated the question. And really, the chances of Hanna recognizing Emma after all this time were nil.

"Maybe. I'm a pretty hard taskmaster and keep her busy most of the time."

Her eyebrows shot up. "What? Is she some gorgeous beauty you're afraid I'll be jealous of?"

"Nope. I mean, yes, she's very pretty, but—" With a glance at the driver, who was looking at them in the rearview mirror with a frown, he pulled Hanna to him and kissed her lips soundly. "She has nothing on you, honey."

"Then let me meet her."

Why couldn't the woman let it go? It would be one thing if this was real. But she didn't need to meet everyone in his life at this point. She'd already spent a week living at his parents' house.

The car turned onto Rockefeller Plaza, and Will leaned forward and pointed. "There's the studio. You ready?"

Her already light skin turned a shade paler. "No. But let's get it over with."

One of the producer's assistants from *The Price of Love*, her name was Celine, if Will remembered correctly, stood on the sidewalk to greet them and ushered them inside. "You're late. We'll have to do a rush job on makeup now."

"Traffic was bad. Sorry."

The woman glanced back as she power walked down a long hallway and into a waiting elevator. "It's New York. Traffic is always bad."

Will guided Hanna to follow, keeping a hand on the small of her back for show and support. "I didn't expect to see you here. Assumed someone from *ALIVE* would meet us."

"Monty wanted us to represent, make sure the show's image is protected and all. You understand."

He didn't really, but then again, the show business stuff was never really his forte.

She punched in the floor number and turned toward him. "You really put a wrench in my schedule by delaying this, you know. I was already in town last Sunday and had to fly all the way back to LA."

Celine had never been his favorite while the show was filming. Some things never changed. He shrugged, not willing to engage her and make the day worse.

Hanna squirmed under his hand, and he took a step closer and squeezed her waist.

The elevator door blissfully opened, and they stepped out into the hall. "Down this hallway, second door on the left, is where you get ready. I'll go get makeup and hair and tell them to hurry so you can have time to brief with the producer."

At least they'd have a minute or two alone. Hanna looked like she might faint any moment, which seemed odd because she always exuded confidence on the set of the show.

Entering the room, Will closed the door behind them and led her to the small froufrou couch. "Everything okay? You don't look so good."

She covered her midsection with a hand and nodded. "Yeah. Just nerves I think. My stomach isn't feeling too hot."

He wasn't a praying man anymore, but if there was a God up there that cared a lick, it would be great timing to step in and help. Hanna getting sick now or, worse, on stage would be the worst possible scenario. "Do you need something? Can I help?"

She shook her head. "No, I—I think it's just nerves."

"You always seemed so in control on set before. What gives, Hanna?"

Sitting back, his adorable little fake fiancée closed her blue eyes and took a few long deep breaths. "There was always this lady on the crew who made me feel better. I don't even remember her name, but she seemed to appear every time reality hit me and panic set in. After I talked with her, it was like, yeah, I could do this. She always joked that she had a paper bag ready just in case though."

Will reached down and slid a stray yellow strand of hair out of her face. "What did she look like?"

"Oh, I don't know. Red hair, always wore it in a ponytail. Thick-rimmed glasses. Thin. Why? Do you remember her?"

Yes. Yes he did. "There were so many crew members, they blurred together. I mostly remember the few that were assigned to me." William grabbed a chocolate cookie from the plate that sat in front of them and held it up to Hanna. "Here. Eat something. It might help your stomach."

She opened an eye, snatched the cookie, and took a slow, savoring bite. Then another. And another until it was gone. "Mmmmm. That is what I nee—"

Before Will could move or realize what was happening, she lurched forward and heaved.

CHAPTER THIRTY

*H*anna curled up on the couch, back facing Celine and Alec, the *ALIVE* producer, as they discussed what to do.

What an idiot she had been to eat that stupid cookie on a sour stomach. What had she been thinking? More so, what had Will been thinking to give it to her?

He was paying the consequences though, via vomit-à-la-shoe.

She wasn't sure she had ever been so humiliated, except of course after Will's horrific lie that started this whole blasted mess.

God, I really need a break. Something good to come of this. I just. . .I don't know what to do anymore.

It was like one disaster after another just kept piling on.

Could it get any worse?

Alec's deep voice boomed throughout the room. "We can't cancel with less than twenty minutes till airtime. Have you forgotten we're called *ALIVE* because it's a 'live' show, Celine? I know you can postpone on your little reality TV thing whenever you want, but we don't have that luxury here."

Hanna could hear Celine pace. "So, what? You want Hanna to go out there looking green and Will to be shoeless? That'd be just fantastic."

"Makeup can do wonders. And send them both out barefoot.

It'd be a statement, something to get people talking about besides what happens in their bedroom."

She'd had enough. Hanna rolled over and propped up on the cushion. "There is no 'their' bedroom. And we'll go do the interview. I'm feeling better now anyway. I think my breakfast just didn't agree with me. And can't he just borrow someone's shoes?"

Will emerged from the bathroom that was attached to the dressing room. His feet were bare, and his rinsed off but still soggy shoes dangled from his fingers. "They aren't perfect, and they might smell, but I think if we blow dry them off a little, I can still wear them. Can someone ask the driver to bring in my suitcase? I can grab a clean pair of socks out of there at least."

She breathed a relieved sigh. Going on national TV barefoot would have been a new low point.

Ignoring a protesting Celine, Alec kicked into gear, barking orders for a crew member to go get Will's luggage, and ordering someone to call hair and makeup down to fix Hanna.

Which made her sit up finally and glance in the mirror across the room.

Oh no.

Her makeup she'd done so carefully this morning, a rarity, looked like one of her kindergartners had applied it. Her mascara had run, her lips showed no sign of color, and her cheeks sported a splotchy pink design. Her hair looked like she'd forgotten to brush it this morning, all mussed up and tangled from laying down on the small dressing room couch.

It would take a miracle to make her look any kind of presentable in the short time they had.

Maybe Celine was right. Maybe they should cancel.

But within minutes, a fresh pair of socks were on Will's feet, and Hanna was ushered to a chair in front of the large dressing room mirror as if she were royalty, instead of the hot mess she actually was.

Some poor soul was attacking Will's shoe with a hair dryer in the corner. God bless them.

One woman started in on the tangled mess that was Hanna's hair, while another took out her cosmetic tools and went to work on Hanna's face.

Will leaned against the wall behind them, his jaw set in a firm line. "You sure you're okay with this, Hanna?"

She started to nod, which got her a slap on the shoulder from the hair lady. "Yes. My stomach isn't rolling like it was earlier. I just want to get this over with."

Moving one muscle would probably be a disaster. She might lose a toe, eye, or fistful of hair.

Alec stood to the side with his notes. "So, you'll walk out there, and the first section will be improv banter. They'll make a few jokes, and you both just roll with it and don't say anything too stupid, okay?"

She started to nod her head but got a swat on each shoulder from both the hair and makeup women. She settled for an "Mmmhmmm" out of her clenched mouth.

"After that, we'll go a little deeper into your engagement and the whole 'Holy Hanna' scandal. This isn't tabloid TV. We'll keep it clean."

Will gave a thumbs-up. "That's why we picked you guys."

"Not saying the questions won't be pointed, but just be honest and entertaining. After all, that's what our viewers want. To see a show."

A show. As in fiction, fake, and unreality. She could definitely give them that.

Alec excused himself, saying he had to get out front and that Celine would come get them when it was time.

The miracle workers put the final touches on their subjects and hustled off to their next victims.

Will stood and slid on his sports coat over his white dress shirt. The man looked downright yummy when he dressed up.

Her heart threatened to jump right out of her chest. "I'm still nervous. Can you imagine if we would've had to do this in bare feet?"

He held out a foot and wiggled it. "But I have handsome toes, so I guess you're the one missing out, aye?"

She would have been offended at his blatant mimicking of her Minnesota accent except for the adorable wink he sent her afterward, "I have seen your bare feet, and I don't think anyone is missing out."

He chuckled and helped her out of the chair then motioned for her to twirl.

She did so, allowing the floral tea-length skirt his mom had helped her choose to flare out a bit. It reminded her of the dress hanging in Lilith's closet. The one she'd never wear.

The nerves came back, but Hanna stood up straight. She would ignore them and get this over with.

At least she had the shoes and outfit Lilith and Carly helped her pick out. She'd never have brought the brown leather high-heel boots for herself in a million years. She had to admit, though, they were pretty amazing, especially with the tan sweater and dark red top to match. It wasn't an outfit she'd have picked, but it totally matched her personality. Simple, a bit vintage, with a bit of surprising funk. Yeah, that was her. Although the "funk" part was questionable many days.

Will let out a low whistle. "You look stunning, my dear."

"Your pretend dear, you mean?"

"Today, you're my dear. Let's go put on a show together, shall we?"

Celine poked her head in. "You're on in five. You both ready finally?"

The woman needed to take some "nice" pills.

This was it. Their big interview. Could she do it?

There wasn't a choice. She had to. For Dad. For Lilith and Harrison.

For herself.

And maybe, just a little, for Will, too.

"Yup, we're ready."

～～

The intro music, some funky Jamaican-meets-country-western number, blared overhead as Hanna held tight to Will's hand just outside the main studio set. She wasn't sure who was on before them. Her mind was too occupied with trying not to throw up again.

It had been a long time since she'd done the whole interview thing. She should be used to it after all the billions she'd given while on the set of *The Price of Love*.

But the bright lights, the crew rushing around, the cameras everywhere, it all overwhelmed her yet again, just like it had the first day on set almost a year ago now. She wasn't a cursing woman, but a few choice words she would have loved to call Carly for making her do the show had run through her brain that day.

Her?

An eligible bachelorette to some bigwig CEO?

Not likely. She was a country bumpkin dressed up in a rich woman's wardrobe, the best that Macy's had to offer. At that moment, when *The Price of Love*'s producers had swarmed and issued commands and frowned at her poor choice of makeup, she would have given anything for some jeans and a Vikings sweatshirt. But everything changed the moment they introduced her to William.

She closed her eyes, cutting out her surroundings, and let herself remember, for the first time since realizing that William was really a big mean wolf.

They didn't do the whole ride-up-in-a-limo thing like other shows.

No, each woman drove up to a big mansion in rented red convertibles. Which had only upped her nerves even more. What if she ran into something? What if she ran into *him*?

Her hands shook on the tan leather steering wheel as she crept up the driveway, knowing that a snail would probably pass her at any moment.

She'd stopped the car in front of a huge fountain decorated with flowers and the most handsome man she'd ever laid eyes on.

William.

And then she'd done something that to this day she still rolled her eyes at.

There was no controlling it. The biggest belly laugh ever flooded out of her. Her? Little ol' Hanna from Embarrass? In a red Corvette, getting ready to meet one of the most handsome men on earth to see if he wanted to marry her? And to top it off, he probably had more money than all the residents in the northern half of Minnesota combined.

If that wasn't hysterical, then Minnesota was just a little chilly in the winter.

Like a gentleman, he'd walked to the car and opened the door for her, offering a hand to help her out. He shut the door and lifted his eyebrow. Obviously, this was the part where she should say something. But all laughing had ended the moment she'd laid her hand in his. It was as if someone had equipped her voice box with a MUTE button.

He squeezed her hand and smiled. "It's nice to meet you. I'm Will."

A camera had inched in close on each side, and she squelched the enormous desire to shove them away. Instead, the sound of his voice had jarred the button. "I'm. . .Hanna."

A wink and another hand squeeze, and he nodded his head and escorted her toward the fountain. "It's wonderful to meet you, Hanna. I look forward to talking to you inside."

Like an idiot, she nodded and all but ran for the mansion door, wondering if she'd make the record for the quickest a girl was sent home.

Obviously, that had never happened.

A whisper in her ear jolted her back to the present. "They're getting ready for a commercial break. We're on next."

She blinked and felt her body sway, only to be steadied by the man who had, at one time, stolen her heart.

The producer signaled commercial, and the crew ran into action. This was it. Their moment to right the wrong.

Will nudged her with his elbow. "You'll wanna see their previous guest."

Glad for the diversion, she peeked around the cameraman who stood in front of her only to come face-to-face with her teenage heartthrob, the only "rebellious" crush she'd ever had on a movie star growing up.

Her skin turned clammy; her head swirled in breathless lack of oxygen. She leaned into Will even more to keep upright.

Mr. Gorgeous, complete with tattooed arms, shaggy hair, and thick-rimmed glasses he probably didn't even need, arched an eyebrow and said in that horrifically handsome voice that only Johnny Depp had, "Good luck out there, girl."

CHAPTER THIRTY-ONE

*Y*ou are not jealous of Johnny Depp.

Will could tell himself that a thousand times, and he still wouldn't believe it. Hanna had almost fainted at the sight of the man.

Why did women have to do that, anyway? It wasn't like he would have gone gaga over the sight of some sexy female star.

"Do you need a towel to wipe up your drool?"

She straightened her back and lifted her chin. "No, I'm fine. I just had a little, uh, crush on him when I was younger. Brought back memories, is all."

Sure.

The music cued again, and the voice of the hostess rose above the applause of the audience. A crew member turned a mobile TV their direction so they could see the set. "Next we have a special treat for you. Eight months ago, we cheered on William Preston, CEO of skincare and cosmetic giant Foster and Jones, which, by the way, produces the fantastic face cream I use *every* morning, as he chose Holy Hanna Knight as his future bride on *The Price of Love.* But then a wee bit of a scandal arose after a pesky little interview William gave."

The host, Mike, laughed. "A wee bit? I couldn't walk ten feet without hearing about those two for like three months afterward. It was worse than when Tom and Katie split."

"Okay, fine. The huge, gigantic, overblown scandal, is that better?" She flung her skinny little arms wide and pretended to hit Mike in the face.

"Hey, hey. Overblown is in the eye of the beholder. A lot of people said that if either of them had at least come out and explained themselves, it wouldn't have been so bad."

Kate put her hands on her hips, acting affronted by Mike's comment. "Excuse me, but their love life is no one else's business. Whether they hooked up"—she used air quotes while she said "hooked up" and winked at a camera—"or not is no one's business but their own."

Mike sat back and shook his head. "Kate, you've been in show business long enough to know that you can't get in front of a camera and expect no one to care about your sex life. It's just a fact of life."

"Well, we're excited to have Will and Hanna on our set today to tell *their* side of the story."

The theme music to *The Price of Love* started to play, their cue to enter the stage. Will escorted Hanna, letting his eyes adjust to the bright lights and his ears to the cheering crowd. Show business was not his thing. He hated this. But it had to be done, and he had to be smart and on his game for Hanna.

He owed her at least that.

Mike, a big man of football stature that could squash him like a bug if he wanted, stood and shook his hand, a big smile on his face despite his not-so-supportive comments a few moments ago.

Will switched with Hanna and gave petite Kate a hug. To his surprise when he released, she gave him a hard sucker punch to the gut.

He fought a second for his breath. "Did you just punch me?"

The petite brunette hopped onto her high-top chair, crossed her legs at the knee with her navy skirt resting just above, and sat back looking very proud of herself. "Yup. That was for Hanna, who I doubt would ever do it, and for every other woman in America who wishes they had the opportunity."

Oh, this was not looking like such a stellar idea now. He hadn't known Kate was a Will hater. "I—" What did a guy say to that?

Hanna put an arm around his side and pretended to help him to his seat, even though he wasn't hurt enough to need it. "Thanks, Kate. But don't worry. Will and I are good now."

Mike laughed and leaned forward, elbow on his knee. "The question is, Hanna, how good?"

She laughed, playing the part perfectly. "If you're referring to what I think you're referring to, not *that* good. But good enough that I'm wearing a ring again, and we're talking about wedding dates."

Kate clapped and squealed like a silly schoolgirl then reached for Hanna's left hand. "You have to show me the rock!"

Hanna extended her hand, a sweet smile gracing her lips. "I know, everyone says it's not big enough. In Will's defense, I'm the one who picked it out. Honestly, I adore it more than the original I got at the end of the show. It's just like my mother's was, except a little bigger. And,"—she leaned forward as if speaking with Kate only—"it'll still inflict some damage if I need to keep this one in line."

The audience laughed, as did Kate and Mike.

Mike slapped his hands on his knees, commanding everyone's attention. "Okay, girly stuff out of the way. We all want to know. What happened to you two? No one would ever give a statement, so we all had our own guesses. We want it straight out of the horse's mouth though. Why did you guys split? And what brought you back together?"

Will started to reply with the words he'd rehearsed over and over for the last week, all politically correct, giving no real details but enough to stop more questions, but Hanna beat him to it. He only hoped she wouldn't screw this up.

"What split us up is pretty well known. Will and I fell in love on TV. That's a hard thing for anyone. But the press likes to brand people a certain way, and I was very adamant that my faith and values stayed intact throughout the show. But William made some poor decisions with his words in an interview, and the press and social media ran with it. Honestly, I was crushed." She paused and closed her eyes and took a breath. Will prayed she wouldn't cry. But she just took a long breath, opened her eyes, and put on the superwoman face he'd come to adore. "My virtue is important to me, and I'd worked hard to make sure that on and off camera my actions were something I could stand before God and be proud of, so for him to insinuate something untrue, it was very difficult for me to handle."

Kate leaned over and patted her knee. "Do I need to punch him again?"

Hanna laced her fingers through his and shook her head, much to Will's relief. "No. Not yet anyway." She butted him with her shoulder playfully and smiled. He had to remind himself it was just a fake put-on and not the real deal. "I had shut him out to take time to process, and honestly, as much as I knew the media was running with the story like a pig swimming in mud, I just wanted away from it all. But then Will showed up, all handsome and apologetic on his own accord. We'd both gotten overwhelmed with the whole media thing, and I think time apart helped put things into perspective."

Will rubbed his thumb over her hand. "We realized that all relationships have issues. While I said something monumentally stupid, Hanna had it in her heart to forgive me, and in the end, we're in love. And true love, given enough time and patience, can overcome a lot of things."

Kate arched her eyebrows and tapped a finger to her chin. "Okay, so just to make sure all the air is clear. Are you, um, sharing night-time accommodations while you're together?"

Will smiled and squeezed Hanna's hand. "I can answer that. We are definitely n—"

Hanna surprised him and everyone else in the studio by inter-rupting him. "Actually, we both feel like our sleeping arrangements are private. What I do and don't do in my bedroom, as well as who I share my bed with and when, is my business alone. It is between God and me. I've made my stance on the matter very clear in the past, and have decided that answering any more questions on the matter is just beating the proverbial dead horse."

Shock surged through Will's veins. He'd expected her to vehe-mently deny any hint of bedroom-esque activities with him. And rightly so, since there hadn't been, unless one counted their midnight chats in his parents' bonus room.

Or the one night on the kitchen counter.

Sweat beaded on his neck at the memory.

Kate lifted her fisted hand. For a minute, Will feared she was going to attempt hitting him again. This time he'd be ready.

Instead, she directed it toward Hanna. "Fist bump, girl. If Mike can fist-bump his sports buddies he has on here, me and you can give a good fist to that."

Hanna laughed and clashed knuckles with their hostess.

Mike cleared his throat. "Okay, so respecting your privacy and all, I am going to assume this means that poor Will here is going to still be left to himself at night. So does this call for a speedy wedding, then? Your dad taking out the shotgun and all just in case?"

Will shook his head. "I'm giving Hanna all the time she needs. The last year has been pretty crazy. On top of that, she has a wedding to plan. A girl can't be rushed in these things, you know."

The host held out his own fist. "Man, you better know it. You're learning fast."

The mammoth host's fist crashed into his own. Will was going to be lucky to walk away from this thing without a broken bone.

Kate clapped her hands. "Okay, now it's my favorite time. We knew our audience would be going crazy with questions, so we're going to select a few to ask them live. How about that?"

Will shot a glance at Hanna. This had *not* been an agreed-upon part of the show, but there wasn't a thing he could do about it now.

Mike looked at the card in his hand, *ALIVE* printed in dark, bold letters on the outside. "First up we have Donna, from right here in Brooklyn."

A woman on the far right of the audience stood up, and a crew member handed her a microphone. She put a hand on her ample hip and stared him down over the rim of her equally large glasses. "Yes. My question is for Will-the-jerk. I read an article this morning that said the only reason you're getting back with Hanna is to save your job. Is that true? Are you lying *to* her instead of just *about* her this time?"

Heat poured into Will's face. He hadn't even taken the time to check media sources this morning. Why had no one else told him? And who had leaked that information?

He blubbered around a moment, until Hanna sat forward. "I'll speak for Will. It's not true at all. We've had countless talks about his job and the impact all this has had on it. We're both very aware of the situation, so there has been no lying to me being done. Will loves his job, and as it is with any man or woman for that matter, his career is important to him. I respect him for that, and honestly, if he was some guy who job hopped and didn't care about providing for a family, I'm not sure I'd love him like I do. So to answer your question, the accusation is entirely false."

Will wanted to plant the longest, most passionate kiss on her lips right now. Fake or not, she'd stuck up for him, and with style and grace at that. *Well done, Hanna. Well done.*

Kate held up a finger. "So, Will, just to clarify. Is something going on with your employment that we're unaware of?"

He smiled and shook his head. "Last time I checked, I am still gainfully employed as the CEO of Foster and Jones. If they've fired me without my knowledge, well, that'd be just as much of a shock to me as it would be news to you. Although, last week one magazine said I was abducted by aliens, so who knows?"

The audience all roared with laughter at that.

Mike checked his card again. "Okay, our next question is from Shirley."

A middle-aged woman stood up and took the offered microphone. She wore a floral skirt that went to the floor, and had short, tightly permed hair. With an arm around her middle, she looked directly at Hanna. "How can you stand up there and profess that you're a Christian woman when all you have done is brought shame to us all? You go on a sin-ridden show, flaunt your body around like you didn't have a care in the world for modesty, and then get yourself tangled up with a man who doesn't even profess to know Jesus. I've sent you countless letters that have gone unresponded to. And now I'm here, once and for all, to ask you to either repent or leave the religion you so obviously have turned your back on."

Will turned to find Hanna's face pure white, her eyes wet with tears. She opened her mouth to respond but, instead, tore off her microphone, flung it on the chair, and walked off stage.

Shirley lifted her chin high in a smug air of victory.

Will fumed. How dare that woman speak to Hanna like that. This was the issue he had with "Christians." They were so full of themselves they missed the giant pile of wood sticking out of both their eyes. He took a few steps toward the audience, ignoring the cameras, all thought of anything politically correct flying out the window. His eyes burned into the woman until her uppity expression turned scared. "Ma'am. The words I would love to say to you right now are not fit for daytime television. So I'll leave you with the words of a man much wiser than you or I. 'Let him who is without sin cast the first stone.' Unless you're saying you're without sin and equal to or better than Jesus, I suggest you shut your da—" He paused, making himself skip the curse word out of respect for Hanna only. "—your mouth and leave my fiancée alone."

Turning, he smiled at the shocked Kate and Mike, shook both of their hands, waved at the audience, and excused himself from the set as they called another commercial break.

CHAPTER THIRTY-TWO

The trip to the airport and the plane ride back to Nashville were quiet. Hanna didn't feel like talking about it. And Will seemed to respect that.

Celine had been quiet when Hanna reached the dressing room. She'd obviously watched it all. Hanna expected to be reamed out about how she walked off stage, but instead, she'd gotten a surprising hug and a half smile.

Will had just told her to get her things so they wouldn't miss their flight.

In all her nightmares, she hadn't expected the interview ending like that. Puking on stage? Stuttering the whole time? Tripping and falling flat on her face? Yeah, all those had been plausible. But having her faith questioned and denounced in front of the whole national viewing audience—and not even having the courage to defend herself—she just couldn't face what harm she'd done.

As they stepped outside the Nashville airport, a black limo waited for them at the curb. Will opened the back door and allowed her to slide in first then talked to the driver for a minute before sliding in himself.

"Sorry about the limo. Emma had requested an SUV, but evidently there was a mix-up."

"It's fine."

The limo pulled out and after a few minutes merged onto I-40.

The silence had been golden at first, but now it was getting a little awkward. She leaned her head against the window and watched as cars drove past and the Nashville skyline appeared ahead of them. All these people, living normal, halfway private lives. She used to be one of them.

Would she ever be that again? Would she always live looking behind her shoulder for cameras or fearful of how every action she took would be interpreted by people on Facebook or Twitter?

She was living a lie. A big, fat, sinful lie. The Shirley lady was right. How could she stand up there and call herself any kind of Christian and continue the life she was living?

And even if she and Will *were* engaged, his faith in Jesus was obviously lacking, if there at all. Would God even bless a relationship like that?

But it didn't even matter. They had no relationship. Just a business deal. That was it.

The thought brought her back to the present, and she glanced over at Will. "You ready for your board meeting tonight?"

He sat with his head laid back, eyes closed, and shook his head. "Not even a little bit."

She reached over and smoothed a hand up and down his arm. He'd ditched the sports coat as soon as they got to the airport. Smiling, she remembered the first flirtatious remark she'd ever said to him. It had been on their second date on the show, and he'd worn this tight-fitting T-shirt that showed off his muscles fabulously.

She'd squeezed his upper arm and said something about being surprised at his muscles, that most CEOs she knew of were either scrawny from not having time to work out or chubby from sitting at a desk all day.

He'd laughed, picked her up using those amazing muscles of his, and spun her around, telling her something about how he'd had about six months warning before he'd appear on the show and had been working out to prepare. He then forbid her ever to look at a "before" picture of him.

Hanna had of course used her phone to look up "before" pictures.

He was surprisingly right. While he'd still been handsome, a layer of squishiness covered him. It had made him look more—real. Like a normal guy who wasn't chiseled for TV. That picture was one of the reasons she'd finally let go of the tight rein she'd held on her heart.

Now, her heart had been stomped on and was slowly healing.

And Will still had his mouthwatering muscles. "You're going to do fine."

His chest lifted and fell with a deep breath. "I just wish I knew exactly what was going on so I could plan."

Hanna understood. Will was a planner. She'd been able to tell during the whole show. He'd been more focused on staying on schedule than the producers were. This morning's debacle hadn't helped the matter.

She turned toward him and laid her head on the seat beside him. "I'm sorry for screwing up the interview."

He peeked open an eye. "It wasn't your fault."

"I shouldn't have run out."

"She shouldn't have been such a b—" He bit back the word she knew he wanted to say. "Such a not-very-nice woman."

"Thanks for that."

"I call 'em like I see 'em."

Hanna shook her head. "No, I mean for respecting me enough to try not to use the words you know I hate."

Turning fully toward her, he lifted a hand and fingered a strand of her hair. "I'll probably still say them from time to time. But I'm trying."

He spoke like this was longer term than just a temporary acting gig. Why did her heart want to sing at the thought? She chose to ignore it though. He probably didn't realize how it sounded. "And I'll forgive you if you do."

Sliding closer, he cupped the back of her neck with his hand. The strong warmth trickled down her body and puddled in her stomach. His face inched forward, his familiar scent even stronger and making it difficult to think. She bit her lip. "Will."

His mouth was just a breath away. "Yes?"

Putting a hand to his chest, she could feel the quick thud of his heartbeat under her palm. "There isn't anyone watching."

He moved his mouth to rest on her ear and nibbled the soft tip, sending shivers of pleasure through her. His soft whisper thrilled her. "I know."

His lips captured the spot right under her ear and left a trail of kisses all the way to her lips.

Heat soared through her as his mouth finally met hers. She trembled, her hands moving on their own, around his neck, pulling him closer.

Time stood still for a moment. For that second, she forgot about the lie, both Will's and now their own. She forgot about the crazy woman in the audience. About social media. The tabloids. About pretty much everything.

For this small place in time, she just enjoyed the man that, despite every logical thought that screamed the opposite, she loved with all her heart.

The admission to herself that she loved him made all other cares fly away. She let her hands roam his hair and pressed soft but hungry kisses of her own against his lips, then slid down to his neck.

He groaned her name and pressed his hands against her lower back, thrilling her even more.

A moment later, the limo lurched and metal screeched, and now entwined, they both went tumbling to the ground as something slammed into the vehicle.

CHAPTER THIRTY-THREE

*W*ill blinked as someone opened the rear limo door. A man with a black hat poked his head in. Stan, the driver. "Everyone okay back here?"

He tried to push up from the floor of the limo, but his legs were intertwined with Hanna's.

She lay half underneath him, her hands pressing on her head, her face screwed up in confusion. "What—what happened?"

They had a kiss that turned Will's brain to mush and literally brought them to their knees. Something he didn't let happen very often. "Someone hit us, I think. You okay?"

She disengaged a leg, freeing him to upright himself and help her sit up. "Yeah. My head just hurts a little."

Stan looked a strange shade of white under all his black attire. "I'm so sorry, ma'am. The car, it came out of nowhere. We had a green light and—"

Will held up a hand to turn off his rambling explanation. "Let's just get Hanna out of here and make sure she's okay."

"I'm—I'm fine. Really. Just a little confused."

Confused wasn't a good sign. Had she hit her head that hard? "Let's make sure they are sending an ambulance just in case."

The driver nodded. "Police and ambulance are on their way. The other guy hit us head-on, so he's banged up pretty good."

This day was going from bad to much, much worse by the minute. "You go see to him, then. I'll help Hanna."

"Yes, sir."

Will looked back to Hanna, who was resting on an elbow and trying to use her other hand to pull up on the seat. "Hold on there, Mighty Mouse. Let me help you."

He reached an arm around her back to help her up.

She leaned into him and, to his surprise and delight, let him support her. "Thanks. Are you okay?"

Other than having ten years shaved off his life? "Yeah. Just worried about you."

"This will just be more bad press, won't it?"

"I don't give a hill of gold about what the press thinks. That you're not hurt is what's important."

Hanna reached a hand up and patted him on the cheek, her mouth curved into a smile that didn't quite reach her eyes. "Thanks for that, too."

He covered her hand with his own and squeezed. "I mean it."

She only nodded and took her hand back.

"You don't believe me."

Her fingers probed at her temples. "Let's just say, I wouldn't blame you for worrying. This was clearly not our fault. But who knows how people will misconstrue it?"

"We have bigger things to focus on right now."

"Like you keeping your job."

His job. The meeting he was likely going to be very tardy for or even miss. He closed his eyes and heard the whir of sirens in the distance, blaring like a warning in his brain. His father's words from years ago, after Will had graduated and landed a coveted job in the science lab at Foster and Jones, emerged from the place he'd stuffed them long ago, complete with a self-absorbed eye roll and all.

"William, I'm proud of you, son. Just remember, a career is great. But don't let it define you. Don't let it become your god. Priorities, son. Remember your priorities."

He never had understood his father's words. Of course his career defined him. He was William, project engineer. Then William, lab manager. Then William, VP of Product Development. And now, twelve short years later, William, CEO.

Today though, as he faced losing it all, that title wasn't as important as the job in front of him. He wanted more than anything in the world to protect the sweet woman who had, in some odd twist of fate, stolen every shred of his heart.

He put a finger beneath Hanna's chin and lifted her gaze to meet his. "No. Like making sure you're all right. You're what's important right now."

Her forehead wrinkled in a combination of confusion and pain. "But William, we—"

The limo door opened and a policeman appeared. "Everyone all right in here?"

Will glanced at Hanna. "We're fine, although she hit her head pretty good, so I'd like to have her checked out."

The officer took a quick inventory of the scene. "Sir, come with me. I'll have a paramedic see to the lady."

Well, at least the man didn't seem to know who they were. That was a plus.

William traded spots with an EMT and followed the policeman.

Outside the limo, he had a better idea of what happened. They were in the middle of a major intersection, and all traffic was being routed around the wreck. A blue SUV had plowed into the front passenger side of the limo. Given the ambulance leaving, Will guessed the driver was already on the way to the hospital.

The officer escorted him to the back of a squad car and peppered him with questions.

Will complied, telling the little he knew, conveniently glossing over "what" they had been doing in the back of the limo. After all, making out with one's fiancée wasn't a crime.

After Will gave him all the information, the officer ripped off a piece of paper and handed it to him.

Scanning the paper, he frowned. "What's this?"

"A citation for not wearing a seat belt."

Anger burned in his throat. This day had been crazy enough, he didn't need some ego-ridden cop to make it worse. He crumpled up the ticket and threw it on the ground then pointed a finger at the cop's chest. "That's crazy, and you know it. We were in a limo. No one wears a seat belt in a limo."

The officer rested his hand on his holster. "Doesn't matter. They require seat belts just like every other on-road vehicle. And I suggest you keep your hands to yourself, sir, unless you'd like to be arrested for assaulting an officer."

Oh, that'd just make it a fine end to his day, indeed. But the words were like being doused with cold water. He let out his hot breath, snagged the ticket from the ground, and shoved it in his pocket. "What about Hanna?"

The cop crossed his arms over his chest and took on a classic *"are you really going to argue with an officer"* stance, feet spread apart and all. "I think everything she's been through is punishment enough, don't you?"

So the policeman did know who they were. And was obviously in Hanna's camp.

Or at least, had a wife who was and intended to earn a few brownie points today.

Will opened his mouth to argue, but the policeman stared him down and then jerked his head to the right. "Tow truck is coming. Stay here until the EMT is done with your friend. I'll be back."

The paramedic escorted Hanna over to him a few minutes later, pronouncing her just fine except a nice egg on her forehead. A little ice would bring the swelling down.

Hanna hugged her arms around her body. "How are we going to get anywhere now? Can you call a cab?"

"Actually, we were almost to my place. It's just a block north. If you're up to it, we can just walk when they let us go."

She glanced around. "You do realize there are people staring and taking pictures, right?"

He hadn't. But now as he focused, they were drawing a crowd. And most all of them had camera phones pointed in their direction.

Will's condo was swanky.

Like, "hey, let's hang money from the ceiling and use hundred-dollar bills as carpet" kind of swanky. He might as well have done so given the gleaming hardwood floors laid in intricate patterns. They had to cost a fortune.

Hanna almost didn't want to set her purse down for fear of breaking or smudging something.

No money hanging from the ceiling was possible though, since the entire living room and kitchen were open to a two-story window view of downtown Nashville. A white spiral staircase, something she'd only seen in movies, led the way to what she assumed were bedrooms.

Will shut the massive double wood door behind him and walked directly to the kitchen. He opened the fridge, a fancy contraption that wasn't the expensive stainless steel she would have expected but instead the same dark walnut front as the cabinet. "You thirsty?"

She shook her head and walked to the window, trying to appear calm in the midst of such extreme opulence. She'd known Will was wealthy. Teased him about it incessantly.

And she'd had her own taste at being spoiled while on *The Price of Love*. But that had been temporary. Like a really long vacation on someone else's bill to places she'd never be able to afford on her own.

This was different. This was Will's everyday life.

Her everyday life had been a classroom full of cute five-year-olds and was now a hay farm in Northern Minnesota. In a farmhouse that creaked every time you walked, decorated with Nanna's doilies and Mom's love of all things ruffles and lace. It was hauling firewood on cold nights to keep the wood-burning furnace going. Normal was shopping at Walmart for jeans and all but living in a Vikings sweatshirt or a pullover sweater for six to eight months out of the year. And digging into her own savings a few times a year because Dad couldn't make the bills, even though she paid him rent monthly.

In the limo today, before all the mess, she'd almost convinced herself that maybe Will was a possibility. That maybe he had changed. That they could work this crazy thing out.

But here.

Here, it was like God was laughing at her, teasing her like dangling filet mignon in front of a dog. Both in religion and in wealth, Hanna and Will were the ultimate oxymoron.

And she was sitting here pretending. The ultimate fraud.

A hand pressed against her shoulder, and she turned to see handsome-as-ever Will.

"I brought you a recovery kit."

She looked down to the small side table beside her. He'd set down a tall bottle of fancy water, a bottle of ibuprofen, and a Ziploc bag full of ice, covered with a paper towel.

He is out of your league, Hanna. OUT OUT OUT OUT OUT!

Smiling through the dull ache in her skull, she dumped a few pills in her palm and swallowed them with the water. "Thanks. I don't think my head hurts enough to need ice though."

"Humor me." He pulled her by the elbow over to the light brown leather couch and gently pushed her down. He propped her feet on the matching oversized ottoman and brought her the ice. "The paramedic said you needed ice, so ice you shall get, my dear."

Out. Of. Your. League, she reminded her swooning heart. This was not the Will she remembered. "I thought you'd give me a tour."

He stood there, looking all handsome in his gray slacks and black button-down shirt, a few buttons undone on the top to taunt a girl. "There's not much to tour. It's a pretty small place. This, as you can see, is the living room. The kitchen is behind you. Over in the corner is the dining room. I like the whole open-area concept." He stopped to hand her the ice bag and motioned for her to apply it.

So he'd continue, she complied.

"You passed the french doors to my office coming in, and on the other side is the bathroom if you need it. On second thought, I don't keep that one stocked unless I know I'm having guests. Just use mine upstairs if you need. There are two bedrooms up there. You can stay in the guest room tonight."

One would have thought *he* was the one who cracked his head on the limo floor. "Uh, yeah, no. There's still time to get a hotel."

He plopped down in the leather recliner beside the couch and propped a foot up on his knee. "I thought you decided not to care what people thought."

"Doesn't mean I want to add fuel to the flames though."

"You already did just by coming here right now."

True enough. She hadn't honestly cared, considering the way her head throbbed and the immense desire to get out of the view of cameras. "I can't sleep here, Will."

"Will it help if I'm not here? I need to get headed to the meeting soon. And I'm so far behind, honestly, I'll probably just work through the night. I have a couch I've slept on in my office plenty of times."

It would be crazy to waste money on a hotel when he wouldn't even be here. "Fine. But a hotel tomorrow, okay?"

He nodded. "I'll have Emma make the reservation."

"When do I get to meet her, by the way?"

Will smiled and stood. "Later this week, maybe I'll bring you by the office. One day at a time, okay?"

Hanna sat back and closed her eyes, letting the cold relief of the ice pack have full impact on her head. She desperately wanted to address the gigantic elephant in the room.

They were pretend engaged.

But their kisses in private where everything but feigned.

They needed to plan how to break up. But she was afraid she'd gone and fallen in love again.

She really wanted to push all good sense out the window and elope with him tonight.

But they were 100 percent wrong for each other.

So many elephants.

So many things to be said.

Will slid out of the recliner and onto his knees in front of her. "We'll figure this out. I have no idea how. But—" He reached forward and brought her to him then kissed her lips with a gentleness she'd never known he possessed. His lips lingered on hers for a few moments, unmoving, just tantalizing her senses and making all reason flee. "But we will. I promise."

She had every reason not to trust him.

Every reason to argue about how this wasn't a problem he could snap his fingers and solve.

But despite it all—

She trusted him.

CHAPTER THIRTY-FOUR

*W*ill walked through the condo parking garage and clicked the button on his key fob to unlock the Audi sedan. He started the car and checked the clock on the dash.

Less than an hour until the board meeting.

Shifting into REVERSE, he backed out of his purchased parking spot and exited the parking garage, preparing to combat rush-hour Nashville traffic. He was used to it. But usually he was on his way home going the opposite direction.

He wasn't a nervous man. His father had instilled in him the art of having confidence in one's abilities without being too cocky. At the time, his dad had thought he was grooming another lawyer like himself. But as much as he and his dad didn't see eye to eye most days, the philosophy had served him well as he rocketed up the corporate ladder.

But today, his future hung in the balance.

He'd tried to be confident with Hanna. She'd looked like a lost, scared puppy.

The truth was, though, he wasn't sure he'd have a job after this meeting. He might be at the office all night, packing up his things.

If the sales numbers weren't showing any improvement or, worse yet, really showed a decline as Doug's report had shown, no amount of maneuvering on his end could save his tail.

The thought should crush him.

And on a level, it did.

But the accident, and maybe the kiss preceding it, had caused a major disruption in his mind-set.

As cliché as it was, as they were flying through the air, the whole two feet of it, his life passed before his eyes.

If he died today, would he be proud of the life he'd led? What legacy did he have? What would he miss?

The truth, now that he had a second to grasp it in stand-still traffic, was that he'd be ticked off for squandering all his time and effort on Foster and Jones. Yes, he loved his job. But he'd let it define him.

He wasn't just William Preston.

He was William Preston, CEO of a multi-billion-dollar corporation.

Whoop-de-do.

He'd rather be Will, husband, with a wife to come home to every night. A wife who needed him to help take out the trash and mow the lawn, or at least hire a guy to mow it. Who needed him to hold her while she cried and to support her dreams.

He'd rather be Dad to a kid or two or three he could build tree forts for and change diapers for. Okay. Maybe not the latter. But he would totally study up on tree fort building. Or even a playhouse if they had a little girl.

He'd rather be a friend to someone who cared for him for more reasons than the fact he had the power to fire them or give them a raise.

And, as eternity flashed before his eyes, he realized that he missed something he never thought possible.

God.

How could that be? He'd effectively given God the finger years ago, telling Him off and going his own way.

But the thought remained.

A small part of his heart still yearned for the faith he'd once had. For the trust in something, or someone, bigger. For a purpose beyond just making money. Beyond achieving a level in a career. Beyond appeasing stockholders and board members.

He'd had that purpose once. Felt and believed it with all his heart. He'd been young and full of zeal. Even when Claire had gotten really sick, he'd been the one to make silly faces at her to make her smile. To assure her how *big* God was and how she was going to be just fine. He promised her that.

But she'd still died.

God had made him break his promise.

And since then, he made it a point to both not make promises and not rely on God.

Yet, hadn't he just made another promise to Hanna?

A promise he had no clue how to keep?

As he pulled into Foster and Jones' parking lot, he gripped the steering wheel until his knuckles turned white.

He didn't need God. He would keep this promise on his own. He *was* William Preston. He fixed things. Give him a problem, he'd find a solution. No divine help needed. All it took was good, sound, analytical thinking.

His brush with death, if one could call it that, had only brought back bad memories. That was all.

But it had done one other thing.

It made William realize he had much more he wanted to live for.

The first order of business. . .

I've got to keep my job.

CHAPTER THIRTY-FIVE

*W*e must ask for your resignation."

William sat at the head of the large conference room table, board members in suits lining each side. The words Sam Deddrick, the director to his right, had just issued, the whole scene really, was a déjà vu from a nightmare he'd had soon after receiving the promotion. In fact, it almost seemed prophetic.

Doug sat at the opposite end, his eyes steeled on William, the haughty know-it-all look on his face.

Careful to school his features, Will nodded and searched for the best words to address this situation. There was no way he was going down without a fight. While asking for a resignation is effectively saying, *"You're fired, but we want to give you the chance to quit so it doesn't look so bad even though everyone will know that we canned you,"* he was still determined to fix this. "We just gave the official interview this morning. There is no way to gauge the impact on sales at this point. That was the whole point of this, wasn't it? To fix what went wrong? To get sales back up?"

Sam cleared his throat. "The numbers are looking more dismal by the day, from what we've seen of the most recent forecast. But it's not just about that. There have been a few things that have come up. . . ."

William narrowed his eyes. Something didn't sound right. "What do you mean, a few things?"

"Internal auditors are questioning some changes you signed off on. Their final report isn't in yet, as you know, but with this development and last quarter's loss, we feel like now might be the right time to part ways amicably."

Changes? He went through all the process changes he'd made in the last year, and nothing detrimental crossed his mind, much less even remotely illegal. "I don't understand. What changes?"

Sam looked down the table at Doug then back again. "Most are in accounting."

Accounting? Suddenly, the light blazed brighter in Will's mind. Accounting wasn't his forte. He knew quite a bit, but he'd cut his corporate teeth on the operations side. He'd relied heavily, perhaps too heavily, on Doug's advice the past year or so. Especially while he was on the TV show and handling all the press that followed.

Had Doug set him up?

Surely not. The guy was a little odd and more than a little rude and overbearing, but this didn't seem like him.

He pushed back his seat and stood, then took his time to study each and every director that lined both sides of the table, looking them each directly in the eye. Finally, his gaze rested on Doug, who sat expressionless with his chin in a hard set.

What should he do? He wasn't a throw-in-the-towel kind of guy.

There was only one person he could trust to help him with this. And as much as he hated the thought of admitting his failure, he had no other choice.

But in order to fix this, he had to buy himself time. Which meant committing what could be the worst career suicide move on the books.

He picked up his yellow steno notepad and pen that cost a fortune and pushed in his chair. "You asked for my resignation, but I'm not going to give it. There has been no evidence presented showing my guilt or even details on what I'm guilty of. I've done nothing but give my best to this company, and that included nothing illegal. I'd like to ask the board to give me a week to address whatever the concerns the auditors have and try to get to the bottom of what's going on."

Doug stood. "I don't think that's a good idea. This company has been through enough the past few years, we don't need a hint of any other scandal."

Sam cleared his throat. "I understand your concerns, Doug, but personally, I'm on the fence about this. If we jump the gun, we'll look just as bad in the public eye, not to mention stockholders. All in favor of reconvening in one week for a final vote—"

About two-thirds of the hands raised.

"All not in favor—"

The remaining hands, including Doug's, shot up.

Sam stood and turned to William. "You have one week to present your case, along with the auditors, to the board. I suggest you use it wisely."

A knock sounded on the door, and Emma peeked her head in. "Boss? Can I come in?"

He motioned her with his hand. "I thought you left awhile ago."

"I thought you were leaving right behind me."

He shrugged. He'd only said it to get some time alone with his thoughts. His assistant was a hoverer. "Lied."

She settled in one of the chairs across from his desk. "So did I."

Good ol' Emma. The girl had spunk. It was what he liked about her. But right now, he just needed to be left alone to think.

And to make a dreaded phone call. "I just have a lot to do; I'm sorry."

"You didn't tell me how the oh-so-urgent meeting went."

He drummed his fingers on top of the folder containing notes he'd gotten from the auditors. Most of the changes they had flagged had been small and seemingly innocuous on their own, at least to him.

Every single one of them had been suggestions made to him by Doug.

But he was smart enough not to mention that just yet.

The suggestions had been made verbally—and William had been the idiot who initiated every one of them. He'd trusted his CFO, even when he, too, had questioned a few of the suggestions.

But his mind had been other places—specifically on a blond from Minnesota and a TV show that was supposed to jump-start the company back into the black.

The auditor had explained that none of them individually were *bad* per say, but they added up to a suspicious trail and, when looked at together, weakened controls.

Never had Will felt so ill equipped to handle his job.

"They asked for my resignation."

Her eyes turned to wide circles. "Did you give it?"

He probably should have. Most people would have. But William wasn't a quitter. He was a fixer. This was a problem, and somehow, someway, he'd find a resolution that didn't involve never being able to find a job for the rest of his life and a possible jail sentence. "No. And I don't plan to."

"So, what? They think you're cooking the books?"

"A bright one, you are."

"But—wouldn't you make them actually look good if you were going to do that?"

It was the same question he'd been contemplating. "You would think. I don't think they entirely know what to think of it all. I'm trying to put myself in their shoes. They have an ex-CEO who is being indicted for accounting fraud. They have sales that had finally started to take a turn up but are now plunging into a nose-dive like a plane with all engines failing. And an inexperienced CEO they weren't entirely sure of in the first place, who has now made some changes that look fishy. I think they are just trying to deploy their parachutes and get out before the whole thing does a fiery crash landing."

She frowned. "You don't think they think I'm part of any of this, right?"

Now there was an interesting thought. What if determined, bright Emma had been involved? She was his asset. The one person in this company who had his back and always stood by him. Even in the whole craziness of *The Price of Love*, she'd agreed to be his eyes and ears. Had she set him up?

Surely not. "You aren't, are you?"

Standing quickly, she jabbed her hands against her hips. "If you think that, then I might as well quit today."

He held up a hand. "I don't. Not really, anyway. I'm just trying to figure all this out."

"Aside from investigating your *innocent* assistant, what do you plan on doing next?"

He eyed the phone, knowing the call he had to make but dreading it. He'd been sitting here for the last thirty minutes trying to get up the courage. The only man who could help could also make the rest of his life miserable because of it.

William sighed and picked up the phone, twirling it in his hand then fisting the handset with a firm, determined grip. He'd do what he had to do to clear his name. Sometimes you had to stand up, be a man, and fight your own fights. And other times—as a wise man once taught him—you had to know when to call in reinforcements.

"I'm calling my father."

CHAPTER THIRTY-SIX

*H*anna stood at the bottom of the white spiral staircase. How did they get furniture up there, anyway?

But nature called. She'd tried the downstairs bathroom, and Will had been right. No toilet paper, no hand towels, no soap, nothing.

Plus, if she was going to stay in the guest bedroom, she might as well get her things settled in.

Being in someone else's house, by herself, was uncomfortable. She tried to treat it as a hotel room, but yeah. That was not gonna work.

Little things reminded her of Will. The small, rather old family picture on the mantel, with his parents, him, and Claire. His jacket thrown over the couch. Dishes in the sink he'd obviously done nothing with before they'd gone to New York. Typical bachelor.

The trip up the twirly stairs made her aching head spin. Good thing she brought her overnight bag up with her on this trip, because she doubted she'd make it back down and up again without passing out.

There was a loft area with a small futon couch and a bookcase. She walked over and fingered a few titles. Just what she'd expected. A few old books on business and a large collection of vintage classics.

Two doors led off from the loft. One of those doors better be the guest room, because if he considered this flimsy couch thingy a guest room, the man had another thing coming.

She entered the first room and immediately smelled him.

William.

Really, the whole house held a whiff of him, but this room had to be his bedroom. The woodsy, masculine scent that made her want to nuzzle his neck every time he was near, even at *so very* inappropriate moments, permeated every square foot of this massive space. She could probably fit the whole top floor of Dad's house in here.

She took a step back. The right thing to do would be to shut the door and go explore the other room where she'd be sleeping. Nosing around in Will's bedroom rated up there with wrestling alligators on the safety meter.

But he'd said the only other bathroom was his anyway. So she could totally blame her need to pee.

Before she could change her mind, Hanna flicked on the light switch, lifted her chin, and marched into his room as if it were a normal, everyday occurrence.

She stopped in the middle of the room.

Oh.

Goodness.

Gracious.

It was all just so—

William. One hundred percent the Will she knew inside. That's what his room screamed. Downstairs showed off the Will the world knew. The one she'd met on the show.

Tailored. Sophisticated. Wealthy. Planned. Crisp, perfect, handsome lines.

Up here, it was still all that.

But with warmth and Will's classic charm. She could close her eyes and picture him in this room with ease.

The bed wasn't made. She could see the spot where he'd thrown the dark gray microsuede comforter up as he'd rolled out of bed. His pillow was scrunched into an odd form. The other side of the large bed was crisply made though, as if untouched for a long period of time.

The opposite wall hosted the biggest TV she'd ever seen hanging from the wall.

Against another wall stood a black chest of drawers, a recliner sitting by its side.

And on top of the dresser was. . .

She took a step closer and picked up the frame.

A picture of her. The one from the show. She was dolled up nicer than she had been the whole show, thanks to the help of the makeup and hair departments and no doubt a bit of photo editing.

What was she supposed to think of this? Will kept a picture of her in his bedroom.

Will. . .who she was fake engaged to.

Will. . .who kissed her until she thought she would dissolve into a puddle.

Will. . .who she was afraid she was actually, truly, despite all the reasons she shouldn't, falling in love with.

Putting the frame back down, a shiny object caught her gaze.

Picking it up, she blinked. Her coin. After all this time, she'd assumed it was long gone.

Maybe it was just a copy—

Turning it to the back, she gasped.

There it was. The pink smiley face she'd added to it.

On the last episode, she'd decided to be a little different. Determined that, whatever the outcome, God had a man for her. So she'd taken a pink Sharpie and drawn a smiley face on hers.

She had been so sure the future would hold smiles.

Ha.

She'd been so full of it.

If only she'd known then. . .

Yet, she smiled when she saw the coin. The thought of William holding on to her treasure, putting it in such an intimate spot as on his dresser, made her heart do a little ballet twirl in her chest.

She laid it back on the dresser, careful to put it exactly how she'd found it so Will would be none the wiser.

Unable to hold back her need to find a bathroom any longer, she crossed to the open door on the other side of the room. Ignoring the sight of a pair of boxers half hanging out of the hamper, she completed her business.

As she turned on the faucet to wash her hands, a light chime rang throughout the house.

What? Did he have it wired to play music when you washed your hands or something?

She turned off the water, dried her hands, and heard it again, along with a loud knock.

Ah, yeah. The doorbell. Duh.

She was halfway down the spiral staircase when reality slapped her.

The doorbell. Should she open it? Probably not.

But what if it was Will, and he forgot his keys or something?

Or maybe an attendant for the building needing something? Or a neighbor coming to say hi?

Or an ex-lover coming to reunite?

Oh, now she *had* to open the door.

Taking the rest of the stairs by two despite her head's complaint at the rush, she got to the condo door and pushed an eye to the peephole.

Doug. What could he want? Other than to ignite more flames on the whole media thing, he'd done nothing to help the situation when he showed up last time. Although, he had helped get her back into her room. He could have left her out in the hallway in her pj's, so that was something at least.

She unlocked the door and opened it for him. "To what do I owe this visit?"

No suave, "I'm awesome so you should hop into bed with me" grin graced his face this time. Normally that would elate her, but the frown it had been replaced with was even more dangerous.

He pushed around her and walked into the room. She shut the door and wrapped her arms around her middle. "Doug, what's wrong?"

He turned, his expression grim and hard to read. "There's something you should know, Hanna."

CHAPTER THIRTY-SEVEN

*H*anna stared at Doug for several seconds in complete silence.

Why was he here?

What should she *know*?

Was this about William? His job? Was he fired?

And if he was, why was Doug here instead of Will?

Something felt fishy. And if anyone knew about fish issues, it was Hanna.

Walking around him, she tightened her fists and headed for the kitchen. Whatever was to come of this, she would be the one to control the conversation and then kick him out as soon as she'd gotten out of him whatever tidbit he'd come to tell her. "Would you like a water or something to drink?"

Doug ran his fingers through his hair, leaving a path of crazy hair that looked about as nervous as he did. "I think you need to sit down, Hanna."

"Oh, come on. It can't be that bad, otherwise Will would have come himself. Unless he died or something." She sucked in a breath. Surely not— She shot around to search his face. "He didn't, right? He's okay, isn't he?"

He held up a hand. "He's healthy as a horse. But he isn't okay."

Confusion swirled like a whirlpool threatening to suck her under the water. "Just spit it out, Doug. What's going on?"

"Will was asked to resign today."

Hanna blew out a breath but remained standing and firm. She'd known it was a possibility, but her heart ached for William. His job was everything to him. Yes, it could consume him at times. He spent countless hours on his laptop or tapping a text to his assistant or on conference calls, even while he was away with her. There was no one more dedicated to his job than William Preston.

To have it yanked out from underneath him was going to be devastating.

But this wasn't "new" news. So why send Doug instead of just making a phone call?

She tossed a water bottle from the fridge in Doug's direction and grabbed one for herself. "Okay. So William knew this might happen. It stinks. I think they're making a big mistake, but that doesn't change anything." He was still fake engaged to her, job or no job. And if they broke up now, she'd just look like a loser dumping a guy when he was down on his luck.

William wouldn't turn the cards on her like that—would he?

The press would paint her as the exact kind of woman *The Price of Love* was designed to weed out.

A money-grubbing vixen who bailed at the first sign of money trouble.

Which was almost comical because she was pretty close to the opposite. She had a hard time accepting that he *had* the kind of money that funded a condo like this and allowed him to jet off across America on a whim.

Doug took a swig of the water and sat down at one of the barstools on the other side of the counter. "There's more, Hanna."

She just stared at him and raised her eyebrows, waiting for him to explain.

"I'm sure you know he was worried about being fired because of the dip in sales."

"Yes, we'd discussed it several times. We'd hoped the engagement and then the interview this morning would help, but obviously, there wouldn't be time for that yet."

Doug tipped his head to the side. "So that's what the engagement was all about? A play by Will to keep his job?"

That, and to save her reputation. But she didn't know how much Doug knew. "No. I love him, Doug. We never really called off the engagement in the first place, and when Will came back and apologized, I forgave him. We both knew what was at stake, but our feelings for each other are very real."

At least she could now say that statement with 100 percent truth. Her feelings for Will were undeniable, even though still inadvisable.

Screwing the cap back on the water bottle, Doug looked up, his expression somber. "Well, this is going to hurt even more, then, and I'm sorry for that."

He was officially making her nervous. "Enough, Doug. Just say what you came to say and leave."

"Fraud. Will wasn't fired due to the sales numbers but because of his part in a massive accounting scandal."

He—what?

Confusion threatened to swallow her whole. Hanna closed her eyes and shook her head. It wasn't possible. Will wasn't like the Bernie Madoffs of the world.

Not *her* Will.

Right?

Doug walked to her and put a hand on her shoulder. "Look. I'm sorry to—"

She pushed his hand off and shoved him. Hard. "No. You're lying. Now keep your hands off me and get out."

He wisely took a step back. "I know this is a shock."

"It's not true. I don't know what's going on here, but it wasn't William. He's not like that."

Doug reached into the hidden pocket of his suit coat and handed her a thick envelope. "I checked it myself. The numbers were just too off this month to refute. Now, these aren't public yet, and we're going to try and keep this pretty hush-hush and fix it internally. No need to have another scandal on their hands."

The old CEO. The one busted for accounting fraud by the Feds a few years back. She knew pretty much zilch about all that corporate lingo stuff, had only skimmed over the news with some reference to socks—or SOX?—and SEC and a bunch of other things that made no difference to a budding kindergarten teacher at the time. But it hadn't been good. That's all she knew.

And now William was messed up with all that?

It just couldn't be.

She grabbed the envelope and used it to point to the door. "Good-bye, Doug."

He stuffed his hands into his pockets and took his sweet time getting to the exit. "I included some cash in the envelope for you to get home on. I'm afraid you'll need it. And—I need those papers back. Obviously, we can't risk this information getting into the wrong hands."

Her fingers tightened around the envelope that featured the Foster and Jones logo and address. She should just give it back to him, let Will explain himself first. Wasn't that the proper thing to do?

No, the proper thing to do would be to pray about it. That's what her dad would lecture.

But God would want her to know what Will was really up to,

right? He was all about truth.

And Hanna wanted to know the truth more than anything.

Ignoring Doug, she slid her finger under the envelope flap and opened it. The first thing she saw was green.

There had to be at least twenty hundred-dollar bills there.

Two thousand dollars would take her home and back much more than once.

She glanced to the right and remembered Will's office. Fitting that she sit in there to find out just what exactly he may or may not have been up to, right?

No longer giving a flip about his privacy or that she was leaving Doug standing in the hallway, she marched in and plopped into Will's big, brown leather chair. She stacked the bills in front of her on the desk that was mostly clean except for a few file folders.

This was it. Time to find out what Will was all about.

She unfolded the loose sheets of paper and scanned the top page.

She was no genius when it came to numbers and had been lucky to get a C in accounting in college.

But even she could tell that something wasn't right. This quarter's numbers were much higher.

She scanned the rest of the pages, but the numbers and various charts meant nothing to her. But they'd obviously meant something to Doug. And if they really had fired Will, then they meant something to the board of directors as well.

Flinging the pages across the room toward the door, Hanna buried her face in her hands, ignoring Doug as he quietly picked up the scattered papers then slipped out the front door, wordlessly.

Good riddance.

What was she going to do? Spend the money on the next flight back to Embarrass? Wait around to give Will a piece of her mind?

Neither sounded enticing. Her life was spiraling downward

quickly, and it looked like the only way to stop was with a big, fiery train wreck.

Lord help her.

Hanna sat back and gripped the wad of cash. What a great thought. God helping her. She didn't blame the Big Guy. She could take a mental review of the past twelve months and see no less than one hundred times she'd done something stupid that was probably directly against what God would have had her do if she'd asked Him.

Why should He bail her out now?

No, she had to set this right on her own. She was treading water and sinking fast.

It was time to abandon ship and swim home.

CHAPTER THIRTY-EIGHT

The next flight out of Nashville to Minneapolis was a red-eye that left at 10:00 p.m., which suited her perfectly. She would need to tell the cabbie to put a rush on it, and it would be late and dark, so hopefully she wouldn't have to worry about anyone noticing her escape. She'd have to stay in a hotel tonight and take another flight in the morning to Duluth, but she refused to stay in Nashville any longer than she had to.

And even if she did run into any gawkers, she'd just ignore them. The damage could get no worse than the truth already made it.

After putting a call in for a cab to come pick her up, she slumped up the stairs and grabbed her bag. She passed by Will's door and paused.

Debating for a moment, she set down her suitcase and marched into his room to his dresser, grabbed her coin off the top, and shoved it into her pocket. Slipping the glittery diamond off her finger, she put it in the place where the coin had once been.

She'd given him her heart, and he'd wrecked it twice now.

Fool me once, shame on you. Fool me twice, shame on me. Fool me three times. . .not going to happen.

Retrieving her bag, she focused only on the steps in front of her, not allowing herself to be taken in again by the opulence of her surroundings.

Downstairs, she made her way to the yellow cab at the curb.

"You the lady headed for BNA?"

The young man took her bag as she nodded. "Yes, thanks for getting here so fast. My flight leaves at ten, so I don't have a lot of extra time."

"Sure thing. You mind sharing a cab though? A guy just asked if I was going that direction, and I told him I'd check with you to see if you'd want to split the bill."

Anything to save cash. "Sure. No problem at all."

The cabbie motioned behind her, and she turned to see a portly man, probably in his fifties, walk up. "Thanks, ma'am. I sure do appreciate it. A friend was supposed to pick me up and bailed on me at the last minute."

She nodded. At least he didn't look dangerous or anything. "No problem. I'm in a hurry myself though, so—"

He held up a hand and walked double speed to the taxi and opened the door for her. "Say no more, we'll get going."

Hanna smiled. A gentleman. Phew. "Thanks." She slid in to the other side to make room for him to sit beside her. A bit awkward, but she'd survive.

Hopefully, the man wouldn't recognize her, but he didn't seem like he'd be up on reality TV and the drama that goes on afterward.

He sat beside her, and the cab took off a moment later.

"I guess I should introduce myself. I'm Seth. And you are?"

She was tempted to make something up, but she'd had way too much lying of late. It was time for the truth. "Hanna. My name is Hanna."

"So, Hanna, you leaving home or going home?"

She forced a smile. "Going home. Definitely going home. And you?"

He lifted the laptop case in his hand. "Leaving. On business.

Takes me all over the country most weeks. Where's home for you?"

"Northern Minnesota. Making it to Minneapolis tonight, then catching an early flight north in the morning." The faster she could be home to her safe spot, the better.

He turned slightly and laughed. "Now, that's just crazy. I'm headed to the Twin Cities tonight, too. Although I'll be staying there for a few days before I jet off again. You on the ten o'clock flight, too?"

This was almost God ordained or something. A friendly person to talk to on the cab ride, half the fare, and a familiar face on the flight home. Not that she was in the mood to talk to anyone, but anything that would get her mind off her woes would be great.

"Yup, that's my flight. How weird is that?"

"I personally think that God doesn't make coincidences."

"Are you a—you know—Christian?" Oh, lovely. She'd asked it like she was some atheist who was shocked at being in the presence of a believer. If he handed her a tract. . .

"Born and raised. And you?"

Could one really be born a Christian? Hm. Not in *her* denomination. "My parents were Christians, and I accepted God when I was pretty little." Like, four years old. Sometimes it felt like she'd been born a Christian. It's all she'd ever known.

And how far she'd fallen. . .

The landing wasn't very pretty.

"Ah, we're similar, then. You married?"

Oh no. If he hit on her. . . "No, just getting out of a relationship though." *And not looking for a rebound man with a potbelly who is probably old enough to be my dad.*

"Gotcha."

"What about you?" It seemed the appropriate thing to ask.

"Married for thirty years now." He looked down at his cell phone and laughed. "That's her now, wanting to know if I got a ride okay."

He tapped a few buttons on his phone, and Hanna looked away to give him his privacy.

"That's wonderful. She sounds very thoughtful." It really was. Because if he *did* try to hit on her, it gave her permission to punch him on behalf of his wife.

They rode the rest of the way making inconsequential small talk. It was apparent he worked a lot and had little time for TV or anything to do with celebrities. What a nice change to chat with someone who didn't have an opinion on what she'd done with her life.

He'd texted his wife a few more times during the ride.

Ugh. She was jealous. Even when she was with Will, he rarely took the time to communicate with her like that. And how dumb was that? She was jealous over the lack of text messages from her former fake fiancé.

He was probably too busy figuring out how to rig sales numbers to steal company money.

Once they were at the airport, Seth paid for the entire carfare, despite her insistence that she pay half. They stayed together and checked in, went through security, then sat next to each other at the gate.

They were about forty-five minutes early, and only a few others dotted the terminal.

After grabbing some keep-me-awake coffee, Seth folded his leg and propped his foot on his knee. "So, you said you were newly single. That why you were in Nashville?"

She sipped the hot drink, feeling it loosen her tongue. "Yes. We were giving it a go one more time, but it just didn't work out."

"He cheating on you or something?"

Ha. She probably would have handled that news better, honestly. "No. He—well, he's a businessman, and I found out that he'd done some not-so-scrupulous things."

"Yeah, that's not good. I commend you for getting out now."

Hanna pressed a finger to the side of her eye, willing the tears to stay in there, just until tomorrow. When she was home at the farmhouse, on her twin-size childhood bed, then she'd bawl her eyes out.

But not yet.

"It was. . .I loved him. I really did. But some things you just can't forgive, you know?"

"Did you find out yourself, or did he get fired or something?"

"I had no clue. I'd have sworn he was innocent, but now that I look back. . .yeah. He didn't have the greatest track record in the honesty department. I should have seen the writing on the wall, but he was just so. . .so charming. He could charm a fish onto a hook."

The picture of Will with that gigantic fish he'd caught popped into her mind.

Seth leaned toward her and placed a pudgy hand over hers. "Well, I'm sorry you had to go through that. But you seem like a bright young lady. You'll be just fine."

Hanna smiled as the preboarding flight announcement came over the intercom. "Thanks. I really appreciate that."

It actually made her feel just a little better to talk with someone. She had a date with her cell phone and a call to Carly once she got settled into her hotel room tonight, but this helped her stave off the need to talk until then.

And thankfully, no reporters had shown up.

Maybe God was looking out for her after all.

⁓

Will stood in his condo, his head pressed against the glass, watching people flit here and there in a rush to get to wherever they planned to go. Usually the sight exhilarated him, but today, he just didn't care.

His dad had flown into town on Wednesday, and they'd spent the last twenty-four hours going over the auditors' notes and brainstorming solutions.

Or, his dad had anyway.

William had been in a dense fog since Tuesday morning, when he'd come home to find that Hanna had disappeared off the face of the earth.

No amount of words could explain it to him. And even so, no words were given to him to try.

He'd come home at five in the morning, expecting to have a sleeping Hanna in his guest room.

Instead, he'd found nothing. She'd left without a trace, leaving only two half-empty water bottles on the counter and her diamond ring on his dresser where her coin used to sit.

The coin he'd treasured every day since she'd given it to him and he'd chosen to accept only hers.

Even when she'd first turned her back on him, albeit for good reason, he'd kept it right there as a reminder of what his stupidity had lost him and the cost of his arrogance.

But this time, he was trying to right his wrongs. Working his hardest to be worthy of her affection.

That night, sitting in his dark office, he'd realized he was in love with her. As crazy as it was, as undeserving as he was, she'd gotten into his heart during that stupid TV show and been there ever since.

William slammed a fist against the reinforced glass.

Now she was gone, and the pain might very well be the death of him.

At first, he worried a reporter had gotten in. Had she gotten scared and left? But her cell went directly to voice mail, and a phone call to her father had gone unanswered. He'd gotten ahold of Carly, only to receive a few unladylike words yelled in his ear and a phone slammed. So he doubted that was the case.

This week could officially go down as the worst one of his life. He'd lost his pride, his heart, and now, probably his job.

Couldn't get much worse than that.

Shoving his hands in his pockets, he strode to his office and sagged into a leather chair, the one where he'd always said he did his best thinking.

Today, it took all his energy to conjure up a coherent thought.

He picked up a handful of files and was tempted to trash them. What did it matter? He did nothing wrong, but so far, even his illustrious father hadn't been able to find a way to clear his name. All roads pointed to William. Even if he hadn't been trying to commit fraud, he'd made some extremely stupid decisions.

On the latter, he could agree.

But fraud?

No way.

The only clear thing was. . .those same roads were wide and all but highlighted in yellow with sticky notes next to them saying "Hey, this is William, and I'm trying to cook the books, okay?"

No one was stupid enough to be so blatantly obvious about corporate fraud. But the board didn't see it that way.

And William was destined for the unemployment line.

He wasn't even sure if CEOs were eligible for unemployment compensation.

Leaning forward, he pressed his forehead against the top of his desk. God must be punishing him. A cruel, cruel punishment for his desertion years ago.

God had just stayed quiet, biding His time until now to unleash His fury on William Preston.

What he wasn't sure of was if he should repent or shake his fists at God for being so callous.

Repentance made him want to laugh. God had been the one in the wrong, not William.

But shaking his fists at God could incur more wrath. He'd prefer the wrath to stop, actually.

Someone cleared their throat from the doorway, and William lifted his head to see his father leaning against the french door, eyes dark. "You've got yourself in a pickle, William."

No, really? What had been the clue? "I know. I wasn't ready for the big career leap. You've told me that a thousand times. If I'd wanted your opinion, I'd have asked for it."

Harrison pushed off the door and walked toward the desk then stopped, arms folded against his broad chest. "Actually, I was going to commend you. I've been spending time looking through all those files you gave me. Looks like you've done a remarkable job. Some of the changes you implemented were nothing short of genius. Except, of course, the ones in question."

Will shrugged, uncomfortable with the rare show of praise. "The company was headed for bankruptcy when I took over. Changes had to be made, one way or another."

"I have a theory for you."

Will nodded toward one of the office chairs. "I'm all ears."

His father sat and folded a leg up over his knee. "I don't think you were the only one framed."

"Meaning?"

"Greg Kasinzisky. Your predecessor. I think someone set him up, too."

That didn't seem possible. The auditors had found proof going back over fifteen years, which coincided with the gradual decline of the over hundred-year-old company. It had been subtle and started before the whole accounting debacle of Enron and the implementation of SOX audits. Even they hadn't caught it, though. The clever maneuvering of funds had been nothing short of genius on Greg's part, if not horrifically illegal and unethical.

The man had maintained his innocence and, to date, hadn't been officially arrested and charged with fraud, but the prosecution was still gathering information for their case. They were taking their time, making sure they had all their ducks in a row before they actually filed charges. From what Will understood, it could still be up to another year before it was done and Greg was in jail.

"Dad, that's crazy. The two scenarios are completely different. And Greg has all but admitted his guilt."

"Call it an educated gut feeling."

Will mulled the ridiculous idea over for a moment. It was crazy but not entirely impossible. "Any educated guesses on who would have done it?"

His dad unfolded his legs, leaned forward, and propped his elbows on his knees. "Who is the one person who was there that long, who has access to everything, and who would have a vested interest in getting both you and Greg booted from your job?"

The answer was as clear and logical as if someone had flown a plane across the sky, a trailing sign billowing in the wind emblazoned with the man's name on it.

CHAPTER THIRTY-NINE

*H*anna had grown up surrounded by snow almost eight months out of every year. In fact, she'd been born at home during a blizzard.

But right now, as she stood at the front window inside the quiet farmhouse, she despised the white, irritating flakes that drifted to the ground and accumulated at a crazy pace.

Mostly because it reminded her of the blizzard that had brought William back in her life again. And everyone knew how *that* had turned out.

Five days. Five very long days since she'd flown home. Her dad had welcomed her as she'd known he would. Lots of soup and hugs and grunts about how his shotgun would come in handy should that young man decide to show his face up here again.

Not that he'd ever shoot anyone. At least not on purpose.

She hoped anyway. . . .

Letting the lace drape drop back over the window, Hanna stuffed her hands into her jeans pockets and walked into the kitchen.

Memories of spilled mayonnaise and William lifting her up in the dark pricked at her.

This wasn't good at all. The thought of William should disgust her, but her heart rebelled. Even her lips had a mind of their own, aching when she thought of their last kiss.

She grabbed her Bible off the kitchen table and walked back into the living room. She clicked the TV off and settled onto the couch, her feet tucked beneath her.

Her fingers caressed the familiar leather cover then turned the pages, her gaze skimming over passages she'd been spoon-fed with since birth.

What a fraud she was.

She'd gone on that stupid show, determined to keep her faith intact. Maybe even show the world that Christians weren't all that bad.

It was almost laughable now. Christians hated her. The world laughed at her. And God. . .

She wasn't even sure God wanted to lay claim to her soul anymore.

What a lovely mess she'd made.

A beating thudded on the front door followed by the sound of it opening. A rush of frigid air swarmed the first floor. Hanna set the Bible aside and hugged the thick, cable-knit sweater closer to her.

Carly stood in the entryway looking like a stuffed snowman in her flake-covered parka and holding a large grocery bag. "I brought a ton of chocolate, because by the looks of this storm, I might be stuck here tonight."

"Thanks for coming in this."

"You send out an SOS and best friends come running, snow or no snow. It's the rule, you know."

While Carly spread out her gifts from heaven, Hanna added another log to the fire in the wood-burning stove and prodded it with the poker, relishing the heat the burning timber gave. Which just brought back another memory of William, looking at the stove as if it were a mass of metal from outer space. Heating a house with wood had been this hilarious oddity to him. Made perfect sense to her now having seen the fireplace in his condo that needed only the push of a button to ignite the cutesy little flame that would barely melt snow, much less heat a house or cook a fish.

And she could cook a mighty nice Northern on this stove.

Plopping down on the couch next to where the queen of chocolate had curled up, she snagged a handful of M&M's and popped a few in her mouth. "I needed this."

Carly picked up the Bible from the coffee table. "A little light reading this afternoon?"

"Not hardly. Just sitting here holding it made me feel like a fraud. It's been months since I've even cracked it open." Not to mention the last time she'd honest to goodness sat down and prayed. The quick "Don't let me screw up while I go do my own thing" prayers didn't count, she assumed.

"So, what? You're feeling guilty?"

Hanna tucked her knees under her chin, wrapping her arms around her legs. "You know all those notes I got?"

"The ones I told you I'd happily burn for you?"

"Yeah, those. And all the people on Facebook and the like. I always thought they were sanctimonious jerks who meddled with other people's business so they could conveniently ignore the giant tree stumps lodged in their own eyes."

Carly shrugged. "Sounds about right to me."

"I'm starting to think they were right." An M&M slapped her on the cheek. "Hey!"

"They weren't right, and you know it. How could you even say that?"

The mistakes she'd made in the last year stood out in her memory like giant red stamps that read *FAILED*. "Nothing has gone right. I've made stupid decision after stupid decision. I'm a fraud, Carly. I went on there thinking I'd be this glaring light for Jesus and all I've done is brought shame. God probably hates me right about now. I just wish I could make it right. But everything feels so empty now."

"I won't argue about your guilt, even though I think it's a little misplaced. We all screw up though. I mean, seriously. Look at Peter."

Hanna frowned. Was Carly dating someone she didn't know about? She'd been MIA for a while but... "Who's Peter?"

Carly rolled her eyes. "Uh, the apostle? Jesus' right-hand man? Guy who tried to walk on water? If you'll remember, he screwed up, too."

Oh. That Peter. "What does the apostle Peter have to do with me?"

"Let's see, if I remember right, Jesus forewarned that he'd deny Him, but Peter said, uh, yeah, no I won't. Then he was even big and bad and chopped off a guy's ear trying to defend Jesus. But when it came down to it, he denied he even knew Him. Three times. He left, I'm sure, feeling like a total failure. Then what does Jesus do? Gives him a second chance. I think there are a lot of parallels. You had a lot of good intentions going into *The Price of Love* regardless of how wise or unwise it was. You totally maintained your witness, despite what some people might say, even if you weren't always perfect along the way. But I think maybe where you went wrong was hiding when the pressure got high. You got scared and snuffed out your light so no one would look at you and hurt you anymore. You gave them the power to wound you instead of seeking the One who had the power to rescue you."

"So, what? I should have just taken off my sword and sliced off all their ears?"

Carly snorted. "No, but I might have. Seriously though, what's that verse about a gentle answer turning away wrath?"

Years of Bible memorization in Sunday school kicked in. "Proverbs 15:1. 'A gentle answer turns away wrath, but a harsh word stirs up anger.'"

"Yes, that's it. Instead of hiding from people, or even, as much as it pains me to say it, shaking your fists at them, maybe the right answer was to respond with a gentle, truthful answer. Does that sound too cheesy?"

Hanna pressed fingers to her eyes to stop the tears threatening to fall again. "Not cheesy at all."

She closed her eyes, blinders falling off and the reality of her mistakes so clear it was like they were highlighted in yellow marker.

She'd hidden instead of standing up for herself. But—fighting back with anger, like she really, really wanted to do, wasn't going to solve a thing.

Had Will been a jerk and made a huge mistake? Oh yeah.

Had the world laughed at her and made fun? Check.

Had Christians totally come out to flog her in a self-righteous, indignant attitude? Definitely.

Well, actually, not all of them, now that she thought about it. She'd gotten quite a few e-mails and notes of encouragement. But the others were the ones that rang in her memory.

Carly tossed another chocolate candy in her mouth. "Remember what Jesus told Peter?"

She'd heard the story a million times. *"Feed my sheep,"* Jesus had said. Three times, the same number of times Peter had denied Him. "I'm fresh out of sheep, girl. I do feed a few cows every day, though."

"My point is, God's given you a platform, whether you like it or not. Get over the fact you made mistakes. Repent and move on. It's not about you anyway. It's about bringing God glory. Ask Him how He wants you to feed His sheep. I bet He has an answer."

Her words echoed in Hanna's ears. *"It's not about you anyway."* Oh yeah. How true was that? She'd gone through so many emotions because of what was going on with her. When had she made it less about God and more about herself?

The moment she'd heard Will's interview, that's when. Her thought hadn't been about how God would look, even though that was how she portrayed it to those she confided in.

No, her anger had been for herself. How could he humiliate *her*?

The price of her selfishness was astonishing. Her career, her future, her family's reputation, her testimony, Will. . .they'd all been her victims.

Well, maybe not Will. He'd made his bed.

Carly grabbed her Diet Coke. "You know, Will called me the other day."

Hanna snapped her hand back from the bag of M&M's she'd been reaching for. "No he didn't."

"Yup." She took a swig then set the can back on the coaster. "We had an interesting conversation."

The candy forgotten, Hanna sank back on the couch, her pulse flying. "What did he say? What did *you* say?"

"He wanted to know why you left. I may have, uh, said a few things my momma would have washed my mouth out with soap for. Totally regretted it later, especially now talking about gentle answers and all, but let's just say, I let the man have it."

"Carly—"

"What? He deserved it."

True. He was a swindler and a manipulator. But why did her heart still hurt so much? Why did she want to cry over losing him instead of, like last time, yell at the thought of ever having to see him again?

Nothing made sense.

Carly leaned forward and looked into her eyes. Her mouth flopped open. "Oh. My. Goodness. You're still in love with him, aren't you? After all he's done?"

Hanna fell back, her head cushioned by the polyester pillow. "I'm so stupid. I *know* he isn't good for me. Every logical reason to despise him is right in front of my face. But I just can't stop thinking about him. Wondering what he's doing. How he's doing. My crazy heart wants nothing more than to hop on that bumpy plane and fly back to Nashville. Ugh."

A throw pillow caught her in the gut. "I can't believe you'd let this guy get to you again. He's bad for you, Hanna."

She grabbed the fluffy weapon and stuffed it under her head. "I know, I know. Something just doesn't feel right about all this." She pressed her fists to her eyes. "I'm so confused."

A ding sounded from Carly's phone, but her friend just clicked off the volume.

"Aren't you going to check it?"

"It's just a Facebook message. It can wait."

That girl and her social media. Hanna used to be the same way. . . until the obscene number of messages she kept getting, most of them cruel, almost drove her over the edge. Deleting her whole account had been the best thing she'd ever done for her sanity at the time. "Go on. You know you're dying to read it. I'm fine." She popped another M&M. "I've got chocolate."

"Since you insist." Whipping out her phone faster than a bird catches a fish, Carly tapped the screen.

Silence followed.

Carly's face went pale. "Uh, you need to read this, Hanna." She held the phone out.

"No. Whatever it is, I don't even want to know." She'd sworn to herself she wouldn't get sucked into the drama this time. Wouldn't spend hours and hours printing off e-mails and clipping horrible magazine articles. In fact, she hadn't even checked her e-mail once since she'd been home.

While she wouldn't run and hide, she wouldn't dive into the muck on purpose either.

"It's not about you. Well, not *all* about you anyway. A friend messaged me a link."

Carly shoved the phone into Hanna's hand, leaving her no choice. "Fine."

She skimmed the headline.

FOSTER AND JONES CEO FIRED AFTER FIANCÉE TATTLES.

What? She didn't tattle on anyone. She ran her finger up the screen to read more.

Yesterday, we released the story that Holy Hanna Knight had accused her fiancé, William Preston, reality TV star and CEO of the skincare giant Foster and Jones, of accounting fraud. Last night, the board of F&J met and voted unanimously to oust William Preston as CEO, and appointed CFO Doug Perry as interim CEO until a permanent decision can be made.

Details of the allegations have not been released. Stay tuned on this developing story.

Bile rose in her stomach, threatening to purge the chocolate she'd just inhaled. "This can't be. Doug said Will was already fired, and I never talked to any reporter."

"Well, evidently you did."

"I only told you, my dad, and—"

Two people came to mind. Doug Perry himself—and that way-too-nice guy she'd shared a taxicab with. "I—I have to call Will."

Carly reached out and grabbed her hand. "Honey, you can't. You need to just leave it alone. He can sort through his own problems. He's the one who committed fraud, remember?"

Ignoring her, she grabbed her own cell from the end table and pushed the numbers she knew by heart.

With each ring of the phone, her heart raced faster. What would she say to the man whose dreams she'd just crushed?

~~~~

Hot anger poured over William as he stood, ringing phone in hand, looking at the caller ID.

How dare she call him right now.

Not only had Hanna left in his lowest moment, without a word of explanation, she might as well have spit in his eyes by telling such a ridiculous story.

Did she really think that of him?

Or did she make it all up, stringing him along all this time, planning her moment of revenge?

He clicked the IGNORE button on his phone and threw it on the black leather couch.

"William, you've got to talk to her sometime."

He turned to face his dad, who, even though his presence was pointless now, refused to leave. "It's no use. She got what she wanted. I am humiliated and ruined. Nothing she can say will change that."

The board meeting the night before flashed in his mind, complete with Doug's fake humble acceptance of Will's job.

The promise of a full SEC investigation loomed.

He could end up in jail, just like Greg would.

"Listen, why don't you come back to New Jersey for a little while? Clear your thoughts. Let your mom worry over you for old times' sake."

Will snorted. "What? No more lectures on how I need to buck up and face it like a man?"

"Sometimes a man has to learn that he can't go through it alone."

He rested a hand on the clear floor-to-ceiling window of the condo he fully planned on putting up for sale immediately. He had a meeting with a realtor in a few hours, in fact. "Sometimes a man has to know when he's beaten. She won. I lost. End of story."

"It isn't a game, Will. There is no winning or losing. Right now, I'd say you're both pretty pathetic."

Leave it to ol' pops to cheer a guy up. The nameless faces on the street below beckoned to him. He needed to escape. Being nameless sounded great right now. "I think I'll go for a walk. Feel free to head back home to Mom. There isn't much that can be done here to help anything."

"By the way, I talked with Greg this morning."

He shoved his hands in his jeans pockets. Just great. The last thing he needed was to be associated with that tainted ex-CEO any more than the media was already linking them on their own. "What did he want?"

"Expressed his empathy."

William turned away from the window. "He still saying he's innocent?"

"I wish you'd talk to him, Will. You already know what I think."

He did. And the more Will mulled it over, the more it made sense.

Doug had been itching to complete his climb of the corporate ladder for years. But Greg had been named CEO all those years ago. The board felt he had more operations knowledge than Doug.

And when they made the unprecedented choice to name Will to the position at such a young age, the man had made no secret of the fact he was ticked.

Something had always felt slimy about the guy.

"There's no proof. And now that I'm not in the office anymore and don't have access to documents, there never will be."

His dad lifted a piece of paper. Will hadn't noticed him holding it before. "Speaking of, I was wondering where you got this from."

William frowned and took the paper. It looked to be a page out of the quarterly sales forecast, but the numbers, even though missing a few pages, didn't look like the ones he'd seen. "Where did you find this?" He'd given back all paper documents related to Foster and Jones early this morning, hoping that it showed cooperation and goodwill on his part. No doubt it wouldn't be long before the SEC came and searched his place anyway. They wouldn't find anything, that he knew for darn sure.

"In your office. It was on the floor behind the door."

Strange. He tossed it back on the glass coffee table. "It doesn't matter. It's over with anyway. Lock up if you leave."

He strode out of the room, ignoring his father's pleas for him to listen.

Listening would get him nowhere. Being a good guy had gotten him nowhere, too.

All he had was a broken heart, a ruined career, and a stupid condo that felt colder than Northern Minnesota in a blizzard.

CHAPTER FORTY

*H*anna dug the shovel into the last bit of snow on the porch and flung the white fluffy stuff to the side, where it fluttered to rest with the other foot of snow she'd shoveled.

Couldn't it be June yet?

Not possible according to her calendar that had just flipped over to March.

What a dreary, dreary winter. They'd had more snow this year than the last five years combined.

The temperature was the only thing she missed about Nashville. She'd give almost anything to be able to walk around with only a light jacket again.

The rumbling of an engine sounded in the distance. Probably her dad back from his trip into the nearby town of Virginia. Their snowblower had finally bitten the dust after years of trusty service, and he wanted to get a new one before the next snow.

She turned to greet him but, instead, found an oversized black SUV pulling into their long driveway. She squinted but couldn't make out the driver through tinted windows.

Eyeing the rifle propped against the front door, she stood straighter, trying to ignore the fact that she looked like the biggest country bumpkin in the world with her snow pants and her dad's way-too-big-for-her flannel jacket on. Not to mention the hat with oversized earflaps.

Crud. She'd forgotten about the hat.

The SUV parked in the spot her dad had plowed earlier, and a man in khakis and a large black wool coat stepped out.

Recognition hit her like a snowball in the face.

Harrison. William's dad.

She'd only have been more surprised if Elvis himself had stepped out of that truck.

She took a few steps forward. "Mr. Preston. What are you doing here?"

The older man, his sprinkled gray hair poking out from under a black stocking cap, walked toward her with a determined stride, stopping a few feet away. "I was hoping we could talk."

She wanted to say no, but the man had always been nothing but kind to her. He'd welcomed her into his home and his family so freely, she could do nothing other than offer him the same courtesy. "Sure. Let's go inside where it's not so cold."

He nodded and followed her up the front walk. "I'd appreciate that. I thought Jersey was cold, but I do believe you all have a leg up on us in that department."

She smiled as she opened the door. "At least it's about five degrees right now. It could be much worse."

Her former future father-in-law stepped inside and tugged off his tan leather gloves and black hat, leaving static-filled hair sticking up all over. The man always looked so pressed and neat. It was hard not to snicker at his crazy hat hair.

"Five degrees is as worse as I'd like to see it, thanks."

She motioned him to have a seat on the sofa. "Would you like something to drink?"

He nodded. "Anything warm would be great."

"I have coffee, hot chocolate, or hot tea. Take your pleasure."

Crinkles formed around his eyes as he smiled and winked. "I'll take whatever you're having."

"Hot chocolate it is." She walked to the kitchen and put the teakettle on the stove to warm the water.

She turned to get the chocolate out of the pantry but almost screamed when she found Harrison standing in the kitchen, leaning against the island. Her hand fluttered to her chest. "Goodness. I didn't hear you walk in."

He just smiled. "Sorry about that."

After grabbing the chocolate, she took out two coffee cups. "So, I'm surprised the cold affects you so much. Jersey gets their fair share of snow and cold."

"We're actually from LA originally. We lived there while William was growing up. We didn't move out East until his junior year of high school. It's been over sixteen years now and I'm still not used to the cold."

The teakettle started to sing, so she fixed their drinks and handed him a cup. "Okay, let's stop skirting around with small talk about the weather."

"Nothing small about this weather, girl."

She smirked. "True. But seriously. Will and I are done. There's nothing you can do about that."

"I'm not here about you and Will—not as a couple, that is."

The hot sweet liquid slid down her throat, warming her stomach. "Then what are you here for?"

"You heard about Will's job?"

She clutched the cup to keep from dropping it. "I'm sorry about that. I—I know it looks like I outed him, but I promise, it wasn't my intent. I don't know if it was—" Should she tell him about Doug's visit? No. Not yet. No use dragging him into it just yet. "I shared a cab with a guy to the airport. He happened to be on my same flight. I didn't mention names, but it was late and I was upset. I may have let it slip that my fiancé was involved in accounting fraud. But I swear I didn't say who."

He stood up straighter, the friendly glint on his face gone, replaced by a serious, lawyer-like expression. "But Will says you didn't know anything about his being accused of fraud. He hadn't told you yet." Unbuttoning his jacket, he took a folder out he'd kept hidden, laid it on the tiled island, and slid it across to her. "I think this might have been part of what you saw. What I want to know is, where'd you find it, and where's the rest of the report?"

She opened the folder to find—

One of the papers Doug had let her look at. Those stupid papers she almost wished she had never given in and looked at. "Where did you find this?" She was sure Doug had taken them all when he left.

"It was on the floor behind the door. Will keeps it open all the time and rarely looks behind it."

That's right. She'd thrown the papers. Doug must have missed a sheet.

She took her mug and walked over to the kitchen table and sat down. "Doug. Doug stopped by and said he thought I should see the report. That I should know the truth about Will. I thought he'd already been fired until the news last week."

Harrison took the bench across the table. "What I'm trying to figure out is how this paper made you think Will was committing fraud?"

Hanna frowned. "What do you mean? Everyone knew the company was struggling. I'm no business expert, but there's no way those numbers could have been accurate."

"I don't know what numbers you saw, but Foster and Jones was still showing a steep decline in profits for the current quarter."

That made no sense. "But Doug said—" The moment the name slipped from her lips, understanding dawned. "He lied."

Harrison reached over the table and covered her hand with his. "We need your help, Hanna."

"No. I don't know what you have in mind, but I'm sorry. The answer is no, regardless. I'm done with this mess. I have to put my life back together, and every time I step back into it, every time I try to make it better, it just gets exponentially worse. I can't. Do you understand?"

He tapped the folder on the table. "What I understand is that you're a chicken."

She straightened her back. "Excuse me?"

"You heard me. You're a chicken. This seems impossible, and instead of doing the right thing, you run away like someone has cut off your head."

"Maybe I am like a chicken. My head is about to be chopped off, and I'm running away to preserve it."

Setting the folder down, Harrison folded his arms and leaned forward to look her in the eye. "Hanna, I'm far from perfect myself. I've messed up a lot, but right now, I'm a father seeing my son hurting and on the verge of giving up on his life. I won't let that happen. I don't think God wants me to let that happen. If you can sit here and tell me that God's okay with you washing your hands of this mess you and Will both made and not dealing with the consequences, then fine. I'll be on my way, and you can keep holed up here, licking your wounds and feeling sorry for yourself. But if you want a chance to see the truth, to see the real William Preston, and to right a whole boatload of wrongs, then I've got a plane ticket with your name on it, headed out at eight tonight."

Emotions warred in her heart.

Was he right? Was she being a chicken and hiding from her self-made problems yet again?

She'd been the one to agree to that show in the first place, knowing full well that scandals almost always came out of it. Good grief, she'd even signed a contract stating the show could portray her in whatever light they wished, good or bad, and indemnifying them of any consequences.

And pretending to be engaged to solve a problem, that had been just icing on the cake.

But. . .she looked at the folder. "Is it true, though? Did William commit fraud?"

Harrison laughed. "Will couldn't cheat anyone out of money if his life depended on it. You may not know it, but once upon a time, he was a young kid, sold out for Jesus, and wouldn't steal a piece of bread from a bird even if he were starving. No, Will isn't a crook. But I think we can both take a wild guess at who is."

Doug.

As she'd suspected herself.

Suddenly, the truth was clear. While a future for her and Will wasn't exactly a possibility, he was not a thief, and if Harrison thought she had the power to help him, she had to try.

"Fine. I'll go."

The front door opened and her dad marched in, stomping snow off his boots. "We got visitors, Hanna-girl?"

She stood and swallowed the knot in her throat. Dad wasn't going to be happy. "Uh, yeah. Mr. Preston, Will's dad, is here."

Her dad came around the corner, a smile on his lips. "Harrison, good to finally meet you." He held out his hand, and the two men shook hands then hugged, complete with hard slaps on the back as if they were old friends.

Hanna glanced between the two, more confused than a fish

circling a plastic, neon-pink worm. "I don't understand. Do you two know each other?"

Her dad came over and squeezed her shoulders. "Of course we do, sugar. You think I'm going to let you traipse off across the country with my blessing without talking to the young man's dad?"

"Your dad called me well over a year ago, before they even started filming your season of *The Price of Love.*"

She groped behind her for the chair and, finding it, allowed herself to fall into it. "I'm so confused right now. Why would you do that?"

"You were all bent on going, and I know you're an adult and all, but I took myself up to the library and did a little research on William Preston. Called up his dad and we had a right nice chat. Been talking, what, 'bout once a week or so since?"

Harrison nodded. "Your dad's a good guy. Promised to take me ice fishing one of these days."

Her dad ignored her and looked at his—friend? "I know you're in a hurry, but next time, you'll have to plan to stay longer."

Had these two retirees been abducted by aliens or something? She looked around. Maybe she was on one of those What-Would-You-Do shows. . .now that would be classic. "Dad, you knew about this?"

He just grinned. "Gave him directions and everything. Also told him not to bring a sissy car like his son did. Now, go pack. You don't have a lot of time if you're going to make it to the airport in time."

The room was almost a haze as she walked to the back stairs, still thoroughly confused.

As she put her foot on the first step, a thought slammed into her. The fake engagement. Her dad knew, but—

Turning, she faced the two. "Harrison, did you know—?"

He nodded. "The whole time."

"And your wife?"

"We keep no secrets from each other."

She blinked, the truth settling in. "But—but she made me buy the dress. . . ."

He flushed red. "That was her idea, not mine. A bit of expensive wishful thinking, we'll call it. It's still hanging up in our closet, just in case."

The thought of the expensive, over-the-top dress hanging there, never to be worn, made her sad.

But unfortunately, it would never be.

Even if *she* wanted it now, Will would never forgive her for ruining his career.

CHAPTER FORTY-ONE

Will sipped his coffee, ignoring the buzz around him at Starbucks.

He'd never actually come and sat down here before, had just breezed in and out on his way to the office when he wasn't running late.

But his realtor had three showings on his condo today, so he had to make himself scarce.

How does one do that when they were jobless?

He took another sip of the startling black brew. They went to the local coffee shop, evidently.

His phone vibrated, and he checked the screen.

A text from Emma.

You at home?

He sighed. He wouldn't have a home for long. No. Starbucks down the street.

Setting the phone on his knee, he sat back in the chair and looked around at the nameless faces. All milling around, some in a hurry, some settled in at what was probably their remote office. All with some sort of purpose. A place to go. A place to be. A place to go home to.

Will was losing both his "go" and "be" places.

He was giving up his "home to" place as a way to cut back on expenses. Sure, he had plenty of money in the bank.

But not many people hired unemployed CEOs who were suspects for fraud.

No, he needed to cut back. Conserve. Figure out what to do next.

He closed his eyes. This was why people committed suicide, he decided. Not that he would ever contemplate that. But he could see how someone given to depression, who felt this utter loss of meaningful life, could think it better just to end it.

His phone vibrated on his leg again. I'M ON MY WAY OVER. JUST DOWN THE STREET. BRINGING SOME GUESTS.

Guests?

What was Emma up to now?

SHOULDN'T YOU BE AT WORK?

His eyes darted from the front glass door back to his phone. He'd rather just be alone, but another part of him was curious.

A text came in. I QUIT. EXPLAIN IN A MINUTE.

Just great. He hoped she didn't have some crazy plan to start their own business or something.

He was through leading companies. Maybe he'd try to go back to R&D somewhere, eventually, after the storm had settled.

That is, if they didn't throw him in jail for something he didn't do.

The door jingled as it opened.

He looked up to see Emma with—

"Greg?"

He stood to meet his predecessor, the man he'd tried hard to distance himself from. He hadn't wanted the previous CEO's indiscretions to leak over onto him.

The distance had obviously done no good.

Greg sat down across the table, and Emma to the side, between them. "Afternoon, Will."

William glanced at his former assistant. "Emma, what's going on?"

"Your dad will be here in a few minutes. I'll let him explain."

She might as well have been speaking Latin. Her words made no sense. "Dad left to go back to Jersey days ago. Why would he be back?"

"Let's just say, he never planned to go home."

"What are you talking abo—"The door jingled again, cutting off his question.

William looked up to see his dad standing beside—

Hanna. The woman he thought he was falling in love with, who ended up serving his head on a platter to the very media she'd despised.

<center>~~~</center>

Hanna stood beside Harrison, her stomach twisted in a knot of nerves.

William sat at a table with a man she didn't recognize and a woman who looked oddly familiar.

"Ella?"

The woman stood and smiled. "It's actually Emma. I am—I mean—was Will's executive assistant."

That didn't make any sense. "But you were on the set. You were part of the crew." She'd been the one gleaming light during the taping of *The Price of Love*. She'd given Hanna pep talks, talked her nerves down, and been so kind. She'd even given her fashion tips on how to wear her hair.

Emma motioned them to sit at the small table. "Will wanted someone on the inside, so I came on to make sure he didn't get fooled by some crazy woman only in it for his money."

"But, that's the point, right? For him to try and figure out on his own who was in it for his money?"

William held up a hand. "None of it matters now. Dad, what is she doing here?"

Hanna sat up straighter. She hadn't expected Will to be happy, but neither had she anticipated the glint of anger in his eyes. It had always been reversed. "Will, I—"

Harrison patted her shoulder. "I think we need to all discuss this in private. Will, how long until we can get in your condo?"

He frowned. "I don't see what there is to talk about."

The man rankled her. They were all trying to help, and he was sitting here like a spoiled brat. "Listen, if he's going to be like this, I'm just going home."

Will stood, his eyes narrowing at her. "I'm not sure why you'd come in the first place after you—"

"After I what? Humiliated you? Ruined your life? Oh, sounds a little familiar, I think."

"This is different."

"Is it?"

Gentle answers, Hanna. Yeah, a lot harder than it sounded.

Harrison cleared his throat. "This isn't the time or place. Will, call your agent and see if you can get back in."

Will looked from her to his dad then back to her. His demeanor seemed to calm a little. "Fine." He jabbed a few numbers on his phone and confirmed that the showings had just finished.

Hanna tried not to laugh at their sour-looking group that entered the fancy, upscale condo. The last time she left, she swore she'd never be back, would never, ever be sucked back in by Will and his aura that had a way of capturing her against her better judgment.

They all took a seat on the swanky leather couch that was more handsome than it was comfortable.

Only Harrison remained standing. "I know you're all a little skeptical, so hear me out. I think we can help each other if we work together. Now, I've done a little digging—"

Will's dad spent the next hour detailing his hypothesis—that

Doug was behind both Greg's demise as well as Will's, and was also instrumental in the media craze that seemed to follow Will and Hanna since the show—giving all the evidence he had gathered to support it.

None of it was concrete or actionable. Almost all of it was circumstantial. But no one in the room was left with any doubt by the time he was finished.

Greg sat forward, his elbows on his knees. "I've thought it was Doug all along. My lawyers have tried everything to pin it on him, but the man covered his tracks well."

Harrison nodded. "That he did, although he got a little desperate with Will. He was no longer able to bide his time and wanted it to be an immediate blow. His demise, however, came when he made a fatal error." He lifted the page from the report Doug had given Hanna and handed it to Greg. "You see this?"

Greg glanced at the sheet and frowned. "It's just a page from the quarterly forecast—and one out of the middle at that. You can't tell much from this."

"Check out the date."

"Two months ago. That's not out of the norm, though, for a preliminary forecast."

Harrison nodded. "Except that Hanna here saw the whole thing, which included numbers showing a pretty significant forecasted profit. Doug used it to convince Hanna that Will was cooking the books. My hypothesis is that these were the actual numbers, and Doug did some fancy accounting using the loopholes he convinced Will to go along with to actually make things look worse—in an effort to get him fired."

Will stood. "It doesn't matter. He'll lie and say Hanna misunderstood him. That paper proves nothing."

His dad sat down on one of the barstools he'd pulled over. "Like

I said, we need more evidence. That's where Hanna comes in."

Hanna lifted her chin. She already knew what was coming and had already agreed to it.

She just wasn't sure Will would.

Her ex-fiancé looked between her and his dad. "What are you talking about?"

"Doug doesn't know any of us have even seen this piece of paper. In fact, he probably doesn't even know it's missing yet. But he is well aware that Hanna has seen the entire report."

"And how does that help us?"

Harrison looked his son in the eye. "Hanna's agreed to wear a wire and get Doug to confess."

CHAPTER FORTY-TWO

*W*ill looked from his dad to Hanna, stunned. "Absolutely not."

Hanna stood, her hands on her irritatingly curvy hips. "Why not?"

He took a step toward her. "It's too dangerous. I may be ticked off at you right now, but I'm not going to be responsible for you getting hurt." He turned. "Dad, I can't believe you'd even suggest this. If Doug really is behind all this, he's dangerous. Who knows what he'll do?"

"I've already talked to the detective working on Greg's case and the SEC and made them aware of our suspicions. They agreed it isn't enough right now but will support us in getting the additional information. We'll have police close by in case anything happens."

He shook his head. "When did you all do this? Why wasn't I involved?"

"Frankly, son, you were too busy feeling sorry for yourself and sulking."

He balled a fist and took a step toward his father. "That's uncalled for."

"It's true. Now, we're going ahead with this whether you like it or not. The question is, will you help?"

Will looked from Hanna to his father.

He didn't really have a choice. "Fine. When will we do it?"

Hanna tucked a blond curl behind her ear, her hand trembling slightly. A sign she was more nervous about this than she let on. "This afternoon. We didn't want to drag it out any longer. Plus, I want to get back home as soon as I can."

Will looked at her, frustrated at the intense burning in his gut at the idea of her in harm's way. He wanted to wrap her in his arms and refuse to allow it.

At the same time, he wanted to throttle her for what she'd done to him. The familiar questions plagued him again. Had it been payback? Had she been leading him on, planning the ultimate revenge?

If so, she'd given an Oscar-winning performance.

But then why was she back now?

He grabbed her elbow and urged her toward the spiral staircase. "I need a moment alone with Hanna."

Hanna glanced at Will's dad, as if gaining permission.

Harrison nodded. "We'll finish laying out the details down here. We don't have a lot of time though, so make it quick."

Will led his ex-fiancée up the staircase and into his bedroom, shutting the door behind them.

"Will, we could have just gone to your office. This isn't really appropriate."

Glancing at the bed, he ran a hand through his hair. She was right. But it was done now. "There is a houseful of people right below us. Believe me when I tell you, your virtue is safe."

She harrumphed. "My virtue was in danger long before now."

He walked to his dresser and picked up the ring, still in the exact spot she'd put it. "I want my coin back."

"We're done being fake engaged, Will. I'm sorry. I know I should have explained, but—"

"I agree. It was a sham from the start. But you gave me that coin, and I gave you this ring. I told you when we were done you could keep it, and I meant it. I'd just like to keep the coin as well."

He turned to look at her, and their eyes met.

They stood silent for several seconds before Hanna stuffed a hand in her jeans pocket and produced the small gold coin then tossed it in the air to him.

He caught it in his hand then held out the ring in his palm. "Forgive me if I don't throw a five-grand diamond to you."

She shook her head. "Keep it."

"No. I told you it was yours when I bought it."

Her hands rested on those crazy, enticing hips. "What am I going to do with an engagement ring I don't need?"

He shrugged. "Pawn it if you want. I don't care."

She pressed a finger against the corner of her eye. "Did I ever tell you why I picked that one?"

"Not that I recall."

"It looks just like my mom's. About twice the size, but the shape and design are similar. We buried it with her, so—it was just sweet to see it. But honestly? Taking it home with me would be more bitter than sweet, and I could never bring myself to sell it. So please. Keep it. You'll be doing me a favor."

He looked at the ring then at her. His heart caught as if having a little hiccup. How was he going to let this irritating woman go?

Then he remembered what she'd done.

Setting the ring and the coin on the dresser, he stuffed his hands in his pockets. "You sure about tonight? You don't have to, you know." Part of him hoped she would apologize to him. Then maybe he could scrounge up enough mercy to forgive her.

She stared at her hands she fiddled with in front of her. "I—I just need to do this. It's the right thing to do."

No apology. No remorse. Just duty. Probably her *Christian* duty.

Well, he'd let her do it, and then they would be done with each other for good.

He'd tried to make good.

She'd have paid her penance.

Wilanna, as the press had dubbed them, would be no more, once and for all.

CHAPTER FORTY-THREE

*H*anna smoothed a hand over the front of her blouse, the tiny bud of a microphone pinned underneath shifting at her touch. She couldn't have been more uncomfortable if she had a gun strapped to her thigh with a garter.

Her rifle from back home in her hands would feel more natural than this.

The elevator dinged as she made it to the tenth floor of the office building that held the corporate headquarters of Foster and Jones.

The doors parted before her, revealing a large, mostly bare room. A sleek desk took up most of the space, with a couple of chairs scattered off to the side, their curvy plastic style offering no allure of comfort. The Foster and Jones logo blazed on the otherwise bare wall.

It was time.

She lifted her chin and hugged the folder close to her chest.

She could do this. She owed Will this much at least. Regardless of everything that had happened over the last year, she'd not only allowed her own life to go into a tailspin but had also brought him down with her.

Time to right the wrong so she could move on.

A thin brunette with long hair and funky red glasses sat at the large round desk, her eyes on the computer. She smiled, but her attention never left the screen. "May I help you?"

"I'm here to see Doug Perry, please."

The receptionist's smile dimmed as she finally looked up. Then she blinked as Hanna's identity dawned on her. "Is he, uh, expecting you?"

"No, but I'm sure he'll want to see me. Please tell him Hanna Knight is here to speak with him."

The receptionist grabbed the phone and pressed a few buttons. "Yes, I have, uh, Hanna Knight to see Mr. Perry."

Hanna leaned over the desk, her confidence building. "Please tell him it's urgent and it would be regrettable if he didn't have time."

The woman, Cheri, if she remembered Will and Emma's advice correctly, repeated Hanna's words.

A moment later, she hung up the phone. "His assistant will be out to take you back shortly. You may have a seat while you wait."

Hanna turned toward one of the hideous-looking blobs of plastic, but the door to the right opened before she could sit.

A pert blond in a skirt a few inches too short for a place of business, in Hanna's opinion, motioned her to follow. "Ms. Knight, this way please."

She followed the woman. As she walked, she felt eyes from the cubicles she passed staring at her, but she lifted her chin and kept her focus on the corner office approaching.

Will's former office.

She wished she would have had a chance to see him in it.

But that ship had sunk last week, her big mouth sending it to the bottom of the ocean as sure as the *Titanic's* glacier disaster.

Approaching the open door, she took a deep breath, adjusted the bottom of her blouse, and threw up a quick prayer. *God, give me courage. . .and help me not to make it worse.*

The perky blond entered first and announced Hanna's arrival, gesturing her to follow.

Doug sat in the large black chair, elbows on the armrests, hands clasped between him. His face was set in that pompous look that made her want to plant her fist against his overly large nose.

While she'd feel so much better, it probably wouldn't help Will.

"Well, if it isn't Hanna Knight. To what do I owe the pleasure?" His voice reeked of condescension as he nodded toward the chair across from his desk.

Her back straight, she walked to the chair and sat, crossing her feet at the ankles. "I don't want to take up too much of your time. I know you're busy now, being the head honcho and all." Shoot. She'd meant to try and keep sarcasm out of her voice.

Yeah, failed at that royally.

Doug's eyes narrowed, his look going from cocky to guarded. "What do you want, Hanna?"

Oh, Lord, this is it. Help me, please. "It isn't so much what I want as what I think you're going to want."

His bushy eyebrows shot up. "Is that so?"

She lifted the vanilla-colored folder for him to see. "Do you remember bringing me the latest sales projections at William's condo?"

His face eased, and he sat back. "I have no recollection of doing any such thing. I may have stopped by to check on you, but that was it. I do have to say, though, I wasn't expecting you to give your own interview like you did. Very vindictive. I was impressed."

Ah. That he would lie about showing up was a good sign.

She opened the folder and withdrew the lone piece of paper. Her next words were so important. She was determined not to lie, but at the same time, he couldn't know she was here on William's behalf. He had to think it was for herself. And, to a point, it was.

"Interesting that you don't recall showing me those papers, especially since you left one page behind."

His demeanor changed slightly, as if he didn't want her to know her effect. But his eyes betrayed the fear that she was certain he felt. "Get to your point, Hanna."

She scooted up in her seat. "I lost my job and my dignity, and I'm fairly certain, given time, I could prove you were the main culprit behind it all. I've done a bit of digging myself, and I think you've been a busy man, Doug. Two CEOs accused of fraud, while the CFO somehow gets off squeaky clean? Yeah, something smells fishy. And now I have a lovely piece of paper that, if I were a betting woman, shows a much more accurate representation of what the sales numbers should have been this last quarter—that is, until you did whatever fancy footwork you do and rigged them to look bad."

"You have no proof of that. Now, I have a meeting in—"

She stood and shot him a smile. "It was nice meeting with you. I have a meeting to get to myself. Sam Deddrick was so kind to be able to fit me in later this afternoon."

Doug stood as well, his face turning twelve shades of red. "Give me that piece of paper."

"What? I thought you said it meant nothing. Or did I hit a nerve? Maybe my guess wasn't too far off, hm?"

Dark eyes stared at her in silence. For a moment, Hanna second-guessed herself. If this guy really was the fraud Harrison thought he was, then—what lengths would he go to in order to shut her up?

She couldn't go back now, though. The framework was already in place. Now she just needed to add a bit of cheese to the trap and let the rat meet his demise. "I might, however, be convinced to cancel my appointment, accidentally shred this little piece of paper, and go back and hibernate in Minnesota."

The rat sat back in his chair, his hands steepled in front of him.

"So you're blackmailing me."

"Call it whatever you want. My life has been turned upside down because of what you did. William made his own bed and can lie in it. But you both drug me into this, and I want to be compensated. William is now unemployed, so I figure you're going to have to be the one to pony up."

"And if I refuse?"

"I keep my appointment with Sam. And I've gotten to know a few reporters pretty well. I'm sure they'd love this piece of juicy information, as well."

He paused only a second. "How much?"

They'd talked long and hard about what amount she should name. Too low and he'd know her case was weak. Too high and he would think of another way to hide the problem. It wasn't until this moment, seeing the evil in his eyes, that she became aware of just what other "ways" Harrison had been referring to. "One hundred grand. Equal to about three years of my salary as a teacher. I think it's more than fair."

Haughty laughter escaped his lips. "You think I'm just going to hand over that kind of cash? You're out of your mind. Anyone would be able to tell it was a payoff. I might not be squeaky clean, as you are aware of, but I hide my trails well."

Score. His first admittance of guilt. But she needed more. She wiggled the folder in her hand. "Not well enough, evidently. Surely you can explain it off as feeling like you need to make restitution for what your 'friend' had done. In fact, if someone does get wind of it, they'll probably see you as a kind and gentle benefactor who wants to help a poor teacher who has been the victim of big bad corporate America. The public would love it." She tried not to laugh hysterically as the words flowed from her mouth.

His eyes probed her face, as if trying to find any other option. A moment later, he opened his desk drawer and reached inside.

Air caught in her lungs. Did he have a gun in there? Surely he wouldn't—

But he pulled out a small rectangular black object.

His checkbook. With a flourish of handwriting, he scribbled her name and the obscene amount on the check, ripped it off, and slid it across the desk. "I'd like the paper in return please."

She pushed the folder across the desk as she accepted the check.

He fingered the piece of paper inside then eyed her. "I'm not stupid enough to believe that you brought the original with you. But I trust that you realize blackmailing is also a federal offense, so at this point, if I go down, I'll be taking you with me. In fact, I just might show them a bit of proof of my own that you've been helping me frame Will."

The microphone scratched against her breast. She wished she could move it up a notch to ensure they were getting all of this. "You would have no proof of that, and you know it."

"Oh, a little security video of you and I entering your hotel room would probably be a great starting point."

"That was your doing and not mine, and you know it."

"Of course, sweet one. But no one else will know it, and that's what matters. You see, that's the crux of it all. Reality is twistable."

She slipped the check into the side pocket of her purse. "Like you twisted the truth with Greg and William?"

"Greg? You know nothing about that."

"No, but I'm smart enough to smell a rotten fish when it's hiding in front of me. It doesn't matter anyway, right? Being that reality is completely twistable."

"Greg was an idiot. Any shrewd businessman would have caught on to what I was doing a long time before the SEC did."

"So because he was too stupid to catch on to you, it made it all right for you to steal money from the company and frame him?"

Pushing his chair back, Doug stood and stalked over to her. She stepped back until her body met the wall and couldn't go any farther.

Blood pounded in her ears, and her lungs refused to exhale as his face moved toward her.

Hands pinning both of her arms to the wall, he pushed his forehead against hers. "If you ever, and I mean ever, try to double-cross me, I swear I'll kill you, Hanna. Do you understand me?"

She flinched at both his words and the hot breath that blew in her face. "Yes. Of course."

He inched back and examined her face. For a moment, she feared he would kiss her. As his mouth moved toward her, his eyes full of lust and greed, the door to the office opened.

He swore then let her go.

A second later, shouts filled the room as FBI agents swarmed, guns drawn.

Hanna stood in her spot, her whole body trembling. A man wearing a black jacket with white FBI lettering came over to her and grabbed her by the arm. "Come with me."

He was none too gentle, but he was getting her out of this room, and he had a gun.

She stumbled after him with only a brief look behind her at Doug, whose face was smothered into the carpet, his hands in cuffs.

CHAPTER FORTY-FOUR

*W*ill sipped his coffee and unfolded the *Wall Street Journal* onto the kitchen counter.

A picture of Doug—his suit disheveled and his face red with anger, being stuffed into a police car—along with the Foster and Jones logo were supersized across the front page.

They'd officially graduated from annoying tabloid press and social media trends to the *WSJ*.

Footsteps sounded behind him. "Well, at least you're off the hook, right?"

He turned to see his dad pulling his rolling suitcase behind him. "I'm unemployed but not in jail. I think I'll choose to be thankful for that."

Harrison clapped him on the shoulder. "Very wise, son. Very wise. Do you know what your plans will be?"

That was the question of the day. His realtor had called thirty minutes ago. He already had three offers on the condo, all well over asking price.

He'd ignored all other phone calls, as most of them would be reporters wanting a statement.

"Honestly? I'd love to change my name and go back to being a lowly research engineer. As much as I loved working my way up in management, I kinda miss being in the thick of things. Pathetic, huh?"

Setting his bag upright, his dad took the barstool next to him. "I owe you an apology, William."

His dad? Apologizing for something? Admitting error? That would be a first. Instead of making a comment, William just looked at him, eyebrows raised.

"I've had a lot of expectations for you throughout your life, son. Maybe too many. I yelled whenever you made what I thought was a mistake, because I knew you could do better."

"You were right, most of the time."

"Not always. And I think somewhere along the line I neglected to remind you how much I loved you and how proud I am of you."

Will squirmed in his seat, his hands clutching the newspaper in front of him. A heart-to-heart talk with his dad, opening old wounds, was not what he needed today. "It's fine, Dad."

"No, no it's not. When we lost Claire, I—I was devastated. But watching you turn your back on God was almost worse. I know I'll see my daughter again someday, but to see my son turning away from the only thing I knew could heal his hurting soul. . . William, it tore me in two. But I was grieving, too, and instead of loving you, I focused on what I thought I could change. I tried to discipline you to Jesus. I doubt any parent has actually succeeded with that method."

A lump formed in Will's throat.

He was a grown man. Midthirties. Already hit the pinnacle of his career. He would not sit here and break down in front of his father. "Well, I'm no worse for it, so don't worry about it."

"I disagree. You're lost, William. And I'm not talking about just your career. On top of it all, you just let the best thing that ever happened to you fly back to Minnesota alone."

Hanna's flight had left that morning. He hadn't even bothered to see her off. That chapter of his life was over and needed to be left far in the past. "Hanna's better off in Minnesota."

Which was true. He had nothing to offer her, and she—she'd paid her penance for ruining his career by helping bring Doug to justice. They had no further reason to communicate.

The memory of her smile invaded his thoughts. Her blond hair brushing her shoulders, her laugh that made him want to kiss that little spot on her neck to make her giggle more—

He shook his head.

No. He needed to get her out of his head and move on. That was all. She was like a drug to him, intoxicating his soul to the point he couldn't see or think straight.

"Is she?"

"Of course. Why are you and Mom so hip on getting us back together, anyway?"

Harrison scooted off the stool and collected his suitcase. "Maybe it was a bit of wishful thinking. But seeing you in love with a woman who's in love with Jesus, it gave us hope. That God had finally brought someone who could convince you to let down that wall of steel you'd built around your heart. But, regardless, we want you to know we love you, William. That's never changed since the moment you were born." He glanced at his watch. "My flight leaves in a few hours, and I still have to return my rental car. Don't be a stranger, okay?"

Will nodded, no fitting words readily coming to mind. Instead, he stood and clapped his dad into a hug.

For a brief second, he was fifteen again, trying to be tough as he hugged his dad at Claire's funeral.

After a moment, he lowered his arms and stepped back. "Have a safe flight, Dad." Nice, safe, emotionless words.

Harrison smiled. "Thanks." He walked toward the door and opened it.

"Dad?"

He turned and looked back.

"Thanks for coming out here to help. I'd probably be in jail or something if you hadn't shown up."

"That's what dads and lawyers are for."

With that he let himself out of the condo.

Will stuffed his hands in his pockets and walked toward the wall of windows that overlooked the city.

The faces of two females filled his mind.

A gorgeous blond who'd probably already landed in Duluth, maybe even back in Embarrass by now.

And a twelve-year-old pixie-faced girl, cheeks sunken in from illness but a sparkle in her eyes even a weak heart couldn't snuff out.

He rested his forehead against the glass.

What was he doing? Life seemed so—pointless.

A verse in the Bible, a book he'd neglected for almost twenty years, flitted in his memory. *"Everything is meaningless."* So completely meaningless.

How appropriate.

Pulling his phone from his pocket, he clicked until Hanna's contact information came up.

Her small picture stared at him. It was one he'd snapped awhile ago. Her hair was in two braids, her smile turned up in an impish grin. It made her look like a teenager rather than an accomplished teacher in her late twenties.

His finger itched to tap her phone number.

Would it hurt to see how she was doing?

Meaningless.

Well, if all was meaningless, he might as well satisfy his curiosity. He tapped the screen and held the phone to his ear.

His heart thudded against his ribs as it rang.

The familiar female voice answered. "Hello?"

Words jumbled in his mouth. "I, uh, just wanted to make sure you made it home okay."

Silence met him. Had she hung up? He moved the phone from his ear and checked. Nope. "Hanna?"

She cleared her throat. "Uh, sorry. Yes. I just got home a few minutes ago."

He walked over to the couch and fell onto the cushions. Memories of sitting on the couch beside her at the little farmhouse rushed to mind. The soft old couch with plaid fabric that showed its age but was comfortable.

Much different than the thick, unforgiving leather number he now stretched out on. "Well, that's good. Your dad doing okay?"

"He's fine."

He should probably just say good-bye and hang up now, but her voice was like a bucket of water being dumped over his dry, thirsty heart. "Weather calmed down there?"

"Yeah. Most of the snow melted in last week's warm snap, but Dad says they're calling for more this weekend."

He smiled. "What's a warm snap for March in Minnesota?"

"It got up to thirty-five a few days. People were walking around without jackets and everything."

Closing his eyes, he let her soft voice soak into his heart. "My dad just left."

"I was wondering if he'd planned to stay a few days or not."

"Nothing left to do. Doug's in jail. Greg and I received word that we are officially cleared this morning. The evidence against Doug is staggering, now that a few lower-level department heads are talking and producing evidence in exchange for immunity. There will be a big turnover at F&J, let's just say that."

"You never said what you're going to do next."

He glanced up at the two-story ceiling, the starkness of it all settling on his soul. "I have no idea."

A moment of silence followed before she spoke again. "Why did you call, Will? Really."

A good question. He wished he knew the answer. "Have you ever read the book of Ecclesiastes?"

"Once or twice."

"It's been awhile, but I was sitting here in my condo, realizing just how pointless life is."

"Will, what are you saying? Are you okay?" Alarm invaded her voice.

He smiled that she would care so much. "Don't worry. I'm not suicidal or anything. I just—I was sitting here thinking about what to do next and nothing made any sense. The only thing I could think of was that verse in the Bible about life being meaningless. And the only desire I could find in my heart was to call and check on you. I figured if it was all meaningless anyway, I might as well call."

"I see."

She didn't really. He could hear it in her voice. "I got three great offers on the condo this morning."

"That's nice. Where will you go now?"

He closed his eyes. "I have no idea."

"You could, you know, try praying about it."

That sounded like something the old Hanna would say, the one she'd been before he'd "corrupted" her in front of the world. "I'm not sure God cares about what I do next."

"Doesn't hurt to try. You know, if everything is meaningless anyway, might as well give it a whirl."

He didn't want to talk about prayer. Not right now. "Can I call you again?"

"Call me?"

"You know, push a few buttons, you answer on the little thing you have held up to your ear. We talk for a bit. That sort of thing."

He could almost see her eye roll. "I know what it means, goof. But why? We don't have anything else to talk about."

The thought of never speaking to her again stabbed his heart until he felt physical pain. "Please, Hanna. No expectations. I promise."

"I guess that would be fine."

Relief flooded him. "Until next time, then."

"Good-bye, Will."

~~~

Hanna pressed END on her phone and sank down onto her bed.

That had been the oddest, scariest call she'd ever had. At one point, she'd almost thought she would need to call Emma to go check on him, make sure he wasn't going to hurt himself.

She had assumed she'd never hear from him again.

The whole flight home her heart had begged her to turn right back around and go to him.

But no. They were done. He had his life to figure out, and she had hers to piece back together.

And now she had the prospect of him calling her again.

How was she ever to put it all behind her?

Dropping to her knees, she dug the shoe box from under her bed and dumped all the clippings and letters on the floor. One by one, she read them.

Memories flooded her.

Yet, the familiar pain in her heart was absent. The articles were just silly now, their untruths borderline comical.

The letters from well-meaning Christians chastising her still weren't fun. But they triggered something new in her now. A part of her heart hurt for *them*. What kind of junk must one be carrying in their own life to lash out in judgment in such a mean, personal way?

Were they only taught about God's judgment, leaving out the part about His grace?

Grace. Such an amazing word.

She fingered a particularly mean letter, one of the few handwritten ones she'd received. Ink in the middle was smudged where her tears had fallen months ago.

Funny thing about grace. It was a two-way street. To be given and received.

Shoving the box aside, she grabbed the letter and headed for her desk. Opening her laptop, she began to type a letter.

Dear Anita,

I received your letter a few months ago. At the time, I was angry with you. Your words, along with the words of thousands of others like you, wounded my soul to the point where I didn't think I'd be able to recover.

But this amazing thing happened.

God showed me that I wasn't beyond His love. That though I'm not perfect, He loves me still, despite what notes such as yours made me feel.

I don't know if you feel guilt over writing that letter, or if you feel totally justified.

I wanted you to know, though, just in case, that I forgive you.

God loves you, Anita, and He loves me, too. I pray that we can both fumble through this life, showing each other the same grace God has given us, and support each other instead of tear each other down.

Blessings and love in Christ,
Not-so-holy-but-trying. . .Hanna

CHAPTER FORTY-FIVE

*W*ill shifted the phone to his other ear and tore open the next box. Moving was not on his list of fun things to do. Talking to Hanna, however, was definitely up there. "How's your dad doing?"

"Pretty good. Glad that the snow seems to be slowing down. Hopefully, we've seen our last big one for the year." Her voice, while still on safe topics like family and the weather, was more comfortable this time.

Like she was getting used to talking to him again.

He liked it.

A lot.

They'd been talking for almost a month now, just a few times a week. He called her each time, never the other way around.

Whether he liked it or not, she had become his meaning. His reason for not going completely crazy. Being unemployed wasn't something he was used to. It wasn't the money. He had plenty saved to live on the rest of his life if he wanted, as long as he invested and spent wisely.

Thus the reason he'd downsized to a townhouse in the suburbs that was much less ostentatious. It suited him better anyway. More comfortable than breakable.

"I was thinking—"

She laughed. "Oh no. The great and powerful William Preston has been thinking. Should I sit down for this?"

"Ha. Ha. And yes, you probably should."

Rustling sounded over the phone. "Okay, so what's up?"

"I, uh, thought maybe I could come up and visit. This summer sometime. Maybe." Oh great. He sounded like a fifteen-year-old asking a girl out on a date for the first time. At least his voice didn't do the whole puberty crack.

"Um. Wow. I mean—"

"You don't have to say yes. I promise I won't be mad." Much.

"It's not that I don't want you to, but—Will, what's your goal for all this? I know you. You always have a plan. I just want to make sure that plan doesn't include a future with me. Because, to be blunt, mine doesn't include a future with you. I need to move on."

Move on? "Then why have you let me call you?"

"Because you needed a friend. And I thought I could maybe be that friend as long as we were long-distance. I see now I was wrong."

Thoughts ping-ponged in his head. Was she finally, officially, breaking up with him?

And was he really being that stalkerish boyfriend who wouldn't accept no for an answer?

Why, yes. Yes, he was. There was just something in her voice. A note of hesitance that said she was trying to convince herself just as much if not more than convince him. "Okay. So you *need* to move on. I get that. But what do you *want*, Hanna? What does your heart say?"

"My heart is what got me in this mess. I no longer trust it or give it a voice."

"What about God?"

The line was silent for a moment. Finally, she cleared her throat. "What about Him?"

"God's in the heart business, isn't He? If you aren't trusting your heart, does that mean you aren't trusting Him either?"

"That was a low blow, Mr. I-haven't-gone-to-church-in-a-decade."

He glanced over where his Bible lay on the side table. He'd actually read it now and then over the last month. There was something about life being ripped from underneath a guy that made him turn back to the idea of a God who was an unmovable foundation. A foundation he'd stepped away from many years ago. "I'm not saying God and I are on buddy-buddy terms. But—let's just say I've been making a few calls His way, just like I have you. Testing the waters."

"That's—amazing. Really, Will. I'm excited for you."

"If I promise not to mention visiting anymore, can I keep calling you, then? As a friend?"

"I—I don't know."

"What if I said God told me to call you."

"You'd be lying, and God would have to bring out the lightning again, buddy."

Will stilled his hand on a box and pressed his forehead to a nearby cabinet. "Please, Hanna. Please let me call."

"Of course. I gotta go though. Dad needs me outside."

"Okay. I'll talk to you later."

Clicking END on his phone, Will let out a breath. At least she hadn't said no completely.

Because like it or not, his heart was officially attached to a blond-haired beauty in Northern Minnesota. He didn't care if he had to sell everything, move up there, and start a career in ice fishing, he'd find a way to show her he was worthy.

He was in love with her, and nothing was going to change that.

As he started to slip his phone into his pocket, it vibrated, announcing an incoming call.

A glance at the caller ID sent every kind of doubt flinging through the air.

The number was a familiar one, belonging to an extension at Foster and Jones.

———～～～———

"William, I'm sure you know why we've asked you here today."

Sitting in the conference room with his former board of directors, Will shifted in his seat and nodded, trying to look like he knew exactly what they were talking about, when in reality, he was as clueless as he was yesterday when he received the phone call inviting him here today.

What the board would want with him at this point, with the company crumbling around its ears and, by all accounts, going under, was anyone's guess. They had been less than forthcoming in their message delivered by, of all people, the receptionist.

"We'd like to formally offer you your job back."

A strange buzzing sounded in William's ears. Was he having a stroke? He could have sworn he'd just heard them offer him his job back, but that made no sense.

He glanced around the room, older men and a few women sitting in suits, eyes all trained on him, expecting a response.

A few weeks ago, he would have jumped at the shot. And if he were smart, he still would.

But all he could think of was Hanna's face, her voice that said she wanted nothing to do with him, yet the tone implying the exact opposite. He'd even called her back and told her about the call.

She'd said she would be praying for him.

A few months ago, he would have laughed at that.

But right now, he felt honored and thankful.

Sam, sitting to his right, cleared his throat. "William? What do you say?"

"I—" What did he say? Words caught in his throat like a fly trapped in a spider's web. If he accepted, he'd have meaning again, right? He could turn the company around, without the fingers of Doug making it impossible at every turn. He could get back his reputation, have his name cleared once and for all.

He finally understood why Hanna had agreed to be pretend engaged with him. To be known as someone you weren't, someone you'd never want to be, was horrible.

To clear his name and right the wrong would be the smart thing to do. The wise thing, even, in the eyes of a lot of people.

But why was his heart screaming at him to tear up the employment contract being handed to him?

Sam cleared his throat. "I know this comes as a shock. But we felt you were the right man for the job two years ago, and we still feel that way. I don't have to tell you, Will, we're in a bad spot. Publicity was horrible, and the stock has tanked. It won't be easy, but you have just the right charisma to get us back on track."

"Why me? I thought you'd want to separate the company from scandal, not invite it back in."

A few exchanges in expressions told him the vote probably hadn't been unanimous. Sam adjusted his tie, glanced at a few others and then back at Will. "You're the right man for the job, Will."

Too many unanswered questions hung in the air. But still, his head screamed, *Take the job, idiot,* while his heart tuned a violin, crooning, *Go get your woman and show her that a heart knows best.*

His heart really needed to learn how to sing in tune.

He pushed back his chair and stood, pushing the employment contract to the middle of the table. "Gentlemen, ladies, I appreciate the offer, but I'm sorry. I must decline. Best of luck to you all."

And with that, he turned on his heel and exited the conference room.

Emma stood in the hall, leaning against the wall. "So?"

He blinked. "What are you doing here? I thought you left when I did."

"Yeah, they asked me to come back, assumed you'd want me for your assistant when you reassumed your position."

Great. He'd not only turned down his own future but hers as well. "I'm sorry, Emma. I didn't realize. I turned them down."

Her lips tilted into a grin. "Good. I was only coming back to help an old friend, anyway. So, when are you headed to Minnesota?"

"How'd you guess?"

"Woman's intuition. Want me to book your flight?"

"You aren't my assistant anymore."

She pushed off the wall and winked. "I know, but I'm your friend. And a friend who is dying to attend the wedding of her former boss. But that won't ever happen if her former boss doesn't turn up the charm and whisk the lady off her feet."

He glanced at his watch, his heart pounding at the prospect. Sometimes, one just had to listen to their heart. And assistant. "Think I can still make a flight tonight?"

"Yeah, but you might want to get a hotel in Duluth before heading to Embarrass."

"Could you—"

She winked and pulled out her iPad from her purse as they walked to the elevator doors. "Already on it."

CHAPTER FORTY-SIX

*T*he only thing worse than Minnesota in a blizzard was Minnesota in mud season.

Hanna gripped her hands on the steering wheel, trying not to frown at her new shoes she'd just splurged on. She wasn't one of those women who had a thousand pairs of shoes in their closet. She had six at most. But that didn't mean she didn't admire them.

And today, she'd made a special trip into town to buy a new pair.

It was all Will's fault and that dad-gum phone call yesterday. He'd talked about hearts and Jesus, said all the right words, and befuddled her mind.

Her *made up* mind that was determined to shut up that heart of hers.

But her heart wasn't so nice. It had pounded and thudded and made its presence known.

To appease it, she'd bought shoes.

Cute little flats with a girly little bow on them and everything. And they were red. Hearts liked red, right?

Her sole purpose was to get her heart—and subsequently her mind—off William Preston.

But then she'd been happily walking out of the store and stepped right into a large pile of Minnesota post-snow-melt mud.

It was so something Will would have done.

And there. Her mind was right back to the man she needed to forget, like, yesterday.

Driving down Highway 21 toward home, she tried to think of anything but him. If Carly wasn't in school, she'd just call her and that would solve the problem. If only—

Suddenly, a flourish of movement bound across the road in front of her.

Air caught in her lungs as she slammed on the brakes, but the deer stood unmoving. At the last moment, she swerved hard to the right.

The truck bumped and slid down the ditch to a stop.

She looked back. The buck, complete with eight-point antlers, looked at her for a moment then took off in the opposite direction.

Her hands shaking, she shifted the truck into REVERSE, hoping she could get enough traction to get back up the ditch.

But her wheels just spun, jerking the cab back and forth with their efforts.

Flinging open the door, she eyed the mud and her new shoes. Eh, they were dirty anyway. She hopped down, ignoring the cold oozing into her shoes.

$59.99 down the drain.

Grabbing a few scraps of wood from the truck bed, she jammed one under each back tire, wedging them as tight as she could.

Climbing back into the cab, she put her hands to the steering wheel and prayed. *Lord, please. Just let me get unstuck and get home. I'll never overspend on new shoes again, I promise.*

She shifted into DRIVE and stepped on the gas, praying all the while that the boards offered just enough traction to get her moving again.

The truck lurched for a foot but then sank and sputtered mud.

A car horn honked behind her.

She looked in the rearview mirror to see an SUV coming to a stop, her pieces of wood resting on its now cracked windshield.

Crud. She knew the spinning would send them flying but had forgotten to check for cars.

More money to come out of her nonexistent savings account. She could just imagine explaining *this* to her insurance guy.

Opening the door, she slid out, ignoring the mud and turning to face the probably ticked-off driver.

Blood rushed to her head at the sight of a man in jeans and adorable flannel standing at the side of the road. "Will?"

He smiled, his hands tucked in his pockets. "You need a little help?"

She wiped a strand of blond hair from her face, only then realizing her hands were covered in mud. "Uh, what are you doing here?"

"Repaying you a favor, I think. You saved my life in a blizzard. Now I get to save you in, well, mud I guess."

A smile tugged at her lips. "Not quite the same."

"It'll have to do. I doubt I'd be any help in a blizzard."

"I—seriously. What are you doing here?"

"Proving a point."

"And that point is?"

He started toward her, but she held up a hand. "You might not want to—"

But it was too late. Two steps into the ditch, William lost his footing, his tennis shoes that probably cost double her new shoes sliding, sending him down the embankment on his hind end, straight toward her.

She took a step to the side to avoid him, but it was too late. His feet tangled with hers, and she went sprawling into the mud beside him.

The world swirled for a moment, but when it came to a stop, Will was beside her.

Even covered in mud, he was way too handsome. Her heart leaped as his hand brushed against her cheek, trying to clear it of mud but probably just making it worse.

"I'm sorry."

She laughed. "I tried to warn you."

"I didn't mean about this. I'm sorry for being a jerk. For assuming I could fix everything. For being overly confident with that reporter. For treating you like anything less than the amazing woman you are."

She leaned into his hand on her face. "I forgive you."

His face moved forward, closing the gap. "I'm in love with you, Hanna Knight. I wanted to come and be your knight in shining SUV, but I guess I'll settle for knight in shiny mud. Will you give me another chance? Please?"

She wanted to say yes. More than anything in this world.

But the price was so steep. "We can't, Will. I want to so bad, but we just won't work. We're in two different places."

He leaned forward, resting his forehead on hers. "Foster and Jones offered me my job back."

She blinked. That's what this was all about? Coming to claim her for his prize and salvage all this mess? Anger warred inside her. No way. She had already boarded that ship and knew right where it headed. Not interested. She swatted away his hand and slid back, slushy mud oozing down the back of her shirt and jeans. It took all she could not to grab a handful and fling it at the man in front of her. "They did? Congratulations."

He scooted closer, a sly grin on his face. "I turned them down."

"If you think—" She paused, her ready rant fizzling in confusion. "You did what?"

"It's not worth it. I knew if I said yes, you'd always think I was coming back to help the company."

"But you love what you do, Will." Was she really trying to convince him to do the very thing she'd just wanted to sling mud in his face for doing?

The thought of him giving up his dream—for her—made her heart want to run in circles, hang the mud.

"I love you. No job, no amount of money, is worth risking losing you, Hanna. You're priceless."

She leaned forward, not caring for their dirty surroundings, only caring that she could no longer deny how *right* the man in front of her was. "I—I love you, too, William Preston."

He closed the small gap and captured her lips with his. He tasted an odd mixture of dirt and nature and Chapstick, but she didn't care. Her hands covered his cheeks as she deepened the kiss, giving her heart away in the process, free of cost.

Dear Reader:

My hope and prayer for all my books is that Jesus will use them to make people laugh when they need it most, but more importantly, that He would use them, in their imperfect, human-written form, to draw His children closer to Him. This book is no different. I named the show in this book *The Price of Love* for a few different reasons. First, it fit with the funny reality TV dating show theme. But it also made me think about Jesus. The true price of love was paid by Jesus on the cross a couple thousand years ago. There is nothing I could ever do to earn the gift of love, of life, He's given. But to accept His gift of eternal life, I have to give up my own life. Every bit of it. Not just the small pieces I feel like giving Him when it's convenient.

In Matthew 16:24–25 (NLT), Jesus says, "If any of you wants to be my follower, you must give up your own way, take up your cross, and follow me. If you try to hang on to your life, you will lose it. But if you give up your life for my sake, you will save it."

Know that you are loved by a God bigger than you can fathom and by an author humbly honored to write stories to glorify Jesus.

- Krista

ACKNOWLEDGMENTS

Huge thanks to –

Jesus. For walking with me through every step of this journey and loving me even (and especially) when I don't deserve it. Which, really, is pretty much every single day.

My husband and kids. You all mean more to me than my words could ever express. Thanks for putting up with my crazy love bugs!

My alley cats. Your support and encouragement means the world to me!

My agent, Sarah. Thanks for living with my crazy long, rambling e-mails and championing my stories. You rock!

My parents. For all your love and support throughout the years! I love you both!

My fabulous editor, Annie, I am forever grateful for the opportunity to work with you! And Linda, for helping me spit-polish this thing!

ABOUT THE AUTHOR

Krista Phillips writes contemporary romance sprinkled with two of her favorite things, laughter and Jesus. And sometimes chocolate for kicks and giggles. She lives in Middle Tennessee with her husband and their four beautiful daughters and is an advocate for congenital heart defect and organ donation awareness. Visit her online at www. kristaphillips.com.